Count Lev Nikolayevich Tolstoy (9 September [O.S. 28 August] 1828 – 20 November [O.S. 7 November] 1910), usually referred to in English as Leo Tolstoy, was a Russian writer who is regarded as one of the greatest authors of all time. He received multiple nominations for Nobel Prize in Literature every year from 1902 to 1906, and nominations for Nobel Peace Prize in 1901, 1902 and 1910, and his miss of the prize is a major Nobel prize controversy. Born to an aristocratic Russian family in 1828, he is best known for the novels War and Peace (1869) and Anna Karenina (1877), often cited as pinnacles of realist fiction. He first achieved literary acclaim in his twenties with his semi-autobiographical trilogy, Childhood, Boyhood, and Youth (1852–1856), and Sevastopol Sketches (1855), based upon his experiences in the Crimean War. Tolstoy's fiction includes dozens of short stories and several novellas such as The Death of Ivan Ilyich (1886), Family Happiness (1859), and Hadji Murad (1912). He also wrote plays and numerous philosophical essays. (Source: Wikipedia)

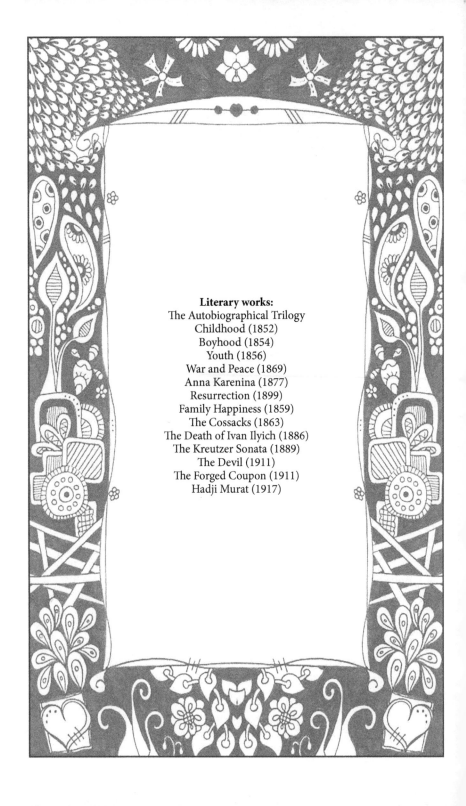

Literary works:
The Autobiographical Trilogy
Childhood (1852)
Boyhood (1854)
Youth (1856)
War and Peace (1869)
Anna Karenina (1877)
Resurrection (1899)
Family Happiness (1859)
The Cossacks (1863)
The Death of Ivan Ilyich (1886)
The Kreutzer Sonata (1889)
The Devil (1911)
The Forged Coupon (1911)
Hadji Murat (1917)

THRONE CLASSICS

SEVASTOPOL
&
THREE DAYS IN THE VILLAGE
AND OTHER SKETCHES
LEO TOLSTOY

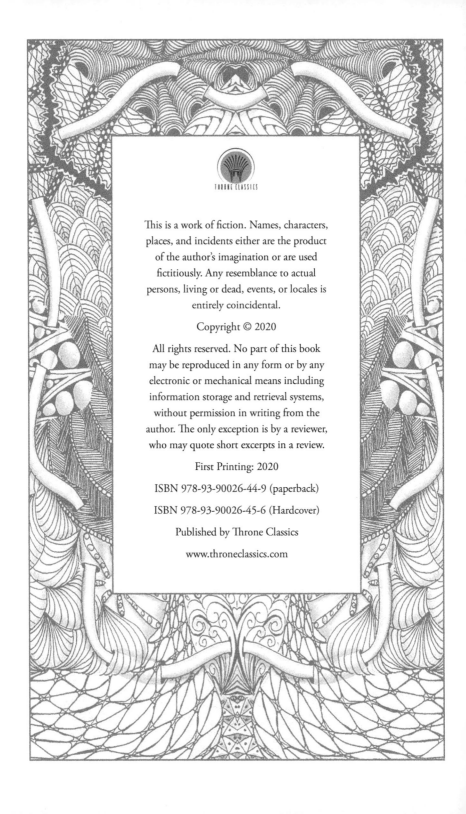

Copyright © 2020

All rights reserved. No part of this book may be reproduced in any form or by any electronic or mechanical means including information storage and retrieval systems, without permission in writing from the author. The only exception is by a reviewer, who may quote short excerpts in a review.

First Printing: 2020

ISBN 978-93-90026-44-9 (paperback)

ISBN 978-93-90026-45-6 (Hardcover)

Published by Throne Classics

www.throneclassics.com

Contents

SEVASTOPOL   **9**

SEVASTOPOL IN DECEMBER, 1854.   9

SEVASTOPOL IN MAY, 1855.   25

SEVASTOPOL IN AUGUST, 1855.   68

THREE DAYS IN THE VILLAGE, AND OTHER SKETCHES   **139**

THREE DAYS IN THE VILLAGE   **139**

FIRST DAY-TRAMPS   139

SECOND DAY-THE LIVING AND THE DYING   147

THIRD DAY-TAXES   157

CONCLUSION-A DREAM   162

SINGING IN THE VILLAGE   170

TRAVELLER AND PEASANT   175

A TALK WITH A WAYFARER   184

FROM THE DIARY   187

FOOTNOTES: 195

About Author   197

SEVASTOPOL
&
THREE DAYS IN THE VILLAGE
AND OTHER SKETCHES

SEVASTOPOL

SEVASTOPOL IN DECEMBER, 1854.

The flush of morning has but just begun to tinge the sky above Sapun Mountain; the dark blue surface of the sea has already cast aside the shades of night and awaits the first ray to begin a play of merry gleams; cold and mist are wafted from the bay; there is no snow—all is black, but the morning frost pinches the face and crackles underfoot, and the far-off, unceasing roar of the sea, broken now and then by the thunder of the firing in Sevastopol, alone disturbs the calm of the morning. It is dark on board the ships; it has just struck eight bells.

Toward the north the activity of the day begins gradually to replace the nocturnal quiet; here the relief guard has passed clanking their arms, there the doctor is already hastening to the hospital, further on the soldier has crept out of his earth hut and is washing his sunburnt face in ice-encrusted water, and, turning towards the crimsoning east, crosses himself quickly as he prays to God; here a tall and heavy camel-wagon has dragged creaking to the cemetery, to bury the bloody dead, with whom it is laden nearly to the top. You go to the wharf—a peculiar odor of coal, manure, dampness, and of beef strikes you; thousands of objects of all sorts—wood, meat, gabions, flour, iron, and so forth—lie in heaps about the wharf; soldiers of various regiments, with knapsacks and muskets, without knapsacks and without muskets, throng thither, smoke, quarrel, drag weights aboard the steamer which lies smoking beside the quay; unattached two-oared boats, filled with all sorts of people,—soldiers, sailors, merchants, women,—land at and leave the wharf.

"To the Grafsky, Your Excellency? be so good." Two or three retired sailors rise in their boats and offer you their services.

You select the one who is nearest to you, you step over the half-decomposed carcass of a brown horse, which lies there in the mud beside the boat, and reach the stern. You quit the shore. All about you is the sea, already glittering in the morning sun, in front of you is an aged sailor, in a camel's-hair coat, and a young, white-headed boy, who work zealously and in silence at the oars. You gaze at the motley vastness of the vessels, scattered far and near over the bay, and at the small black dots of boats moving about on the shining azure expanse, and at the bright and beautiful buildings of the city, tinted with the rosy rays of the morning sun, which are visible in one direction, and at the foaming white line of the quay, and the sunken ships from which black tips of masts rise sadly here and there, and at the distant fleet of the enemy faintly visible as they rock on the crystal horizon of the sea, and at the streaks of foam on which leap salt bubbles beaten up by the oars; you listen to the monotonous sound of voices which fly to you over the water, and the grand sounds of firing, which, as it seems to you, is increasing in Sevastopol.

It cannot be that, at the thought that you too are in Sevastopol, a certain feeling of manliness, of pride, has not penetrated your soul, and that the blood has not begun to flow more swiftly through your veins.

"Your Excellency! you are steering straight into the Kistentin,"[A] says your old sailor to you as he turns round to make sure of the direction which you are imparting to the boat, with the rudder to the right.

"And all the cannon are still on it," remarks the white-headed boy, casting a glance over the ship as we pass.

"Of course; it's new. Korniloff lived on board of it," said the old man, also glancing at the ship.

"See where it has burst!" says the boy, after a long silence, looking at a white cloud of spreading smoke which has suddenly appeared high over the South Bay, accompanied by the sharp report of an exploding bomb.

"He is firing to-day with his new battery," adds the old man, calmly spitting on his hands. "Now, give way, Mishka! we'll overtake the barge." And your boat moves forward more swiftly over the broad swells of the bay, and you actually do overtake the heavy barge, upon which some bags are piled, and which is rowed by awkward soldiers, and it touches the Grafsky wharf amid a multitude of boats of every sort which are landing.

Throngs of gray soldiers, black sailors, and women of various colors move noisily along the shore. The women are selling rolls, Russian peasants with samovárs are crying hot sbiten;[B] and here upon the first steps are strewn rusted cannon-balls, bombs, grape-shot, and cast-iron cannon of various calibers; a little further on is a large square, upon which lie huge beams, gun-carriages, sleeping soldiers; there stand horses, wagons, green guns, ammunition-chests, and stacks of arms; soldiers, sailors, officers, women, children, and merchants are moving about; carts are arriving with hay, bags, and casks; here and there Cossacks make their way through, or officers on horseback, or a general in a drosky. To the right, the street is hemmed in by a barricade, in whose embrasures stand some small cannon, and beside these sits a sailor smoking his pipe. On the left a handsome house with Roman ciphers on the pediment, beneath which stand soldiers and blood-stained litters—everywhere you behold the unpleasant signs of a war encampment. Your first impression is inevitably of the most disagreeable sort. The strange mixture of camp and town life, of a beautiful city and a dirty bivouac, is not only not beautiful, but seems repulsive disorder; it even seems to you that every one is thoroughly frightened, and is fussing about without knowing what he is doing. But look more closely at the faces of these people who are moving about you, and you will gain an entirely different idea. Look at this little soldier from the provinces, for example, who is leading a troïka of brown horses to water, and is purring something to himself so composedly that he evidently will not go astray in this motley crowd, which does not exist for him; but he is fulfilling his duty, whatever that may be,—watering the horses or carrying arms,—with just as much composure, self-confidence, and equanimity as though it were taking place in Tula or Saransk. You will read the same expression on the face of this officer who passes by in immaculate white gloves, and in the face of the sailor who is smoking as he sits on the barricade, and in the faces of the working soldiers, waiting with their litters on the steps of the former club, and in the face of yonder girl, who, fearing to wet her pink gown, skips across the street on the little stones.

Yes! disenchantment certainly awaits you, if you are entering Sevastopol for the first time. In vain will you seek, on even a single countenance, for traces of anxiety, discomposure, or even of enthusiasm, readiness for death, decision,—there is nothing of the sort. You will see the tradespeople quietly engaged in the duties of their callings, so that, possibly, you may reproach yourself for superfluous raptures, you may entertain some doubt as to the justice of the ideas regarding the heroism of the defenders of Sevastopol which you have formed from stories, descriptions, and the sights and sounds on the northern side. But, before you doubt, go upon the bastions, observe the defenders of Sevastopol on the very scene of the defence, or, better still, go straight across into that house, which was formerly the Sevastopol Assembly House, and upon whose roof stand soldiers with litters,—there you will behold the defenders of Sevastopol, there you will behold frightful and sad, great and laughable, but wonderful sights, which elevate the soul.

You enter the great Hall of Assembly. You have but just opened the door when the sight and smell of forty or fifty seriously wounded men and of those who have undergone amputation—some in hammocks, the majority upon the floor—suddenly strike you. Trust not to the feeling which detains you upon the threshold of the hall; be not ashamed of having come to look at the sufferers, be not ashamed to approach and address them: the unfortunates like to see a sympathizing human face, they like to tell of their sufferings and to hear words of love and interest. You walk along between the beds and seek a face less stern and suffering, which you decide to approach, with the object of conversing.

"Where are you wounded?" you inquire, timidly and with indecision, of an old, gaunt soldier, who, seated in his hammock, is watching you with a good-natured glance, and seems to invite you to approach him. I say "you ask timidly," because these sufferings inspire you, over and above the feeling of profound sympathy, with a fear of offending and with a lofty reverence for the man who has undergone them.

"In the leg," replies the soldier; but, at the same time, you perceive, by the folds of the coverlet, that he has lost his leg above the knee. "God be thanked now," he adds,—"I shall get my discharge."

"Were you wounded long ago?"

12

"It was six weeks ago, Your Excellency."

"Does it still pain you?"

"No, there's no pain now; only there's a sort of gnawing in my calf when the weather is bad, but that's nothing."

"How did you come to be wounded?"

"On the fifth bastion, during the first bombardment. I had just trained a cannon, and was on the point of going away, so, to another embrasure when it struck me in the leg, just as if I had stepped into a hole and had no leg."

"Was it not painful at the first moment?"

"Not at all; only as though something boiling hot had struck my leg."

"Well, and then?"

"And then—nothing; only the skin began to draw as though it had been rubbed hard. The first thing of all, Your Excellency, is not to think at all. If you don't think about a thing, it amounts to nothing. Men suffer from thinking more than from anything else."

At that moment, a woman in a gray striped dress and a black kerchief bound about her head approaches you.

She joins in your conversation with the sailor, and begins to tell about him, about his sufferings, his desperate condition for the space of four weeks, and how, when he was wounded, he made the litter halt that he might see the volley from our battery, how the grand-duke spoke to him and gave him twenty-five rubles, and how he said to him that he wanted to go back to the bastion to direct the younger men, even if he could not work himself. As she says all this in a breath, the woman glances now at you, now at the sailor, who has turned away as though he did not hear her and plucks some lint from his pillow, and her eyes sparkle with peculiar enthusiasm.

"This is my housewife, Your Excellency!" the sailor says to you, with an expression which seems to say, "You must excuse her. Every one knows it's a woman's way—she's talking nonsense."

You begin to understand the defenders of Sevastopol. For some reason, you feel ashamed of yourself in the presence of this man. You would like to say a very great deal to him, in order to express to him your sympathy and admiration; but you find no words, or you are dissatisfied with those which come into your head,—and you do reverence in silence before this taciturn, unconscious grandeur and firmness of soul, this modesty in the face of his own merits.

"Well, God grant you a speedy recovery," you say to him, and you halt before another invalid, who is lying on the floor and appears to be awaiting death in intolerable agony.

He is a blond man with pale, swollen face. He is lying on his back, with his left arm thrown out, in a position which is expressive of cruel suffering. His parched, open mouth with difficulty emits his stertorous breathing; his blue, leaden eyes are rolled up, and from beneath the wadded coverlet the remains of his right arm, enveloped in bandages, protrude. The oppressive odor of a corpse strikes you forcibly, and the consuming, internal fire which has penetrated every limb of the sufferer seems to penetrate you also.

"Is he unconscious?" you inquire of the woman, who comes up to you and gazes at you tenderly as at a relative.

"No, he can still hear, but he's very bad," she adds, in a whisper. "I gave him some tea to-day,—what if he is a stranger, one must still have pity!—and he hardly tasted it."

"How do you feel?" you ask him.

The wounded man turns his eyeballs at the sound of your voice, but he neither sees nor understands you.

"There's a gnawing at my heart."

A little further on, you see an old soldier changing his linen. His face and body are of a sort of cinnamon-brown color, and gaunt as a skeleton. He has no arm at all; it has been cut off at the shoulder. He is sitting with a wide-awake air, he puts himself to rights; but you see, by his dull, corpse-like gaze, his frightful gauntness, and the wrinkles on his face, that he is a being who has suffered for the best part of his life.

On the other side, you behold in a cot the pale, suffering, and delicate face of a woman, upon whose cheek plays a feverish flush.

"That's our little sailor lass who was struck in the leg by a bomb on the 5th," your guide tells you. "She was carrying her husband's dinner to him in the bastion."

"Has it been amputated?"

"They cut it off above the knee."

Now, if your nerves are strong, pass through the door on the left. In yonder room they are applying bandages and performing operations. There, you will see doctors with their arms blood-stained above the elbow, and with pale, stern faces, busied about a cot, upon which, with eyes widely opened, and uttering, as in delirium, incoherent, sometimes simple and touching words, lies a wounded man under the influence of chloroform. The doctors are busy with the repulsive but beneficent work of amputation. You see the sharp, curved knife enter the healthy, white body, you see the wounded man suddenly regain consciousness with a piercing cry and curses, you see the army surgeon fling the amputated arm into a corner, you see another wounded man, lying in a litter in the same apartment, shrink convulsively and groan as he gazes at the operation upon his comrade, not so much from physical pain as from the moral torture of anticipation.—You behold the frightful, soul-stirring scenes; you behold war, not from its conventional, beautiful, and brilliant side, with music and drum-beat, with fluttering flags and galloping generals, but you behold war in its real phase—in blood, in suffering, in death.

On emerging from this house of pain, you will infallibly experience a sensation of pleasure, you will inhale the fresh air more fully, you will feel satisfaction in the consciousness of your health, but, at the same time, you will draw from the sight of these sufferings a consciousness of your nothingness, and you will go calmly and without any indecision to the bastion.

"What do the death and sufferings of such an insignificant worm as I signify in comparison with so many deaths and such great sufferings?" But the sight of the clear sky, the brilliant sun, the fine city, the open church, and the soldiers moving about in various directions soon restores your mind to its normal condition of frivolity, petty cares, and absorption in the present alone.

Perhaps you meet the funeral procession of some officer coming from the church, with rose-colored coffin, and music and fluttering banners; perhaps the sounds of firing reach your ear from the bastion, but this does not lead you back to your former thoughts; the funeral seems to you a very fine military spectacle, and you do not connect with this spectacle, or with the sounds, any clear idea of suffering and death, as you did at the point where the bandaging was going on.

Passing the barricade and the church, you come to the most lively part of the city. On both sides hang the signs of shops and inns. Merchants, women in bonnets and kerchiefs, dandified officers,—everything speaks to you of the firmness of spirit, of the independence and the security of the inhabitants.

Enter the inn on the right if you wish to hear the conversations of sailors and officers; stories of the preceding night are sure to be in progress there, and of Fenka, and the affair of the 24th, and of the dearness and badness of cutlets, and of such and such a comrade who has been killed.

"Devil take it, how bad things are with us to-day!" ejaculates the bass voice of a beardless naval officer, with white brows and lashes, in a green knitted sash.

"Where?" asks another.

"In the fourth bastion," replies the young officer, and you are certain to look at the white-lashed officer with great attention, and even with some respect, at the words, "in the fourth bastion." His excessive ease of manner, the way he flourishes his hands, his loud laugh, and his voice, which seems to you insolent, reveal to you that peculiar boastful frame of mind which some very young men acquire after danger; nevertheless, you think he is about to tell you how bad the condition of things on the fourth bastion is because of the bombs and balls. Nothing of the sort! things are bad because it is muddy.

"It's impossible to pass through the battery," says he, pointing at his boots, which are covered with mud above the calf. "And my best gun-captain was killed to-day; he was struck plump in the forehead," says another. "Who's that? Mitiukhin?" "No!... What now, are they going to give me any veal? the villains!" he adds to the servant of the inn. "Not Mitiukhin, but Abrosimoff. Such a fine young fellow!—he was in the sixth sally."

At another corner of the table, over a dish of cutlets with peas, and a bottle of sour Crimean wine called "Bordeaux," sit two infantry officers; one with a red collar, who is young and has two stars on his coat, is telling the other, with a black collar and no stars, about the affair at Alma. The former has already drunk a good deal, and it is evident, from the breaks in his narrative, from his undecided glance expressive of doubt as to whether he is believed, and chiefly from the altogether too prominent part which he has played in it all, and from the excessive horror of it all, that he is strongly disinclined to bear strict witness to the truth. But these tales, which you will hear for a long time to come in every corner of Russia, are nothing to you; you prefer to go to the bastions, especially to the fourth, of which you have heard so many and such diverse things. When any one says that he has been in the fourth bastion, he says it with a peculiar air of pride and satisfaction; when any one says, "I am going to the fourth bastion," either a little agitation or a very great indifference is infallibly perceptible in him; when any one wants to jest about another, he says, "You must be stationed in the fourth bastion;" when you meet litters and inquire whence they come, the answer is generally, "From the fourth bastion." On the whole, two totally different opinions exist with regard to this terrible bastion; one is held by those who have never been in it, and who are convinced that the fourth bastion is a regular grave for every one who enters it, and the other by those who live in it, like the white-lashed midshipman, and who, when they mention the fourth bastion, will tell you whether it is dry or muddy there, whether it is warm or cold in the mud hut, and so forth.

During the half-hour which you have passed in the inn, the weather has changed; a fog which before spread over the sea has collected into damp, heavy, gray clouds, and has veiled the sun; a kind of melancholy, frozen mist

17

sprinkles from above, and wets the roofs, the sidewalks, and the soldiers' overcoats.

Passing by yet another barricade, you emerge from the door at the right and ascend the principal street. Behind this barricade, the houses are unoccupied on both sides of the street, there are no signs, the doors are covered with boards, the windows are broken in; here the corners are broken away, there the roofs are pierced. The buildings seem to be old, to have undergone every sort of vicissitude and deprivation characteristic of veterans, and appear to gaze proudly and somewhat scornfully upon you. You stumble over the cannon-balls which strew the way, and into holes filled with water, which have been excavated in the stony ground by the bombs. In the street you meet and overtake bodies of soldiers, sharpshooters, officers; now and then you encounter a woman or a child, but it is no longer a woman in a bonnet, but a sailor's daughter in an old fur cloak and soldier's boots. As you proceed along the street, and descend a small declivity, you observe that there are no longer any houses about you, but only some strange heaps of ruined stones, boards, clay, and beams; ahead of you, upon a steep hill, you perceive a black, muddy expanse, intersected by canals, and this that is in front is the fourth bastion. Here you meet still fewer people, no women are visible, the soldiers walk briskly, you come across drops of blood on the road, and you will certainly encounter there four soldiers with a stretcher and upon the stretcher a pale yellowish face and a blood-stained overcoat. If you inquire, "Where is he wounded?" the bearers will say angrily, without turning towards you, "In the leg or the arm," if he is slightly wounded, or they will preserve a gloomy silence if no head is visible on the stretcher and he is already dead or badly hurt.

The shriek of a cannon-ball or a bomb close by surprises you unpleasantly, as you ascend the hill. You understand all at once, and quite differently from what you have before, the significance of those sounds of shots which you heard in the city. A quietly cheerful memory flashes suddenly before your fancy; your own personality begins to occupy you more than your observations; your attention to all that surrounds you diminishes, and a certain disagreeable feeling of uncertainty suddenly overmasters you. In spite

18

of this decidedly base voice, which suddenly speaks within you, at the sight of danger, you force it to be silent, especially when you glance at a soldier who runs laughing past you at a trot, waving his hands, and slipping down the hill in the mud, and you involuntarily expand your chest, throw up your head a little higher, and climb the slippery, clayey hill. As soon as you have reached the top, rifle-balls begin to whiz to the right and left of you, and, possibly, you begin to reflect whether you will not go into the trench which runs parallel with the road; but this trench is full of such yellow, liquid, foul-smelling mud, more than knee-deep, that you will infallibly choose the path on the hill, the more so as you see that every one uses the path. After traversing a couple of hundred paces, you emerge upon a muddy expanse, all ploughed up, and surrounded on all sides by gabions, earthworks, platforms, earth huts, upon which great cast-iron guns stand, and cannon-balls lie in symmetrical heaps. All these seem to be heaped up without any aim, connection, or order. Here in the battery sit a knot of sailors; there in the middle of the square, half buried in mud, lies a broken cannon; further on, a foot-soldier, with his gun, is marching through the battery, and dragging his feet with difficulty through the sticky soil. But everywhere, on all sides, in every spot, you see broken dishes, unexploded bombs, cannon-balls, signs of encampment, all sunk in the liquid, viscous mud. You seem to hear not far from you the thud of a cannon-ball; on all sides, you seem to hear the varied sounds of balls,—humming like bees, whistling sharply, or in a whine like a cord—you hear the frightful roar of the fusillade, which seems to shake you all through with some horrible fright.

"So this is it, the fourth bastion, this is it—that terrible, really frightful place!" you think to yourself, and you experience a little sensation of pride, and a very large sensation of suppressed terror. But you are mistaken, this is not the fourth bastion. It is the Yazonovsky redoubt—a place which is comparatively safe; and not at all dreadful.

In order to reach the fourth bastion, you turn to the right, through this narrow trench, through which the foot-soldier has gone. In this trench you will perhaps meet stretchers again, sailors and soldiers with shovels; you will see the superintendent of the mines, mud huts, into which only two men can crawl by bending down, and there you will see sharpshooters of the Black Sea battalions, who are changing their shoes, eating, smoking their pipes, and living; and you will still see everywhere that same stinking mud, traces of a camp, and cast-off iron débris in every possible form. Proceeding yet three hundred paces, you will emerge again upon a battery,—on an open space, all cut up into holes and surrounded by gabions, covered with earth, cannon, and earthworks. Here you will perhaps see five sailors playing cards under the shelter of the breastworks, and a naval officer who, perceiving that you are a new-comer, and curious, will with pleasure show his household arrangements, and everything which may be of interest to you.

This officer rolls himself a cigarette of yellow paper, with so much composure as he sits on a gun, walks so calmly from one embrasure to another, converses with you so quietly, without the slightest affectation, that, in spite of the bullets which hum above you even more thickly than before, you become cool yourself, question attentively, and listen to the officer's replies.

This officer will tell you, but only if you ask him, about the bombardment on the 5th, he will tell you how only one gun in his battery could be used, and out of all the gunners who served it only eight remained, and how, nevertheless, on the next morning, the 6th, he fired all the guns; he will tell you how a bomb fell upon a sailor's earth hut on the 5th, and laid low eleven men; he will point out to you, from the embrasures, the enemy's batteries and entrenchments, which are not more than thirty or forty fathoms distant from this point. I fear, however, that, under the influence of the whizzing bullets, you may thrust yourself out of the embrasure in order to view the enemy; you will see nothing, and, if you do see anything, you will be very much surprised that that white stone wall, which is so near you and from which white smoke rises in puffs,—that that white wall is the enemy—he, as the soldiers and sailors say.

It is even quite possible that the naval officer will want to discharge a shot or two in your presence, out of vanity or simply for his own pleasure. "Send the captain and his crew to the cannon;" and fourteen sailors step up briskly and merrily to the gun and load it—one thrusting his pipe into his pocket, another one chewing a biscuit, still another clattering his heels on the platform.

Observe the faces, the bearing, the movements of these men. In every wrinkle of that sunburned face, with its high cheek-bones, in every muscle, in the breadth of those shoulders, in the stoutness of those legs shod in huge boots, in every calm, firm, deliberate gesture, these chief traits which constitute the power of Russia—simplicity and straightforwardness—are visible; but here, on every face, it seems to you that the danger, misery, and the sufferings of war have, in addition to these principal characteristics, left traces of consciousness of personal worth, emotion, and exalted thought.

All at once a frightful roar, which shakes not your organs of hearing alone but your whole being, startles you so that you tremble all over. Then you hear the distant shriek of the shot as it pursues its course, and the dense smoke of the powder conceals from you the platform and the black figures of the sailors who are moving about upon it. You hear various remarks of the sailors in reference to this shot, and you see their animation, and an exhibition of a feeling which you had not expected to behold perhaps—a feeling of malice, of revenge against the enemy, which lies hidden in the soul of each man. "It struck the embrasure itself; it seems to have killed two men—see, they've carried them off!" you hear in joyful exclamation. "And now they are angry; they'll fire at us directly," says some one; and, in fact, shortly after you see a flash in front and smoke; the sentry, who is standing on the breastwork, shouts "Can-non!" And then the ball shrieks past you, strikes the earth, and scatters a shower of dirt and stones about it.

This ball enrages the commander of the battery; he orders a second and a third gun to be loaded, the enemy also begins to reply to us, and you experience a sensation of interest, you hear and see interesting things. Again the sentry shouts, "Can-non!" and you hear the same report and blow, the same shower, or he shouts "Mortar!" and you hear the monotonous, even rather pleasant whistle of the bomb, with which it is difficult to connect the thought of horror; you hear this whistle approaching you, and increasing in swiftness, then you see the black sphere, the impact on the ground, the resounding explosion of the bomb which can be felt. With the whistle and shriek, splinters fly again, stones whiz through the air, and mud showers over you. At these sounds you experience a strange feeling of enjoyment, and, at the same time, of terror. At the moment when you know that the projectile is flying towards you, it will infallibly occur to you that this shot will kill you; but the feeling of self-love upholds you, and no one perceives the knife which is cutting your heart. But when the shot has flown past without touching you, you grow animated, and a certain cheerful, inexpressibly pleasant feeling overpowers you, but only for a moment, so that you discover a peculiar sort of charm in danger, in this game of life and death, you want cannon-balls or bombs to strike nearer to you.

But again the sentry has shouted in his loud, thick voice, "Mortar!" again there is a shriek, and a bomb bursts, but with this noise comes the groan of a man. You approach the wounded man, at the same moment with the bearers; he has a strange, inhuman aspect, covered as he is with blood and mud. A part of the sailor's breast has been torn away. During the first moments, there is visible on his mud-stained face only fear and a certain simulated, premature expression of suffering, peculiar to men in that condition; but, at the same time, as the stretcher is brought to him and he is laid upon it on his sound side, you observe that this expression is replaced by an expression of a sort of exaltation and lofty, inexpressible thought. His eyes shine more brilliantly, his teeth are clenched, his head is held higher with difficulty, and, as they lift him up, he stops the bearers and says to his comrades, with difficulty and in a trembling voice: "Farewell, brothers!" He tries to say something more, and it is plain that he wants to say something touching, but he repeats once more: "Farewell, brothers!"

At that moment, one of his fellow-sailors steps up to him, puts the cap on the head which the wounded man holds towards him, and, waving his hand indifferently, returns calmly to his gun. "That's the way with seven or eight men every day," says the naval officer to you, in reply to the expression of horror which has appeared upon your countenance, as he yawns and rolls a cigarette of yellow paper.

Thus you have seen the defenders of Sevastopol, on the very scene of the defence, and you go back paying no attention, for some reason or other, to the cannon-balls and bullets, which continue to shriek the whole way until you reach the ruined theatre,—you proceed with composure, and with your soul in a state of exaltation.

The principal and cheering conviction which you have brought away is the conviction of the impossibility of the Russian people wavering anywhere whatever—and this impossibility you have discerned not in the multitude of traverses, breastworks, artfully interlaced trenches, mines, and ordnance, piled one upon the other, of which you have comprehended nothing; but you have discerned it in the eyes, the speech, the manners, in what is called the spirit of the defenders of Sevastopol. What they are doing they do so simply, with so little effort and exertion, that you are convinced that they can do a hundred times more—that they can do anything. You understand that the feeling which makes them work is not a feeling of pettiness, ambition, forgetfulness, which you have yourself experienced, but a different sentiment, one more powerful, and one which has made of them men who live with their ordinary composure under the fire of cannon, amid hundreds of chances of death, instead of the one to which all men are subject who live under these conditions amid incessant labor, poverty, and dirt. Men will not accept these frightful conditions for the sake of a cross or a title, nor because of threats; there must be another lofty incentive as a cause, and this cause is the feeling which rarely appears, of which a Russian is ashamed, that which lies at the bottom of each man's soul—love for his country.

Only now have the tales of the early days of the siege of Sevastopol, when there were no fortifications there, no army, no physical possibility of holding it, and when at the same time there was not the slightest doubt that it would not surrender to the enemy,—of the days when that hero worthy of ancient Greece, Korniloff, said, as he reviewed the army: "We will die, children, but we will not surrender Sevastopol;" and our Russians, who are not fitted to be phrase-makers, replied: "We will die! hurrah!"—only now have tales of that time ceased to be for you the most beautiful historical legends, and have become real facts and worthy of belief. You comprehend clearly, you figure to yourself, those men whom you have just seen, as the very heroes of those grievous times, who have not fallen, but have been raised by the spirit, and have joyfully prepared for death, not for the sake of the city, but of the country. This epos of Sevastopol, whose hero was the Russian people, will leave mighty traces in Russia for a long time to come.

Night is already falling. The sun has emerged from the gray clouds, which cover the sky just before its setting, and has suddenly illuminated with a crimson glow the purple vapors, the greenish sea covered with ships and boats rocking on the regular swell, and the white buildings of the city, and the people who are moving through its streets. Sounds of some old waltz played by the regimental band on the boulevard, and the sounds of firing from the bastions, which echo them strangely, are borne across the water.

FOOTNOTES:

[A] The vessel Constantine.

[B] A drink made of water, molasses, laurel-leaves or salvia, which is drunk like tea, especially by the lower classes.

SEVASTOPOL IN MAY, 1855.

I.

Six months have already passed since the first cannon-ball whistled from the bastions of Sevastopol, and ploughed the earth in the works of the enemy, and since that day thousands of bombs, cannon-balls, and rifle-balls have been flying incessantly from the bastions into the trenches and from the trenches into the bastions, and the angel of death has never ceased to hover over them.

Thousands of men have been disappointed in satisfying their ambition; thousands have succeeded in satisfying theirs, in becoming swollen with pride; thousands repose in the embrace of death. How many red coffins and canvas canopies there have been! And still the same sounds are echoed from the bastions, and still on clear evenings the French peer from their camp, with involuntary tremor, at the yellow, furrowed bastions of Sevastopol, at the black forms of our sailors moving about upon them, and count the embrasures and the iron cannon which project angrily from them; the under officer still gazes through his telescope, from the heights of the telegraph station, at the dark figures of the French at their batteries, at their tents, at the columns moving over the green hill, and at the puffs of smoke which issue forth from the trenches,—and a crowd of men, formed of divers races, still streams in throngs from various quarters, with the same ardor as ever, and with desires differing even more greatly than their races, towards this fateful spot. And the question, unsolved by the diplomats, has still not been solved by powder and blood.

II.

On the boulevard of the besieged city of Sevastopol, not far from the pavilion, the regimental band was playing, and throngs of military men and of women moved gayly through the streets. The brilliant sun of spring had risen in the morning over the works of the English, had passed over the bastions, then over the city, over the Nikolaevsky barracks, and, illuminating all with equal cheer, had now sunk into the blue and distant sea, which was lighted with a silvery gleam as it heaved in peace.

A tall, rather bent infantry officer, who was drawing upon his hand a glove which was presentable, if not entirely white, came out of one of the small naval huts, built on the left side of the Morskaya[C] street, and, staring thoughtfully at the ground, took his way up the slope to the boulevard.

The expression of this officer's homely countenance did not indicate any great mental capacity, but rather simplicity, judgment, honor, and a tendency to solid worth. He was badly built, not graceful, and he seemed to be constrained in his movements. He was dressed in a little worn cap, a cloak of a rather peculiar shade of lilac, from beneath whose edge the gold of a watch-chain was visible; in trousers with straps, and brilliantly polished calfskin boots. He must have been either a German—but his features clearly indicate his purely Russian descent—or an adjutant, or a regimental quartermaster, only in that case he would have had spurs, or an officer who had exchanged from the cavalry for the period of the campaign, or possibly from the Guards. He was, in fact, an officer who had exchanged from the cavalry, and as he ascended the boulevard, at the present moment, he was meditating upon a letter which he had just received from a former comrade, now a retired land-owner in the Government of T., and his wife, pale, blue-eyed Natasha, his great friend. He recalled one passage of the letter, in which his comrade said:—

"When our Invalid[D] arrives, Pupka (this was the name by which the retired uhlan called his wife) rushes headlong into the vestibule, seizes the paper, and runs with it to the seat in the arbor, in the drawing-room (in which, if you remember, you and I passed such delightful winter evenings when the regiment was stationed in our town), and reads your heroic deeds with such ardor as it is impossible for you to imagine. She often speaks of you. 'There is Mikhaïloff,' she says, 'he's such a love of a man. I am ready to kiss him when I see him. He fights on the bastions, and he will surely receive the Cross of St. George, and he will be talked about in the newspapers ...' and so on, and so on ... so that I am really beginning to be jealous of you."

In another place he writes: "The papers reach us frightfully late, and, although there is plenty of news conveyed by word of mouth, not all of it can be trusted. For instance, the young ladies with the music, acquaintances of yours, were saying yesterday that Napoleon was already captured by our Cossacks, and that he had been sent to Petersburg; but you will comprehend how much I believe of this. Moreover, a traveller from Petersburg told us (he has been sent on special business by the minister, is a very agreeable person, and, now that there is no one in town, he is more of a resource to us than you can well imagine ...) well, he declares it to be a fact that our troops have taken Eupatoria, so that the French have no communication whatever with Balaklava, and that in this engagement two hundred of ours were killed, but that the French lost fifteen thousand. My wife was in such raptures over this that she caroused all night, and she declares that her instinct tells her that you certainly took part in that affair, and that you distinguished yourself."

In spite of these words, and of the expressions which I have purposely put in italics, and the whole tone of the letter, Staff-Captain Mikhaïloff recalled, with inexpressibly sad delight, his pale friend in the provinces, and how she had sat with him in the arbor in the evening, and talked about sentiment, and he thought of his good comrade, the uhlan, and of how the latter had grown angry and had lost the game when they had played cards for kopek stakes in his study, and how the wife had laughed at them ... he recalled the friendship of these two people for himself (perhaps it seemed to him to lie chiefly on the side of his pale feminine friend); all these faces with their surroundings flitted before his mind's eye, in a wonderfully sweet, cheerfully rosy light, and, smiling at his reminiscences, he placed his hand on the pocket which contained the letter so dear to him.

From reminiscences Captain Mikhaïloff involuntarily proceeded to dreams and hopes. "And what will be the joy and amazement of Natasha," he thought, as he paced along the narrow lane, "... when she suddenly reads in the Invalid a description of how I was the first to climb upon the cannon, and that I have received the George! I shall certainly be promoted to a full captaincy, by virtue of seniority. Then it is quite possible that I may get the grade of major in the line, this very year, because many of our brothers have already been killed, and many more will be in this campaign. And after that there will be more affairs on hand, and a regiment will be entrusted to me, since I am an experienced man ... lieutenant-colonel ... the Order of St. Anna on my neck ... colonel!..." and he was already a general, granting an interview to Natasha, the widow of his comrade, who, according to his dreams, would have died by that time, when the sounds of the music on the boulevard penetrated more distinctly to his ears, the crowds of people caught his eye, and he found himself on the boulevard, a staff-captain of infantry as before.

III.

He went, first of all, to the pavilion, near which were standing the musicians, for whom other soldiers of the same regiment were holding the notes, in the absence of stands, and about whom a ring of cadets, nurses, and children had formed, intent rather on seeing than on hearing. Around the pavilion stood, sat, or walked sailors, adjutants, and officers in white gloves. Along the grand avenue of the boulevard paced officers of every sort, and women of every description, rarely in bonnets, mostly with kerchiefs on their heads (some had neither bonnets nor kerchiefs), but no one was old, and it was worthy of note that all were gay young creatures. Beyond, in the shady and fragrant alleys of white acacia, isolated groups walked and sat.

No one was especially delighted to encounter Captain Mikhaïloff on the boulevard, with the exception, possibly, of the captain of his regiment, Obzhogoff, and Captain Suslikoff, who pressed his hand warmly; but the former was dressed in camel's-hair trousers, no gloves, a threadbare coat, and his face was very red and covered with perspiration, and the second shouted so loudly and incoherently that it was mortifying to walk with them, particularly in the presence of the officers in white gloves (with one of whom, an adjutant, Staff-Captain Mikhaïloff exchanged bows; and he might have bowed to another staff-officer, since he had met him twice at the house of a mutual acquaintance). Besides, what pleasure was it to him to promenade with these two gentlemen, Obzhogoff and Suslikoff, when he had met them and shaken hands with them six times that day already? It was not for this that he had come.

He wanted to approach the adjutant with whom he had exchanged bows, and to enter into conversation with these officers, not for the sake of letting Captains Obzhogoff and Suslikoff and Lieutenant Pashtetzky see him talking with them, but simply because they were agreeable people, and, what was more, they knew the news, and would have told it.

But why is Captain Mikhaïloff afraid, and why cannot he make up his mind to approach them? "What if they should, all at once, refuse to recognize me," he thinks, "or, having bowed to me, what if they continue their conversation among themselves, as though I did not exist, or walk away from me entirely, and leave me standing there alone among the aristocrats." The word aristocrats (in the sense of a higher, select circle, in any rank of life) has acquired for some time past with us, in Russia, a great popularity, and has penetrated into every locality and into every class of society whither vanity has penetrated—among merchants, among officials, writers, and officers, to Saratoff, to Mamaduish, to Vinnitz, everywhere where men exist.

To Captain Obzhogoff, Staff-Captain Mikhaïloff was an aristocrat. To Staff-Captain Mikhaïloff, Adjutant Kalugin was an aristocrat, because he was an adjutant, and was on such a footing with the other adjutants as to call them "thou"! To Adjutant Kalugin, Count Nordoff was an aristocrat, because he was an adjutant on the Emperor's staff.

Vanity! vanity! and vanity everywhere, even on the brink of the grave, and among men ready to die for the highest convictions. Vanity! It must be that it is a characteristic trait, and a peculiar malady of our century. Why was nothing ever heard among the men of former days, of this passion, any more than of the small-pox or the cholera? Why did Homer and Shakespeare talk of love, of glory, of suffering, while the literature of our age is nothing but an endless narrative of snobs and vanity?

The staff-captain walked twice in indecision past the group of his aristocrats, and the third time he exerted an effort over himself and went up to them. This group consisted of four officers: Adjutant Kalugin, an acquaintance of Mikhaïloff's, Adjutant Prince Galtsin, who was something of an aristocrat even for Kalugin himself, Colonel Neferdoff, one of the so-called hundred and twenty-two men of the world (who had entered the service for this campaign, from the retired list), and Captain of Cavalry Praskukhin, also one of the hundred and twenty-two. Luckily for Mikhaïloff, Kalugin was in a very fine humor (the general had just been talking to him in a very confidential way, and Prince Galtsin, who had just arrived from Petersburg, was stopping with him); he did not consider it beneath his dignity to give his hand to Captain Mikhaïloff, which Praskukhin, however, could not make up his mind to do, though he had met Mikhaïloff very frequently on the bastion, had drunk the latter's wine and vodka, and was even indebted to him twenty rubles and a half at preference. As he did not yet know Prince Galtsin very well, he did not wish to convict himself, in the latter's presence, of an acquaintance with a simple staff-captain of infantry. He bowed slightly to the latter.

"Well, Captain," said Kalugin, "when are we to go to the bastion again? Do you remember how we met each other on the Schvartz redoubt—it was hot there, hey?"

"Yes, it was hot," said Mikhaïloff, recalling how he had, that night, as he was making his way along the trenches to the bastion, encountered Kalugin, who was walking along like a hero, valiantly clanking his sword. "I ought to have gone there to-morrow, according to present arrangements; but we have a sick man," pursued Mikhaïloff, "one officer, as...."

He was about to relate how it was not his turn, but, as the commander of the eighth company was ill, and the company had only a cornet left, he had regarded it as his duty to offer himself in the place of Lieutenant Nepshisetzky, and was, therefore, going to the bastion to-day. But Kalugin did not hear him out.

"I have a feeling that something is going to happen within a few days," he said to Prince Galtsin.

"And won't there be something to-day?" asked Mikhaïloff, glancing first at Kalugin, then at Galtsin.

No one made him any reply. Prince Galtsin merely frowned a little, sent his eyes past the other's cap, and, after maintaining silence for a moment, said:—

"That's a magnificent girl in the red kerchief. You don't know her, do you, captain?"

"She lives near my quarters; she is the daughter of a sailor," replied the staff-captain.

"Come on; let's have a good look at her."

And Prince Galtsin linked one arm in that of Kalugin, the other in that of the staff-captain, being convinced in advance that he could afford the latter no greater gratification, which was, in fact, quite true.

The staff-captain was superstitious, and considered it a great sin to occupy himself with women before a battle; but on this occasion he feigned to be a vicious man, which Prince Galtsin and Kalugin evidently did not believe, and which greatly amazed the girl in the red kerchief, who had more than once observed how the staff-captain blushed as he passed her little window. Praskukhin walked behind, and kept touching Prince Galtsin with his hand, and making various remarks in the French tongue; but as a fourth person could not walk on the small path, he was obliged to walk alone, and it was only on the second round that he took the arm of the brave and well known naval officer Servyagin, who had stepped up and spoken to him, and who was also desirous of joining the circle of aristocrats. And the gallant and famous beau joyfully thrust his honest and muscular hand through the elbow of a man who was known to all, and even well known to Servyagin, as not too nice. When Praskukhin, explaining to the prince his acquaintance with that sailor, whispered to him that the latter was well known for his bravery, Prince Galtsin, having been on the fourth bastion on the previous evening, having seen a bomb burst twenty paces from him, considering himself no less a hero than this gentleman, and thinking that many a reputation is acquired undeservedly, paid no particular attention to Servyagin.

It was so agreeable to Staff-Captain Mikhaïloff to walk about in this company that he forgot the dear letter from T——, and the gloomy thoughts which had assailed him in connection with his impending departure for the bastion. He remained with them until they began to talk exclusively among themselves, avoiding his glances, thereby giving him to understand

31

that he might go, and finally deserted him entirely. But the staff-captain was content, nevertheless, and as he passed Yunker[E] Baron Pesth, who had been particularly haughty and self-conceited since the preceding night, which was the first that he had spent in the bomb-proof of the fifth bastion, and consequently considered himself a hero, he was not in the least offended at the presumptuous expression with which the yunker straightened himself up and doffed his hat before him.

IV.

When later the staff-captain crossed the threshold of his quarters, entirely different thoughts entered his mind. He looked around his little chamber, with its uneven earth floor, and saw the windows all awry, pasted over with paper, his old bed, with a rug nailed over it, upon which was depicted a lady on horseback, and over which hung two Tula pistols, the dirty couch of a cadet who lived with him, and which was covered with a chintz coverlet; he saw his Nikita, who, with untidy, tallowed hair, rose from the floor, scratching his head; he saw his ancient cloak, his extra pair of boots, and a little bundle, from which peeped a bit of cheese and the neck of a porter bottle filled with vodka, which had been prepared for his use on the bastion, and all at once he remembered that he was obliged to go with his company that night to the fortifications.

"It is certainly foreordained that I am to be killed to-night," thought the captain.... "I feel it. And the principal point is that I need not have gone, but that I offered myself. And the man who thrusts himself forward is always killed. And what's the matter with that accursed Nepshisetsky? It is quite possible that he is not sick at all; and they will kill another man for his sake, they will infallibly kill him. However, if they don't kill me, I shall be promoted probably. I saw how delighted the regimental commander was when I asked him to allow me to go, if Lieutenant Nepshisetsky was ill. If I don't turn out a major, then I shall certainly get the Vladímir cross. This is the thirteenth time that I have been to the bastion. Ah, the thirteenth is an unlucky number. They will surely kill me, I feel that I shall be killed; but some one had to go, it was impossible for the lieutenant of the corps to go. And, whatever happens, the honor of the regiment, the honor of the army, depends on it. It was my duty to go ... yes, my sacred duty. But I have a foreboding."

The captain forgot that this was not the first time that a similar foreboding had assailed him, in a greater or less degree, when it had been necessary to go to the bastion, and he did not know that every one who sets out on an affair experiences this foreboding with more or less force. Having calmed himself with this conception of duty, which was especially and strongly developed in the staff-captain, he seated himself at the table, and began to write a farewell letter to his father. Ten minutes later, having finished his letter, he rose from the table, his eyes wet with tears, and, mentally reciting all the prayers he knew, he set about dressing. His coarse, drunken servant indolently handed him his new coat (the old one, which the captain generally wore when going to the bastion, was not mended).

"Why is not my coat mended? You never do anything but sleep, you good-for-nothing!" said Mikhaïloff, angrily.

"Sleep!" grumbled Nikita. "You run like a dog all day long; perhaps you stop—but you must not sleep, even then!"

"You are drunk again, I see."

"I didn't get drunk on your money, so you needn't scold."

"Hold your tongue, blockhead!" shouted the captain, who was ready to strike the man. He had been absent-minded at first, but now he was, at last, out of patience, and embittered by the rudeness of Nikita, whom he loved, even spoiled, and who had lived with him for twelve years.

"Blockhead? Blockhead?" repeated the servant. "Why do you call me a blockhead, sir? Is this a time for that sort of thing? It is not good to curse."

Mikhaïloff recalled whither he was on the point of going, and felt ashamed of himself.

"You are enough to put a saint out of patience, Nikita," he said, in a gentle voice. "Leave that letter to my father on the table, and don't touch it," he added, turning red.

"Yes, sir," said Nikita, melting under the influence of the wine which he had drunk, as he had said, "at his own expense," and winking his eyes with a visible desire to weep.

But when the captain said: "Good-by, Nikita," on the porch, Nikita suddenly broke down into repressed sobs, and ran to kiss his master's hand.... "Farewell, master!" he exclaimed, sobbing. The old sailor's wife, who was standing on the porch, could not, in her capacity of a woman, refrain from joining in this touching scene, so she began to wipe her eyes with her dirty sleeve, and to say something about even gentlemen having their trials to bear, and that she, poor creature, had been left a widow. And she related for the hundredth time to drunken Nikita the story of her woes; how her husband had been killed in the first bombardment, and how her little house had been utterly ruined (the one in which she was now living did not belong to her), and so on. When his master had departed, Nikita lighted his pipe, requested the daughter of their landlord to go for some vodka, and very soon ceased to weep, but, on the contrary, got into a quarrel with the old woman about some small bucket, which, he declared, she had broken.

"But perhaps I shall only be wounded," meditated the captain, as he marched through the twilight to the bastion with his company. "But where? How? Here or here?" he thought, indicating his belly and his breast.... "If it should be here (he thought of the upper portion of his leg), it might run round. Well, but if it were here, and by a splinter, that would finish me."

The captain reached the fortifications safely through the trenches, set his men to work, with the assistance of an officer of sappers, in the darkness, which was complete, and seated himself in a pit behind the breastworks. There was not much firing; only once in a while the lightning flashed from our batteries, then from his, and the brilliant fuse of a bomb traced an arc of flame against the dark, starry heavens. But all the bombs fell far in the rear and to the right of the rifle-pits in which the captain sat. He drank his vodka, ate his cheese, lit his cigarette, and, after saying his prayers, he tried to get a little sleep.

V.

Prince Galtsin, Lieutenant-Colonel Neferdoff, and Praskukhin, whom no one had invited, to whom no one spoke, but who never left them, all went to drink tea with Adjutant Kalugin.

"Well, you did not finish telling me about Vaska Mendel," said Kalugin, as he took off his cloak, seated himself by the window in a soft lounging-chair, and unbuttoned the collar of his fresh, stiffly starched cambric shirt: "How did he come to marry?"

"That's a joke, my dear fellow! There was a time, I assure you, when nothing else was talked of in Petersburg," said Prince Galtsin, with a laugh, as he sprang up from the piano, and seated himself on the window beside Kalugin. "It is simply ludicrous, and I know all the details of the affair."

And he began to relate—in a merry, and skilful manner—a love story, which we will omit, because it possesses no interest for us. But it is worthy of note that not only Prince Galtsin, but all the gentlemen who had placed themselves here, one on the window-sill, another with his legs coiled up under him, a third at the piano, seemed totally different persons from what they were when on the boulevard; there was nothing of that absurd arrogance and haughtiness which they and their kind exhibit in public to the infantry officers; here they were among their own set and natural, especially Kalugin and Prince Galtsin, and were like very good, amiable, and merry children. The conversation turned on their companions in the service in Petersburg, and on their acquaintances.

"What of Maslovsky?"

"Which? the uhlan of the body-guard or of the horse-guard?"

"I know both of them. The one in the horse-guards was with me when he was a little boy, and had only just left school. What is the elder one? a captain of cavalry?"

"Oh, yes! long ago."

"And is he still going about with his gypsy maid?"

"No, he has deserted her ..." and so forth, and so forth, in the same strain.

Then Prince Galtsin seated himself at the piano, and sang a gypsy song in magnificent style. Praskukhin began to sing second, although no one had asked him, and he did it so well that they requested him to accompany the prince again, which he gladly consented to do.

The servant came in with the tea, cream, and cracknels on a silver salver.

"Serve the prince," said Kalugin.

"Really, it is strange to think," said Galtsin, taking a glass, and walking to the window, "that we are in a beleaguered city; tea with cream, and such quarters as I should be only too happy to get in Petersburg."

"Yes, if it were not for that," said the old lieutenant-colonel, who was dissatisfied with everything, "this constant waiting for something would be simply unendurable ... and to see how men are killed, killed every day,— and there is no end to it, and under such circumstances it would not be comfortable to live in the mud."

"And how about our infantry officers?" said Kalugin. "They live in the bastions with the soldiers in the casemates and eat beet soup with the soldiers—how about them?"

"How about them? They don't change their linen for ten days at a time, and they are heroes—wonderful men."

At this moment an officer of infantry entered the room.

"I ... I was ordered ... may I present myself to the gen ... to His Excellency from General N.?" he inquired, bowing with an air of embarrassment.

Kalugin rose, but, without returning the officer's salute, he asked him, with insulting courtesy and strained official smile, whether they[F] would not wait awhile; and, without inviting him to be seated or paying any further attention to him, he turned to Prince Galtsin and began to speak to him in French, so that the unhappy officer, who remained standing in the middle of the room, absolutely did not know what to do with himself.

"It is on very important business, sir," said the officer, after a momentary pause.

"Ah! very well, then," said Kalugin, putting on his cloak, and accompanying him to the door.

"Eh bien, messieurs, I think there will be hot work to-night," said Kalugin in French, on his return from the general's.

"Hey? What? A sortie?" They all began to question him.

"I don't know yet—you will see for yourselves," replied Kalugin, with a mysterious smile.

"And my commander is on the bastion—of course, I shall have to go," said Praskukhin, buckling on his sword.

But no one answered him: he must know for himself whether he had to go or not.

Praskukhin and Neferdoff went off, in order to betake themselves to their posts. "Farewell, gentlemen!" "Au revoir, gentlemen! We shall meet again to-night!" shouted Kalugin from the window when Praskukhin and Neferdoff trotted down the street, bending over the bows of their Cossack saddles. The trampling of their Cossack horses soon died away in the dusky street.

"No, tell me, is something really going to take place to-night?" said Galtsin, in French, as he leaned with Kalugin on the window-sill, and gazed at the bombs which were flying over the bastions.

"I can tell you, you see ... you have been on the bastions, of course?" (Galtsin made a sign of assent, although he had been only once to the fourth bastion.) "Well, there was a trench opposite our lunette", and Kalugin, who was not a specialist, although he considered his judgment on military affairs particularly accurate, began to explain the position of our troops and of the enemy's works and the plan of the proposed affair, mixing up the technical terms of fortifications a good deal in the process.

"But they are beginning to hammer away at our casemates. Oho! was that ours or his? there, it has burst," they said, as they leaned on the window-sill, gazing at the fiery line of the bomb, which exploded in the air, at the lightning of the discharges, at the dark blue sky, momentarily illuminated, and at the white smoke of the powder, and listened to the sounds of the firing, which grew louder and louder.

"What a charming sight? is it not?" said Kalugin, in French, directing the attention of his guest to the really beautiful spectacle. "Do you know, you cannot distinguish the stars from the bombs at times."

"Yes, I was just thinking that that was a star; but it darted down ... there, it has burst now. And that big star yonder, what is it called? It is just exactly like a bomb."

"Do you know, I have grown so used to these bombs that I am convinced that a starlight night in Russia will always seem to me to be all bombs; one gets so accustomed to them."

"But am not I to go on this sortie?" inquired Galtsin, after a momentary silence.

"Enough of that, brother! Don't think of such a thing! I won't let you go!" replied Kalugin. "Your turn will come, brother!"

"Seriously? So you think that it is not necessary to go? Hey?..."

At that moment, a frightful crash of rifles was heard in the direction in which these gentlemen were looking, above the roar of the cannon, and thousands of small fires, flaring up incessantly, without intermission, flashed along the entire line.

"That's it, when the real work has begun!" said Kalugin.—"That is the sound of the rifles, and I cannot hear it in cold blood; it takes a sort of hold on your soul, you know. And there is the hurrah!" he added, listening to the prolonged and distant roar of hundreds of voices, "A-a-aa!" which reached him from the bastion.

"What is this hurrah, theirs or ours?"

"I don't know; but it has come to a hand-to-hand fight, for the firing has ceased."

At that moment, an officer followed by his Cossack galloped up to the porch, and slipped down from his horse.

"Where from?"

"From the bastion. The general is wanted."

"Let us go. Well, now, what is it?"

"They have attacked the lodgements ... have taken them ... the French have brought up their heavy reserves ... they have attacked our forces ... there were only two battalions," said the panting officer, who was the same that had come in the evening, drawing his breath with difficulty, but stepping to the door with perfect unconcern.

"Well, have they retreated?" inquired Galtsin.

"No," answered the officer, angrily. "The battalion came up and beat them back; but the commander of the regiment is killed, and many officers, and I have been ordered to ask for re-enforcements...."

And with these words he and Kalugin went off to the general, whither we will not follow them.

Five minutes later, Kalugin was mounted on the Cossack's horse (and with that peculiar, quasi-Cossack seat, in which, as I have observed, all adjutants find something especially captivating, for some reason or other), and rode at a trot to the bastion, in order to give some orders, and to await the news of the final result of the affair. And Prince Galtsin, under the influence of that oppressive emotion which the signs of a battle near at hand usually produce on a spectator who takes no part in it, went out into the street, and began to pace up and down there without any object.

VI.

The soldiers were bearing the wounded on stretchers, and supporting them by their arms. It was completely dark in the streets; now and then, a rare light flashed in the hospital or from the spot where the officers were seated. The same thunder of cannon and exchange of rifle-shots was borne from the bastions, and the same fires flashed against the dark heavens. Now and then, you could hear the trampling hoofs of an orderly's horse, the groan of a wounded man, the footsteps and voices of the stretcher-bearers, or the conversation of some of the frightened female inhabitants, who had come out on their porches to view the cannonade.

Among the latter were our acquaintances Nikita, the old sailor's widow, with whom he had already made his peace, and her ten-year-old daughter. "Lord, Most Holy Mother of God!" whispered the old woman to herself with a sigh, as she watched the bombs, which, like balls of fire, sailed incessantly from one side to the other. "What a shame, what a shame! I-i-hi-hi! It was not so in the first bombardment. See, there it has burst, the cursed thing! right above our house in the suburbs."

"No, it is farther off, in aunt Arinka's garden, that they all fall," said the little girl.

"And where, where is my master now!" said Nikita, with a drawl, for he was still rather drunk. "Oh, how I love that master of mine!—I don't know myself!—I love him so that if, which God forbid, they should kill him in this sinful fight, then, if you will believe it, aunty, I don't know myself what I might do to myself in that case—by Heavens, I don't! He is such a master that words will not do him justice! Would I exchange him for one of those who play cards? That is simply—whew! that's all there is to say!" concluded Nikita, pointing at the lighted window of his master's room, in which, as the staff-captain was absent, Yunker Zhvadchevsky had invited his friends to a carouse, on the occasion of his receiving the cross: Sub-Lieutenant Ugrovitch and Sub-Lieutenant Nepshisetsky, who was ill with a cold in the head.

"Those little stars! They dart through the sky like stars, like stars!" said the little girl, breaking the silence which succeeded Nikita's words. "There, there! another has dropped! Why do they do it, mamma?"

"They will ruin our little cabin entirely," said the old woman, sighing, and not replying to her little daughter's question.

"And when uncle and I went there to-day, mamma," continued the little girl, in a shrill voice, "there was such a big cannon-ball lying in the room, near the cupboard; it had broken through the wall and into the room ... and it is so big that you couldn't lift it."

"Those who had husbands and money have gone away," said the old woman, "and now they have ruined my last little house. See, see how they are firing, the wretches. Lord, Lord!"

"And as soon as we came out, a bomb flew at us, and burst and scattered the earth about, and a piece of the shell came near striking uncle and me."

VII.

Prince Galtsin met more and more wounded men, in stretchers and on foot, supporting each other, and talking loudly.

"When they rushed up, brothers," said one tall soldier, who had two guns on his shoulder, in a bass voice, "when they rushed up and shouted, 'Allah, Allah!'[G] they pressed each other on. You kill one, and another takes his place—you can do nothing. You never saw such numbers as there were of them...."

But at this point in his story Galtsin interrupted him.

"You come from the bastion?"

"Just so, Your Honor!"

"Well, what has been going on there? Tell me."

"Why, what has been going on? They attacked in force, Your Honor; they climbed over the wall, and that's the end of it. They conquered completely, Your Honor."

"How conquered? You repulsed them, surely?"

"How could we repulse them, when he came up with his whole force? They killed all our men, and there was no help given us."

The soldier was mistaken, for the trenches were behind our forces; but this is a peculiar thing, which any one may observe: a soldier who has been wounded in an engagement always thinks that the day has been lost, and that the encounter has been a frightfully bloody one.

"Then, what did they mean by telling me that you had repulsed them?" said Galtsin, with irritation. "Perhaps the enemy was repulsed after you left? Is it long since you came away?"

"I have this instant come from there, Your Honor," replied the soldier. "It is hardly possible. The trenches remained in his hands ... he won a complete victory."

"Well, and are you not ashamed to have surrendered the trenches? This is horrible!" said Galtsin, angered by such indifference.

"What, when he was there in force?" growled the soldier.

"And, Your Honor," said a soldier on a stretcher, who had just come up with them, "how could we help surrendering, when nearly all of us had been killed? If we had been in force, we would only have surrendered with our lives. But what was there to do? I ran one man through, and then I was struck.... O-oh! softly, brothers! steady, brothers! go more steadily!... O-oh!" groaned the wounded man.

"There really seem to be a great many extra men coming this way," said Galtsin, again stopping the tall soldier with the two rifles. "Why are you walking off? Hey there, halt!"

The soldier halted, and removed his cap with his left hand.

"Where are you going, and why?" he shouted at him sternly. "He ..."

But, approaching the soldier very closely at that moment, he perceived that the latter's right arm was bandaged, and covered with blood far above the elbow.

"I am wounded, Your Honor!"

"Wounded? how?"

"It must have been a bullet, here!" said the soldier, pointing at his arm, "but I cannot tell yet. My head has been broken by something," and, bending over, he showed the hair upon the back of it all clotted together with blood.

"And whose gun is that second one you have?"

"A choice French one, Your Honor! I captured it. And I should not have come away if it had not been to accompany this soldier; he might fall down," he added, pointing at the soldier, who was walking a little in front, leaning upon his gun, and dragging his left foot heavily after him.

Prince Galtsin all at once became frightfully ashamed of his unjust suspicions. He felt that he was growing crimson, and turned away, without questioning the wounded men further, and, without looking after them, he went to the place where the injured men were being cared for.

Having forced his way with difficulty to the porch, through the wounded men who had come on foot, and the stretcher-bearers, who were entering with the wounded and emerging with the dead, Galtsin entered the first room, glanced round, and involuntarily turned back, and immediately ran into the street. It was too terrible.

VIII.

The vast, dark, lofty hall, lighted only by the four or five candles, which the doctors were carrying about to inspect the wounded, was literally full. The stretcher-bearers brought in the wounded, ranged them one beside another on the floor, which was already so crowded that the unfortunate wretches hustled each other and sprinkled each other with their blood, and then went forth for more. The pools of blood which were visible on the unoccupied places, the hot breaths of several hundred men, and the steam which rose from those who were toiling with the stretchers produced a peculiar, thick, heavy, offensive atmosphere, in which the candles burned dimly in the different parts of the room. The dull murmur of diverse groans, sighs, death-rattles, broken now and again by a shriek, was borne throughout the apartment. Sisters of charity, with tranquil faces, and with an expression not of empty, feminine, tearfully sickly compassion, but of active, practical sympathy, flitted hither and thither among the blood-stained cloaks and shirts, stepping over the wounded, with medicine, water, bandages, lint.

Doctors, with their sleeves rolled up, knelt beside the wounded, beside whom the assistant surgeons held the candles, inspecting, feeling, and probing the wounds, in spite of the terrible groans and entreaties of the sufferers. One of the doctors was seated at a small table by the door, and, at the moment when Galtsin entered the room, he was just writing down "No. 532."

"Iván Bogaeff, common soldier, third company of the S—— regiment, fractura femoris complicata!" called another from the extremity of the hall, as he felt of the crushed leg.... "Turn him over."

"O-oi, my fathers, good fathers!" shrieked the soldier, beseeching them not to touch him.

"Perforatio capitis."

"Semyon Neferdoff, lieutenant-colonel of the N—— regiment of infantry. Have a little patience, colonel: you can only be attended to this way; I will let you alone," said a third, picking away at the head of the unfortunate colonel, with some sort of a hook.

"Ai! stop! Oi! for God's sake, quick, quick, for the sake a-a-a-a!..."

"Perforatio pectoris ... Sevastyan Sereda, common soldier ... of what regiment? however, you need not write that: moritur. Carry him away," said the doctor, abandoning the soldier, who was rolling his eyes, and already emitting the death-rattle.

Forty stretcher-bearers stood at the door, awaiting the task of transporting to the hospital the men who had been attended to, and the dead to the chapel, and gazed at this picture in silence, only uttering a heavy sigh from time to time....

IX.

On his way to the bastion, Kalugin met numerous wounded men; but, knowing from experience that such a spectacle has a bad effect on the spirits of a man on the verge of an action, he not only did not pause to interrogate them, but, on the contrary, he tried not to pay any heed to them. At the foot of the hill he encountered an orderly, who was galloping from the bastion at full speed.

"Zobkin! Zobkin! Stop a minute!"

"Well, what is it?"

"Where are you from?"

"From the lodgements."

"Well, how are things there! Hot?"

"Ah, frightfully!"

And the orderly galloped on.

In fact, although there was not much firing from the rifles, the cannonade had begun with fresh vigor and greater heat than ever.

"Ah, that's bad!" thought Kalugin, experiencing a rather unpleasant sensation, and there came to him also a presentiment, that is to say, a very usual thought—the thought of death.

But Kalugin was an egotist and gifted with nerves of steel; in a word, he was what is called brave. He did not yield to his first sensation, and began to arouse his courage; he recalled to mind a certain adjutant of Napoleon, who, after having given the command to advance, galloped up to Napoleon, his head all covered with blood.

"You are wounded?" said Napoleon to him. "I beg your pardon, Sire, I am dead,"—and the adjutant fell from his horse, and died on the spot.

This seemed very fine to him, and he fancied that he somewhat resembled this adjutant; then he gave his horse a blow with the whip; and assumed still more of that knowing Cossack bearing, glanced at his orderly, who was galloping behind him, standing upright in his stirrups, and thus in dashing style he reached the place where it was necessary to dismount. Here he found four soldiers, who were smoking their pipes as they sat on the stones.

"What are you doing here?" he shouted at them.

"We have been carrying a wounded man from the field, Your Honor, and have sat down to rest," one of them replied, concealing his pipe behind his back, and pulling off his cap.

"Resting indeed! March off to your posts!"

And, in company with them, he walked up the hill through the trenches, encountering wounded men at every step.

On attaining the crest of the hill, he turned to the left, and, after taking a few steps, found himself quite alone. Splinters whizzed near him, and struck in the trenches. Another bomb rose in front of him, and seemed to be flying straight at him. All of a sudden he felt terrified; he ran off five paces at full speed, and lay down on the ground. But when the bomb burst, and at a distance from him, he grew dreadfully vexed at himself, and glanced about as he rose, to see whether any one had perceived him fall, but there was no one about.

When fear has once made its way into the mind, it does not speedily give way to another feeling. He, who had boasted that he would never bend, hastened along the trench with accelerated speed, and almost on his hands and knees. "Ah! this is very bad!" he thought, as he stumbled. "I shall certainly be killed!" And, conscious of how difficult it was for him to breathe, and that the perspiration was breaking out all over his body, he was amazed at himself, but he no longer strove to conquer his feelings.

All at once steps became audible in advance of him. He quickly straightened himself up, raised his head, and, boldly clanking his sword, began to proceed at a slower pace than before. He did not know himself. When he joined the officer of sappers and the sailor who were coming to meet him, and the former called to him, "Lie down," pointing to the bright speck of a bomb, which, growing ever brighter and brighter, swifter and swifter, as it approached, crashed down in the vicinity of the trench, he only bent his head a very little, involuntarily, under the influence of the terrified shout, and went his way.

"Whew! what a brave man!" ejaculated the sailor, who had calmly watched the exploding bomb, and, with practised glance, at once calculated that its splinters could not strike inside the trench; "he did not even wish to lie down."

Only a few steps remained to be taken, across an open space, before Kalugin would reach the casemate of the commander of the bastion, when he was again attacked by dimness of vision and that stupid sensation of fear; his heart began to beat more violently, the blood rushed to his head, and he was obliged to exert an effort over himself in order to reach the casemate.

"Why are you so out of breath?" inquired the general, when Kalugin had communicated to him his orders.

"I have been walking very fast, Your Excellency!"

"Will you not take a glass of wine?"

Kalugin drank the wine, and lighted a cigarette. The engagement had already come to an end; only the heavy cannonade continued, going on from both sides.

In the casemate sat General N., the commander of the bastion, and six other officers, among whom was Praskukhin, discussing various details of the conflict. Seated in this comfortable apartment, with blue hangings, with a sofa, a bed, a table, covered with papers, a wall clock, and the holy pictures, before which burned a lamp, and gazing upon these signs of habitation, and at the arshin-thick (twenty-eight inches) beams which formed the ceiling, and listening to the shots, which were deadened by the casemate, Kalugin positively could not understand how he had twice permitted himself to be overcome with such unpardonable weakness. He was angry with himself, and he longed for danger, in order that he might subject himself to another trial.

"I am glad that you are here, captain," he said to a naval officer, in the cloak of staff-officer, with a large moustache and the cross of St. George, who entered the casemate at that moment, and asked the general to give him some men, that he might repair the two embrasures on his battery, which had been demolished. "The general ordered me to inquire," continued Kalugin, when the commander of the battery ceased to address the general, "whether your guns can fire grape-shot into the trenches."

"Only one of my guns will do that," replied the captain, gruffly.

"Let us go and see, all the same."

The captain frowned, and grunted angrily:—

"I have already passed the whole night there, and I came here to try and get a little rest," said he. "Cannot you go alone? My assistant, Lieutenant Kartz, is there, and he will show you everything."

The captain had now been for six months in command of this, one of the most dangerous of the batteries—and even when there were no casemates he had lived, without relief, in the bastion and among the sailors, from the beginning of the siege, and he bore a reputation among them for bravery. Therefore his refusal particularly struck and amazed Kalugin. "That's what reputation is worth!" he thought.

"Well, then, I will go alone, if you will permit it," he said, in a somewhat bantering tone to the captain, who, however, paid not the slightest heed to his words.

But Kalugin did not reflect that he had passed, in all, at different times, perhaps fifty hours on the bastion, while the captain had lived there for six months. Kalugin was actuated, moreover, by vanity, by a desire to shine, by the hope of reward, of reputation, and by the charm of risk; but the captain had already gone through all that: he had been vain at first, he had displayed valor, he had risked his life, he had hoped for fame and guerdon, and had even obtained them, but these actuating motives had already lost their power over him, and he regarded the matter in another light; he fulfilled his duty with punctuality, but understanding quite well how small were the chances for his life which were left him, after a six-months residence in the bastion, he no longer risked these casualties, except in case of stern necessity, so that the young lieutenant, who had entered the battery only a week previous, and who was now showing it to Kalugin, in company with whom he took turns in leaning out of the embrasure, or climbing out on the ramparts, seemed ten times as brave as the captain.

After inspecting the battery, Kalugin returned to the casemate, and ran against the general in the dark, as the latter was ascending to the watch-tower with his staff-officers.

"Captain Praskukhin!" said the general, "please to go to the first lodgement and say to the second battery of the M—— regiment, which is at work there, that they are to abandon their work, to evacuate the place without making any noise, and to join their regiment, which is standing at the foot of the hill in reserve.... Do you understand? Lead them to their regiment yourself."

"Yes, sir."

And Praskukhin set out for the lodgement on a run.

The firing was growing more infrequent.

X.

"Is this the second battalion of the M—— regiment?" asked Praskukhin, hastening up to the spot, and running against the soldiers who were carrying earth in sacks.

"Exactly so."

"Where is the commander?"

Mikhaïloff, supposing that the inquiry was for the commander of the corps, crawled out of his pit, and, taking Praskukhin for the colonel, he stepped up to him with his hand at his visor.

"The general has given orders ... that you ... are to be so good as to go ... as quickly as possible ... and, in particular, as quietly as possible, to the rear ... not to the rear exactly, but to the reserve," said Praskukhin, glancing askance at the enemy's fires.

On recognizing Praskukhin and discovering the state of things, Mikhaïloff dropped his hand, gave his orders, and the battalion started into motion, gathered up their guns, put on their cloaks, and set out.

No one who has not experienced it can imagine the delight which a man feels when he takes his departure, after a three-hours bombardment, from such a dangerous post as the lodgements. Several times in the course of those three hours, Mikhaïloff had, not without reason, considered his end as inevitable, and had grown accustomed to the conviction that he should infallibly be killed, and that he no longer belonged to this world. In spite of this, however, he had great difficulty in keeping his feet from running away with him when he issued from the lodgements at the head of his corps, in company with Praskukhin.

"Au revoir," said the major, the commander of another battalion, who was to remain in the lodgements, and with whom he had shared his cheese, as they sat in the pit behind the breastworks—"a pleasant journey to you."

"Thanks, I hope you will have good luck after we have gone. The firing seems to be holding up."

But no sooner had he said this than the enemy, who must have observed the movement in the lodgements, began to fire faster and faster. Our guns began to reply to him, and again a heavy cannonade began. The stars were gleaming high, but not brilliantly in the sky. The night was dark—you could hardly see your hand before you; only the flashes of the discharges and the explosions of the bombs illuminated objects for a moment. The soldiers marched on rapidly, in silence, involuntarily treading close on each other's heels; all that was audible through the incessant firing was the measured sound of their footsteps on the dry road, the noise of their bayonets as they came in contact, or the sigh and prayer of some young soldier, "Lord, Lord! what is this!" Now and then the groan of a wounded man arose, and the shout, "Stretcher!" (In the company commanded by Mikhaïloff, twenty-six men were killed in one night, by the fire of the artillery alone.) The lightning flashed against the distant horizon, the sentry in the bastion shouted, "Cannon!" and the ball, shrieking over the heads of the corps, tore up the earth, and sent the stones flying.

"Deuce take it! how slowly they march," thought Praskukhin, glancing back continually, as he walked beside Mikhaïloff. "Really, it will be better for me to run on in front; I have already given the order.... But no, it might be said later on that I was a coward. What will be will be; I will march with them."

"Now, why is he walking behind me?" thought Mikhaïloff, on his side.

"So far as I have observed, he always brings ill-luck. There it comes, flying straight for us, apparently."

After traversing several hundred paces, they encountered Kalugin, who was going to the casemates, clanking his sword boldly as he walked, in order to learn, by the general's command, how the work was progressing there. But on meeting Mikhaïloff, it occurred to him that, instead of going thither, under that terrible fire, which he was not ordered to do, he could make minute inquiries of the officer who had been there. And, in fact, Mikhaïloff furnished him with a detailed account of the work. After walking a short distance with them, Kalugin turned into the trench, which led to the casemate.

"Well, what news is there?" inquired the officer, who was seated alone at the table, and eating his supper.

"Well, nothing, apparently, except that there will not be any further conflict."

"How so? On the contrary, the general has but just gone up to the top of the works. A regiment has already arrived. Yes, there it is ... do you hear? The firing has begun again. Don't go. Why should you?" added the officer, perceiving the movement made by Kalugin.

"But I must be there without fail, in the present instance," thought Kalugin, "but I have already subjected myself to a good deal of danger to-day; the firing is terrible."

"Well, after all, I had better wait for him here," he said.

In fact, the general returned, twenty minutes later, accompanied by the officers, who had been with him; among their number was the yunker, Baron Pesth, but Praskukhin was not with them. The lodgements had been captured and occupied by our forces.

After receiving a full account of the engagement, Kalugin and Pesth went out of the casemates.

XI.

"There is blood on your cloak; have you been having a hand-to-hand fight?" Kalugin asked him.

"Oh, 'tis frightful! Just imagine...."

And Pesth began to relate how he had led his company, how the commander of the company had been killed, how he had spitted a Frenchman, and how, if it had not been for him, the battle would have been lost.

The foundations for this tale, that the company commander had been killed, and that Pesth had killed a Frenchman, were correct; but, in giving the details, the yunker had invented facts and bragged.

He bragged involuntarily, because, during the whole engagement, he had been in a kind of mist, and had forgotten himself to such a degree that everything which happened seemed to him to have happened somewhere, sometime, and with some one, and very naturally he had endeavored to bring out these details in a light which should be favorable to himself. But what had happened in reality was this:—

The battalion to which the yunker had been ordered for the sortie had stood under fire for two hours, near a wall; then the commander of the battalion said something, the company commanders made a move, the battalion got under way, issued forth from behind the breastworks, marched forward a hundred paces, and came to a halt in columns. Pesth had been ordered to take his stand on the right flank of the second company.

The yunker stood his ground, absolutely without knowing where he was, or why he was there, and, with restrained breath, and with a cold chill running down his spine, he had stared stupidly straight ahead into the dark beyond, in the expectation of something terrible. But, since there was no firing in progress, he did not feel so much terrified as he did queer and strange at finding himself outside the fortress, in the open plain. Again the battalion commander ahead said something. Again the officers had conversed in whispers, as they communicated the orders, and the black wall of the first company suddenly disappeared. They had been ordered to lie down. The second company lay down also, and Pesth, in the act, pricked his hand on something sharp. The only man who did not lie down was the commander of the second company. His short form, with the naked sword which he was flourishing, talking incessantly the while, moved about in front of the troop.

"Children! my lads! ... look at me! Don't fire at them, but at them with your bayonets, the dogs! When I shout, Hurrah! follow me close ... the chief thing is to be as close together as possible ... let us show what we are made of! Do not let us cover ourselves with shame—shall we, hey, my children? For our father the Tsar!"

"What is our company commander's surname?" Pesth inquired of a yunker, who was lying beside him. "What a brave fellow he is!"

"Yes, he's always that way in a fight ..." answered the yunker. "His name is Lisinkovsky."

At that moment, a flame flashed up in front of the company. There was a crash, which deafened them all, stones and splinters flew high in the air (fifty seconds, at least, later a stone fell from above and crushed the foot of a soldier). This was a bomb from an elevated platform, and the fact that it fell in the midst of the company proved that the French had caught sight of the column.

"So they are sending bombs!... Just let us get at you, and you shall feel the bayonet of a three-sided Russian, curse you!" shouted the commander of the company, in so loud a tone that the battalion commander was forced to order him to be quiet and not to make so much noise.

After this the first company rose to their feet, and after it the second. They were ordered to fix bayonets, and the battalion advanced. Pesth was so terrified that he absolutely could not recollect whether they advanced far, or whither, or who did what. He walked like a drunken man. But all at once millions of fires flashed from all sides, there was a whistling and a crashing. He shrieked and ran, because they were all shrieking and running. Then he stumbled and fell upon something. It was the company commander (who had been wounded at the head of his men and who, taking the yunker for a Frenchman, seized him by the leg). Then when he had freed his leg, and risen to his feet, some man ran against his back in the dark and almost knocked him down again; another man shouted, "Run him through! what are you staring at!"

Then he seized a gun, and ran the bayonet into something soft. "Ah,

Dieu!" exclaimed some one in a terribly piercing voice, and then only did Pesth discover that he had transfixed a Frenchman. The cold sweat started out all over his body. He shook as though in a fever, and flung away the gun. But this lasted only a moment; it immediately occurred to him that he was a hero. He seized the gun again, and, shouting "Hurrah!" with the crowd, he rushed away from the dead Frenchman. After having traversed about twenty paces, he came to the trench. There he found our men and the company commander.

"I have run one man through!" he said to the commander.

"You're a brave fellow, Baron."

XII.

"But, do you know, Praskukhin has been killed," said Pesth, accompanying Kalugin, on the way back.

"It cannot be!"

"But it can. I saw him myself."

"Farewell; I am in a hurry."

"I am well content," thought Kalugin, as he returned home; "I have had luck for the first time when on duty. That was a capital engagement, and I am alive and whole. There will be some fine presentations, and I shall certainly get a golden sword. And I deserve it too."

After reporting to the general all that was necessary, he went to his room, in which sat Prince Galtsin, who had returned long before, and who was reading a book, which he had found on Kalugin's table, while waiting for him.

It was with a wonderful sense of enjoyment that Kalugin found himself at home again, out of all danger, and, having donned his night-shirt and lain down on the sofa, he began to relate to Galtsin the particulars of the affair, communicating them, naturally, from a point of view which made it appear that he, Kalugin, was a very active and valiant officer, to which, in my opinion, it was superfluous to refer, seeing that every one knew it and that no one had any right to doubt it, with the exception, perhaps, of the deceased Captain Praskukhin, who, in spite of the fact that he had considered it a piece of happiness to walk arm in arm with Kalugin, had told a friend, only the evening before, in private, that Kalugin was a very fine man, but that, between you and me, he was terribly averse to going to the bastions.

No sooner had Praskukhin, who had been walking beside Mikhaïloff, taken leave of Kalugin, and, betaking himself to a safer place, had begun to recover his spirits somewhat, than he caught sight of a flash of lightning behind him flaring up vividly, heard the shout of the sentinel, "Mortar!" and the words of the soldiers who were marching behind, "It's flying straight at the bastion!"

Mikhaïloff glanced round. The brilliant point of the bomb seemed to be suspended directly over his head in such a position that it was absolutely impossible to determine its course. But this lasted only for a second. The bomb came faster and faster, nearer and nearer, the sparks of the fuse were already visible, and the fateful whistle was audible, and it descended straight in the middle of the battalion.

"Lie down!" shouted a voice.

Mikhaïloff and Praskukhin threw themselves on the ground. Praskukhin shut his eyes, and only heard the bomb crash against the hard earth somewhere in the vicinity. A second passed, which seemed an hour—and the bomb had not burst. Praskukhin was alarmed; had he felt cowardly for nothing? Perhaps the bomb had fallen at a distance, and it merely seemed to him that the fuse was hissing near him. He opened his eyes, and saw with satisfaction that Mikhaïloff was lying motionless on the earth, at his very feet. But then his eyes encountered for a moment the glowing fuse of the bomb, which was twisting about at a distance of an arshin from him.

A cold horror, which excluded every other thought and feeling, took possession of his whole being. He covered his face with his hands.

Another second passed—a second in which a whole world of thoughts, feelings, hopes, and memories flashed through his mind.

"Which will be killed, Mikhaïloff or I? Or both together? And if it is I, where will it strike? If in the head, then all is over with me; but if in the leg, they will cut it off, and I shall ask them to be sure to give me chloroform,— and I may still remain among the living. But perhaps no one but Mikhaïloff will be killed; then I will relate how we were walking along together, and how he was killed and his blood spurted over me. No, it is nearer to me ... it will kill me!"

Then he remembered the twenty rubles which he owed Mikhaïloff, and recalled another debt in Petersburg, which ought to have been paid long ago; the gypsy air which he had sung the previous evening recurred to him. The woman whom he loved appeared to his imagination in a cap with lilac ribbons, a man who had insulted him five years before, and whom he had not paid off for his insult, came to his mind, though inextricably interwoven with these and with a thousand other memories the feeling of the moment—the fear of death—never deserted him for an instant.

"But perhaps it will not burst," he thought, and, with the decision of despair, he tried to open his eyes. But at that instant, through the crevice of his eyelids, his eyes were smitten with a red fire, and something struck him in the centre of the breast, with a frightful crash; he ran off, he knew not whither, stumbled over his sword, which had got between his legs, and fell over on his side.

"Thank God! I am only bruised," was his first thought, and he tried to touch his breast with his hands; but his arms seemed fettered, and pincers were pressing his head. The soldiers flitted before his eyes, and he unconsciously counted them: "One, two, three soldiers; and there is an officer, wrapped up in his cloak," he thought. Then a flash passed before his eyes, and he thought that something had been fired off; was it the mortars, or the cannon? It must have been the cannon. And there was still another shot; and there were more soldiers; five, six, seven soldiers were passing by him. Then suddenly he felt afraid that they would crush him. He wanted to shout to them that he was bruised; but his mouth was so dry that his tongue clove to his palate and he was tortured by a frightful thirst.

He felt that he was wet about the breast: this sensation of dampness reminded him of water, and he even wanted to drink this, whatever it was. "I must have brought the blood when I fell," he thought, and, beginning to give way more and more to terror, lest the soldiers who passed should crush him, he collected all his strength, and tried to cry: "Take me with you!" but, instead of this, he groaned so terribly that it frightened him to hear himself. Then more red fires flashed in his eyes—and it seemed to him as though the soldiers were laying stones upon him; the fires danced more and more rarely, the stones which they piled on him oppressed him more and more.

He exerted all his strength, in order to cast off the stones; he stretched himself out, and no longer saw or heard or thought or felt anything. He had been killed on the spot by a splinter of shell, in the middle of the breast.

XIII.

Mikhaïloff, on catching sight of the bomb, fell to the earth, and, like Praskukhin, he went over in thought and feeling an incredible amount in those two seconds while the bomb lay there unexploded. He prayed to God mentally, and kept repeating: "Thy will be done!"

"And why did I enter the military service?" he thought at the same time; "and why, again, did I exchange into the infantry, in order to take part in this campaign? Would it not have been better for me to remain in the regiment of Uhlans, in the town of T., and pass the time with my friend Natasha? And now this is what has come of it."

And he began to count, "One, two, three, four," guessing that if it burst on the even number, he would live, but if on the uneven number, then he should be killed. "All is over; killed," he thought, when the bomb burst (he did not remember whether it was on the even or the uneven number), and he felt a blow, and a sharp pain in his head. "Lord, forgive my sins," he murmured, folding his hands, then rose, and fell back senseless.

His first sensation, when he came to himself, was the blood which was flowing from his nose, and a pain in his head, which had become much less powerful. "It is my soul departing," he thought.—"What will it be like there? Lord, receive my soul in peace!—But one thing is strange," he thought,— "and that is that, though dying, I can still hear so plainly the footsteps of the soldiers and the report of the shots."

"Send some bearers ... hey there ... the captain is killed!" shouted a voice over his head, which he recognized as the voice of his drummer Ignatieff.

Some one grasped him by the shoulders. He made an effort to open his eyes, and saw overhead the dark blue heavens, the clusters of stars, and two bombs, which were flying over him, one after the other; he saw Ignatieff, the soldiers with the stretcher, the walls of the trench, and all at once he became convinced that he was not yet in the other world.

He had been slightly wounded in the head with a stone. His very first impression was one resembling regret; he had so beautifully and so calmly prepared himself for transit yonder that a return to reality, with its bombs, its trenches, and its blood, produced a disagreeable effect on him; his second impression was an involuntary joy that he was alive, and the third a desire to leave the bastion as speedily as possible. The drummer bound up his commander's head with his handkerchief, and, taking him under the arm, he led him to the place where the bandaging was going on.

"But where am I going, and why?" thought the staff-captain, when he recovered his senses a little.—"It is my duty to remain with my men,—the more so as they will soon be out of range of the shots," some voice whispered to him.

"Never mind, brother," he said, pulling his arm away from the obliging drummer. "I will not go to the field-hospital; I will remain with my men."

And he turned back.

"You had better have your wound properly attended to, Your Honor," said Ignatieff. "In the heat of the moment, it seems as if it were a trifle; but it will be the worse if not attended to. There is some inflammation rising there ... really, now, Your Honor."

Mikhaïloff paused for a moment in indecision, and would have followed Ignatieff's advice, in all probability, had he not called to mind how many severely wounded men there must needs be at the field-hospital. "Perhaps the doctor will smile at my scratch," thought the staff-captain, and he returned with decision to his men, wholly regardless of the drummer's admonitions.

"And where is Officer Praskukhin, who was walking with me?" he asked the lieutenant, who was leading the corps when they met.

"I don't know—killed, probably," replied the lieutenant, reluctantly.

"How is it that you do not know whether he was killed or wounded? He was walking with us. And why have you not carried him with you?"

"How could it be done, brother, when the place was so hot for us!"

"Ah, how could you do such a thing, Mikhaïl Ivánowitch!" said Mikhaïloff, angrily.—"How could you abandon him if he was alive; and if he was dead, you should still have brought away his body."

"How could he be alive when, as I tell you, I went up to him and saw!" returned the lieutenant.—"As you like, however! Only, his own men might carry him off. Here, you dogs! the cannonade has abated," he added....

Mikhaïloff sat down, and clasped his head, which the motion caused to pain him terribly.

"Yes, I must go and get him, without fail; perhaps he is still alive," said Mikhaïloff. "It is our duty, Mikhaïl Ivánowitch!"

Mikhaïl Ivánowitch made no reply.

"He did not take him at the time, and now the soldiers must be sent alone—and how can they be sent? their lives may be sacrificed in vain, under that hot fire," thought Mikhaïloff.

"Children! we must go back—and get the officer who was wounded there in the ditch," he said, in not too loud and commanding a tone, for he felt how unpleasant it would be to the soldiers to obey his order,—and, in fact, as he did not address any one in particular by name, no one set out to fulfil it.

"It is quite possible that he is already dead, and it is not worth while to subject the men to unnecessary danger; I alone am to blame for not having seen to it. I will go myself and learn whether he is alive. It is my duty," said Mikhaïloff to himself.

"Mikhaïl Ivánowitch! Lead the men forward, and I will overtake you," he said, and, pulling up his cloak with one hand, and with the other constantly touching the image of Saint Mitrofaniy, in which he cherished a special faith, he set off on a run along the trench.

Having convinced himself that Praskukhin was dead, he dragged himself back, panting, and supporting with his hand the loosened bandage and his head, which began to pain him severely. The battalion had already reached the foot of the hill, and a place almost out of range of shots, when Mikhaïloff overtook it. I say, almost out of range, because some stray bombs struck here and there.

"At all events, I must go to the hospital to-morrow, and put down my name," thought the staff-captain, as the medical student assisting the doctors bound his wound.

XIV.

Hundreds of bodies, freshly smeared with blood, of men who two hours previous had been filled with divers lofty or petty hopes and desires, now lay, with stiffened limbs, in the dewy, flowery valley which separated the bastion from the trench, and on the level floor of the chapel for the dead in Sevastopol; hundreds of men crawled, twisted, and groaned, with curses and prayers on their parched lips, some amid the corpses in the flower-strewn vale, others on stretchers, on cots, and on the blood-stained floor of the hospital.

And still, as on the days preceding, the dawn glowed, over Sapun Mountain, the twinkling stars paled, the white mist spread abroad from the dark sounding sea, the red glow illuminated the east, long crimson cloudlets darted across the blue horizon; and still, as on days preceding, the powerful, all-beautiful sun rose up, giving promise of joy, love, and happiness to all who dwell in the world.

XV.

On the following day, the band of the chasseurs was playing again on the boulevard, and again officers, cadets, soldiers, and young women were promenading in festive guise about the pavilion and through the low-hanging alleys of fragrant white acacias in bloom.

Kalugin, Prince Galtsin, and some colonel or other were walking arm-in-arm near the pavilion, and discussing the engagement of the day before. As always happens in such cases, the chief governing thread of the conversation was not the engagement itself, but the part which those who were narrating the story of the affair took in it.

Their faces and the sound of their voices had a serious, almost melancholy expression, as though the loss of the preceding day had touched and saddened them deeply; but, to tell the truth, as none of them had lost any one very near to him, this expression of sorrow was an official expression, which they merely felt it to be their duty to exhibit.

On the contrary, Kalugin and the colonel were ready to see an engagement of the same sort every day, provided that they might receive a gold sword or the rank of major-general—notwithstanding the fact that they were very fine fellows.

I like it when any warrior who destroys millions to gratify his ambition is called a monster. Only question any Lieutenant Petrushkoff, and Sub-Lieutenant Antonoff, and so on, on their word of honor, and every one of them is a petty Napoleon, a petty monster, and ready to bring on a battle on the instant, to murder a hundred men, merely for the sake of receiving an extra cross or an increase of a third in his pay.

"No, excuse me," said the colonel; "it began first on the left flank. I was there myself."

"Possibly," answered Kalugin. "I was farther on the right; I went there twice. Once I was in search of the general, and the second time I went merely to inspect the lodgements. It was a hot place."

"Yes, of course, Kalugin knows," said Prince Galtsin to the colonel. "You know that V. told me to-day that you were a brave fellow...."

"But the losses, the losses were terrible," said the colonel. "I lost four hundred men from my regiment. It's a wonder that I escaped from there alive."

At this moment, the figure of Mikhaïloff, with his head bandaged, appeared at the other extremity of the boulevard, coming to meet these gentlemen.

"What, are you wounded, captain?" said Kalugin.

"Yes, slightly, with a stone," replied Mikhaïloff.

"Has the flag been lowered yet?"[H] inquired Prince Galtsin, gazing over the staff-captain's cap, and addressing himself to no one in particular.

"Non, pas encore," answered Mikhaïloff, who wished to show that he understood and spoke French.

"Is the truce still in force?" said Galtsin, addressing him courteously in Russian, and thereby intimating—so it seemed to the captain—It must be difficult for you to speak French, so why is it not better to talk in your own tongue simply?... And with this the adjutants left him. The staff-captain again felt lonely, as on the preceding evening, and, exchanging salutes with various gentlemen,—some he did not care, and others he did not dare, to join,—he seated himself near Kazarsky's monument, and lighted a cigarette.

Baron Pesth also had come to the boulevard. He had been telling how he had gone over to arrange the truce, and had conversed with the French officers, and he declared that one had said to him, "If daylight had held off another half-hour, these ambushes would have been retaken;" and that he had replied, "Sir, I refrain from saying no, in order not to give you the lie," and how well he had said it, and so on.

But, in reality, although he had had a hand in the truce, he had not dared to say anything very particular there, although he had been very desirous of talking with the French (for it is awfully jolly to talk with Frenchmen). Yunker Baron Pesth had marched up and down the line for a long time, incessantly inquiring of the Frenchmen who were near him: "To what regiment do you belong?" They answered him; and that was the end of it.

When he walked too far along the line, the French sentry, not suspecting that this soldier understood French, cursed him. "He has come to spy out our works, the cursed ..." said he; and, in consequence, Yunker Baron Pesth, taking no further interest in the truce, went home, and thought out on the way thither those French phrases, which he had now repeated. Captain Zoboff was also on the boulevard, talking loudly, and Captain Obzhogoff, in a very dishevelled condition, and an artillery captain, who courted no one, and was happy in the love of the yunkers, and all the faces which had been there on the day before, and all still actuated by the same motives. No one was missing except Praskukhin, Neferdoff, and some others, whom hardly any one remembered or thought of now, though their bodies were not yet washed, laid out, and interred in the earth.

XVI.

White flags had been hung out from our bastion, and from the trenches of the French, and in the blooming valley between them lay disfigured corpses, shoeless, in garments of gray or blue, which laborers were engaged in carrying off and heaping upon carts. The odor of the dead bodies filled the air. Throngs of people had poured out of Sevastopol, and from the French camp, to gaze upon this spectacle, and they pressed one after the other with eager and benevolent curiosity.

Listen to what these people are saying.

Here, in a group of Russians and French who have come together, is a young officer, who speaks French badly, but well enough to make himself understood, examining a cartridge-box of the guards.

"And what is this bird here for?" says he.

"Because it is a cartridge-box belonging to a regiment of the guards, Monsieur, and bears the Imperial eagle."

"And do you belong to the guard?"

"Pardon, Monsieur, I belong to the sixth regiment of the line."

"And this—bought where?" asks the officer, pointing to a cigar-holder of yellow wood, in which the Frenchman was smoking his cigarette.

"At Balaklava, Monsieur. It is very plain, of palm-wood."

"Pretty!" says the officer, guided in his conversation not so much by his own wishes as by the words which he knows.

"If you will have the kindness to keep it as a souvenir of this meeting, you will confer an obligation on me."

And the polite Frenchman blows out the cigarette, and hands the holder over to the officer with a little bow. The officer gives him his, and all the members of the group, Frenchmen as well as Russians, appear very much pleased and smile.

Then a bold infantryman, in a pink shirt, with his cloak thrown over his shoulders, accompanied by two other soldiers, who, with their hands behind their backs, were standing behind him, with merry, curious countenances, stepped up to a Frenchman, and requested a light for his pipe. The Frenchman brightened his fire, stirred up his short pipe, and shook out a light for the Russian.

"Tobacco good!" said the soldier in the pink shirt; and the spectators smile.

"Yes, good tobacco, Turkish tobacco," says the Frenchman. "And your tobacco—Russian?—good?"

"Russian, good," says the soldier in the pink shirt: whereupon those present shake with laughter. "The French not good—bon jour, Monsieur," says the soldier in the pink shirt, letting fly his entire charge of knowledge in the language at once, as he laughs and taps the Frenchman on the stomach. The French join in the laugh.

"They are not handsome, these beasts of Russians," says a zouave, amid the crowd of Frenchmen.

"What are they laughing about?" says another black-complexioned one, with an Italian accent, approaching our men.

"Caftan good," says the audacious soldier, staring at the zouave's embroidered coat-skirts, and then there is another laugh.

"Don't leave your lines; back to your places, sacré nom!" shouts a French corporal, and the soldiers disperse with evident reluctance.

In the meantime, our young cavalry officer is making the tour of the French officers. The conversation turns on some Count Sazonoff, "with whom I was very well acquainted, Monsieur," says a French officer, with one epaulet—"he is one of those real Russian counts, of whom we are so fond."

"There is a Sazonoff with whom I am acquainted," said the cavalry officer, "but he is not a count, so far as I know, at least; a little dark-complexioned man, of about your age."

"Exactly, Monsieur, that is the man. Oh, how I should like to see that dear count! If you see him, pray, present my compliments to him—Captain Latour," says he, bowing.

"Isn't this a terrible business that we are conducting here? It was hot work last night, wasn't it?" says the cavalry officer, wishing to continue the conversation, and pointing to the dead bodies.

"Oh, frightful, Monsieur! But what brave fellows your soldiers are—what brave fellows! It is a pleasure to fight with such valiant fellows."

"It must be admitted that your men do not hang back, either," says the cavalry-man, with a bow, and the conviction that he is very amiable.

But enough of this.

Let us rather observe this lad of ten, clad in an ancient cap, his father's probably, shoes worn on bare feet, and nankeen breeches, held up by a single suspender, who had climbed over the wall at the very beginning of the truce, and has been roaming about the ravine, staring with dull curiosity at the French, and at the bodies which are lying on the earth, and plucking the blue wild-flowers with which the valley is studded. On his way home with a large bouquet, he held his nose because of the odor which the wind wafted to him, and paused beside a pile of corpses, which had been carried off the field, and stared long at one terrible headless body, which chanced to be the nearest to him. After standing there for a long while, he stepped up closer, and touched with his foot the stiffened arm of the corpse which protruded. The arm swayed a little. He touched it again, and with more vigor. The arm swung back, and then fell into place again. And at once the boy uttered a shriek, hid his face in the flowers, and ran off to the fortifications as fast as he could go.

Yes, white flags are hung out from the bastion and the trenches, the flowery vale is filled with dead bodies, the splendid sun sinks into the blue sea, and the blue sea undulates and glitters in the golden rays of the sun. Thousands of people congregate, gaze, talk, and smile at each other. And why do not Christian people, who profess the one great law of love and self-sacrifice, when they behold what they have wrought, fall in repentance upon their knees before Him who, when he gave them life, implanted in the soul of each of them, together with a fear of death, a love of the good and the beautiful, and, with tears of joy and happiness, embrace each other like brothers? No! But it is a comfort to think that it was not we who began this war, that we are only defending our own country, our father-land. The white flags have been hauled in, and again the weapons of death and suffering are shrieking; again innocent blood is shed, and groans and curses are audible.

I have now said all that I wish to say at this time. But a heavy thought overmasters me. Perhaps it should not have been said; perhaps what I have said belongs to one of those evil truths which, unconsciously concealed in the soul of each man, should not be uttered, lest they become pernicious, as a cask of wine should not be shaken, lest it be thereby spoiled.

Where is the expression of evil which should be avoided? Where is the expression of good which should be imitated in this sketch? Who is the villain, who the hero? All are good, and all are evil.

Neither Kalugin, with his brilliant bravery—bravoure de gentilhomme—and his vanity, the instigator of all his deeds; nor Praskukhin, the empty-headed, harmless man, though he fell in battle for the faith, the throne, and his native land; nor Mikhaïloff, with his shyness; nor Pesth, a child with no firm convictions or principles, can be either the heroes or the villains of the tale.

The hero of my tale, whom I love with all the strength of my soul, whom I have tried to set forth in all his beauty, and who has always been, is, and always will be most beautiful, is—the truth.

FOOTNOTES:

[C] Sea.

[D] Military Gazette.

[E] A civilian, without military training, attached to a regiment as a non-commissioned officer, who may eventually become a regular officer.

[F] A polite way of referring to the general in the plural.

[G] A The Russian soldiers, who had been fighting the Turks, were so accustomed to this cry of the enemy that they always declared that the French also cried "Allah."—Author's Note.

[H] This sentence is in French.

SEVASTOPOL IN AUGUST, 1855.

I.

At the end of August, along the rocky highway to Sevastopol, between Duvanka and Bakhtchisaraï, through the thick, hot dust, at a foot-pace, drove an officer's light cart, that peculiar telyezhka, not now to be met with, which stands about half-way between a Jewish britchka, a Russian travelling-carriage, and a basket-wagon. In the front of the wagon, holding the reins, squatted the servant, clad in a nankeen coat and an officer's cap, which had become quite limp; seated behind, on bundles and packages covered with a military coat, was an infantry officer, in a summer cloak.

As well as could be judged from his sitting position, the officer was not tall in stature, but extremely thick, and that not so much from shoulder to shoulder as from chest to back; he was broad and thick, and his neck and the base of the head were excessively developed and swollen. His waist, so called, a receding strip in the centre of the body, did not exist in his case; but neither had he any belly; on the contrary, he was rather thin than otherwise, particularly in the face, which was overspread with an unhealthy yellowish sunburn. His face would have been handsome had it not been for a certain bloated appearance, and the soft, yet not elderly, heavy wrinkles that flowed together and enlarged his features, imparting to the whole countenance a general expression of coarseness and of lack of freshness. His eyes were small, brown, extremely searching, even bold; his moustache was very thick, but the ends were kept constantly short by his habit of gnawing them; and his chin, and his cheek-bones in particular were covered with a remarkably strong, thick, and black beard, of two days' growth.

The officer had been wounded on the 10th of May, by a splinter, in the head, on which he still wore a bandage, and, having now felt perfectly well for the last week, he had come out of the Simferopol Hospital, to rejoin his regiment, which was stationed somewhere in the direction from which shots could be heard; but whether that was in Sevastopol itself, on the northern defences, or at Inkermann, he had not so far succeeded in ascertaining with much accuracy from any one.

Shots were still audible near at hand, especially at intervals, when the hills did not interfere, or when borne on the wind with great distinctness and frequency, and apparently near at hand. Then it seemed as though some explosion shook the air, and caused an involuntary shudder. Then, one after the other, followed less resounding reports in quick succession, like a drum-beat, interrupted at times by a startling roar. Then, everything mingled in a sort of reverberating crash, resembling peals of thunder, when a thunder-storm is in full force, and the rain has just begun to pour down in floods, every one said; and it could be heard that the bombardment was progressing frightfully.

The officer kept urging on his servant, and seemed desirous of arriving as speedily as possible. They were met by a long train of the Russian-peasant type, which had carried provisions into Sevastopol, and was now returning with sick and wounded soldiers in gray coats, sailors in black paletots, volunteers in red fezes, and bearded militia-men. The officer's light cart had to halt in the thick, immovable cloud of dust raised by the carts, and the officer, blinking and frowning with the dust that stuffed his eyes and ears, gazed at the faces of the sick and wounded as they passed.

"Ah, there's a sick soldier from our company," said the servant, turning to his master, and pointing to the wagon which was just on a line with them, full of wounded, at the moment.

On the cart, towards the front, a bearded Russian, in a lamb's-wool cap, was seated sidewise, and, holding the stock of his whip under his elbow, was tying on the lash. Behind him in the cart, about five soldiers, in different positions, were shaking about. One, though pale and thin, with his arm in a bandage, and his cloak thrown on over his shirt, was sitting up bravely in the middle of the cart, and tried to touch his cap on seeing the officer, but immediately afterwards (recollecting, probably, that he was wounded) he pretended that he only wanted to scratch his head. Another, beside him, was lying flat on the bottom of the wagon; all that was visible was two hands, as they clung to the rails of the wagon, and his knees uplifted limp as mops, as they swayed about in various directions. A third, with a swollen face and a bandaged head, on which was placed his soldier's cap, sat on one side, with his legs dangling over the wheel, and, with his elbows resting on his knees, seemed immersed in thought. It was to him that the passing officer addressed himself.

"Dolzhnikoff!" he exclaimed.

"Here," replied the soldier, opening his eyes, and pulling off his cap, in such a thick and halting bass voice that it seemed as though twenty soldiers had uttered an exclamation at one and the same time.

"When were you wounded, brother?"

The leaden and swimming eyes of the soldier grew animated; he evidently recognized his officer.

"I wish Your Honor health!" he began again, in the same abrupt bass as before.

"Where is the regiment stationed now?"

"It was stationed in Sevastopol, but they were to move on Wednesday, Your Honor."

"Where to?"

"I don't know; it must have been to the Sivernaya, Your Honor! To-day, Your Honor," he added, in a drawling voice, as he put on his cap, "they have begun to fire clear across, mostly with bombs, that even go as far as the bay; they are fighting horribly to-day, so that—"

It was impossible to hear what the soldier said further; but it was evident, from the expression of his countenance and from his attitude, that he was uttering discouraging remarks, with the touch of malice of a man who is suffering.

The travelling officer, Lieutenant Kozeltzoff, was no common officer. He was not one of those that live so and so and do thus and so because others

70

live and do thus; he did whatever he pleased, and others did the same, and were convinced that it was well. He was rather richly endowed by nature with small gifts: he sang well, played on the guitar, talked very cleverly, and wrote very easily, particularly official documents, in which he had practised his hand in his capacity of adjutant of the battalion; but the most noticeable trait in his character was his egotistical energy, which, although chiefly founded on this array of petty talents, constituted in itself a sharp and striking trait. His egotism was of the sort that is most frequently found developed in masculine and especially in military circles, and which had become a part of his life to such a degree that he understood no other choice than to domineer or to humiliate himself; and his egotism was the mainspring even of his private impulses; he liked to usurp the first place over people with whom he put himself on a level.

"Well! it's absurd of me to listen to what a Moskva[I] chatters!" muttered the lieutenant, experiencing a certain weight of apathy in his heart, and a dimness of thought, which the sight of the transport full of wounded and the words of the soldier, whose significance was emphasized and confirmed by the sounds of the bombardment, had left with him. "That Moskva is ridiculous! Drive on, Nikolaeff! go ahead! Are you asleep?" he added, rather fretfully, to the servant, as he re-arranged the skirts of his coat.

The reins were tightened, Nikolaeff clacked his lips, and the wagon moved on at a trot.

"We will only halt a minute for food, and will proceed at once, this very day," said the officer.

II.

As he entered the street of the ruined remains of the stone wall, forming the Tatar houses of Duvanka, Lieutenant Kozeltzoff was stopped by a transport of bombs and grape-shot, which were on their way to Sevastopol, and had accumulated on the road. Two infantry soldiers were seated in the dust, on the stones of a ruined garden-wall by the roadside, devouring a watermelon and bread.

"Have you come far, fellow-countryman?" said one of them, as he

71

chewed his bread, to the soldier, with a small knapsack on his back, who had halted near them.

"I have come from my government to join my regiment," replied the soldier, turning his eyes away from the watermelon, and readjusting the sack on his back. "There we were, two weeks ago, at work on the hay, a whole troop of us; but now they have drafted all of us, and we don't know where our regiment is at the present time. They say that our men went on the Korabelnaya last week. Have you heard anything, gentlemen?"

"It's stationed in the town, brother," said the second, an old soldier of the reserves, digging away with his clasp-knife at the white, unripe melon. "We have just come from there, this afternoon. It's terrible, my brother!"

"How so, gentlemen?"

"Don't you hear how they are firing all around to-day, so that there is not a whole spot anywhere? It is impossible to say how many of our brethren have been killed." And the speaker waved his hand and adjusted his cap.

The passing soldier shook his head thoughtfully, gave a clack with his tongue, then pulled his pipe from his boot-leg, and, without filling it, stirred up the half-burned tobacco, lit a bit of tinder from the soldier who was smoking, and raised his cap.

"There is no one like God, gentlemen! Good-bye," said he, and, with a shake of the sack on his back, he went his way.

"Hey, there! you'd better wait," said the man who was digging out the watermelon, with an air of conviction.

"It makes no difference!" muttered the traveller, threading his way among the wheels of the assembled transports.

III.

The posting-station was full of people when Kozeltzoff drove up to it. The first person whom he encountered, on the porch itself, was a thin and very young man, the superintendent, who continued his altercation with two officers, who had followed him out.

"It's not three days only, but ten that you will have to wait. Even generals wait, my good sirs!" said the superintendent, with a desire to administer a prick to the travellers; "and I am not going to harness up for you."

"Then don't give anybody horses, if there are none! But why furnish them to some lackey or other with baggage?" shouted the elder of the two officers, with a glass of tea in his hand, and plainly avoiding the use of pronouns,[J] but giving it to be understood that he might very easily address the superintendent as "thou."

"Judge for yourself, now, Mr. Superintendent," said the younger officer, with some hesitation. "We don't want to go for our own pleasure. We must certainly be needed, since we have been called for. And I certainly shall report to the general. But this, of course,—you know that you are not paying proper respect to the military profession."

"You are always spoiling things," the elder man interrupted, with vexation. "You only hinder me; you must know how to talk to them. Here, now, he has lost his respect. Horses this very instant, I say!"

"I should be glad to give them to you, bátiushka,[K] but where am I to get them?"

After a brief silence, the superintendent began to grow irritated, and to talk, flourishing his hands the while.

"I understand, bátiushka. And I know all about it myself. But what are you going to do? Only give me"—here a ray of hope gleamed across the faces of the officers—"only give me a chance to live until the end of the month, and you won't see me here any longer. I'd rather go on the Malakhoff tower, by Heavens! than stay here. Let them do what they please about it! There's not a single sound team in the station this day, and the horses haven't seen a wisp of hay these three days." And the superintendent disappeared behind the gate.

Kozeltzoff entered the room in company with the officers.

"Well," said the elder officer, quite calmly, to the younger one, although but a second before he had appeared to be greatly irritated, "we have been travelling these three weeks, and we will wait a little longer. There's no harm done. We shall get there at last."

The dirty, smoky apartment was so filled with officers and trunks that it was with difficulty that Kozeltzoff found a place near the window, where he seated himself; he began to roll himself a cigarette, as he glanced at the faces and lent an ear to the conversations.

To the right of the door, near a crippled and greasy table, upon which stood two samovárs, whose copper had turned green in spots, here and there, and where sugar was portioned out in various papers, sat the principal group. A young officer, without moustache, in a new, short, wadded summer coat, was pouring water into the teapot.

Four such young officers were there, in different corners of the room. One of them had placed a cloak under his head, and was fast asleep on the sofa. Another, standing by the table, was cutting up some roast mutton for an officer without an arm, who was seated at the table.

Two officers, one in an adjutant's cloak, the other in an infantry cloak, a thin one however, and with a satchel strapped over his shoulder, were sitting near the oven bench, and it was evident, from the very way in which they stared at the rest, and from the manner in which the one with the satchel smoked his cigar, that they were not line officers on duty at the front, and that they were delighted at it.

Not that there was any scorn apparent in their manner, but there was a certain self-satisfied tranquillity, founded partly on money and partly on their close intimacy with generals, a certain consciousness of superiority which even extended to a desire to hide it.

A thick-lipped young doctor and an officer of artillery, with a German cast of countenance, were seated almost on the feet of the young officer who was sleeping on the sofa, and counting over their money.

There were four officers' servants, some dozing and others busy with the trunks and packages near the door.

Among all these faces, Kozeltzoff did not find a single familiar one; but

74

he began to listen with curiosity to the conversation. The young officers, who, as he decided from their looks alone, had but just come out of the military academy, pleased him, and, what was the principal point, they reminded him that his brother had also come from the academy, and should have joined recently one of the batteries of Sevastopol.

But the officer with the satchel, whose face he had seen before somewhere, seemed bold and repulsive to him. He even left the window, and, going to the stove-bench, seated himself on it, with the thought that he would put the fellow down if he took it into his head to say anything. In general, purely as a brave "line" officer, he did not like "the staff," such as he had recognized these two officers to be at the first glance.

IV.

"But this is dreadfully annoying," said one of the young officers, "to be so near, and yet not be able to get there. Perhaps there will be an action this very day, and we shall not be there."

In the sharp voice and the mottled freshness of the color that swept across the youthful face of this officer as he spoke there was apparent the sweet young timidity of the man who is constantly afraid lest his every word shall not turn out exactly right.

The one-armed officer glanced at him with a smile.

"You will get there soon enough, I assure you," he said.

The young officer looked with respect at the haggard face of the armless officer, so unexpectedly illuminated by a smile, held his peace for a while, and busied himself once more with his tea. In fact, the one-armed officer's face, his attitude, and, most of all, the empty sleeve of his coat, expressed much of that tranquil indifference that may be explained in this way—that he looked upon every conversation and every occurrence as though saying, "That is all very fine; I know all about that, and I can do a little of that myself, if I only choose."

"What is our decision to be?" said the young officer again to his companion in the short coat. "Shall we pass the night here, or shall we proceed with our own horses?"

His comrade declined to proceed.

"Just imagine, captain," said the one who was pouring the tea, turning to the one-armed man, and picking up the knife that the latter had dropped, "they told us that horses were frightfully dear in Sevastopol, so we bought a horse in partnership at Simferopol."

"They made you pay pretty high for it, I fancy."

"Really, I do not know, captain; we paid ninety rubles for it and the team. Is that very dear?" he added, turning to all the company, and to Kozeltzoff, who was staring at him.

"It was not dear, if the horse is young," said Kozeltzoff.

"Really! but they told us that it was dear. Only, she limps a little, but that will pass off. They told us that she was very strong."

"What academy are you from?" asked Kozeltzoff, who wished to inquire for his brother.

"We are just from the academy of the nobility; there are six of us, and we are on our way to Sevastopol at our own desire," said the talkative young officer. "But we do not know where our battery is; some say that it is in Sevastopol, others that it is at Odessa."

"Was it not possible to find out at Simferopol?" asked Kozeltzoff.

"They do not know there. Just imagine, one of our comrades went to the headquarters there, and they were impertinent to him. You can imagine how disagreeable that was! Would you like to have me make you a cigarette," he said at that moment to the one-armed officer, who was just pulling out his cigarette-machine.

He waited on the latter with a sort of servile enthusiasm.

"And are you from Sevastopol also?" he went on. "Oh, good Heavens, how wonderful that is! How much we did think of you, and of all our heroes, in Petersburg," he said, turning to Kozeltzoff with respect and good-natured flattery.

"And now, perhaps, you may have to go back?" inquired the lieutenant.

"That is just what we are afraid of. You can imagine that, after having bought the horse, and provided ourselves with all the necessaries,—a coffee-pot with a spirit-lamp, and other indispensable trifles,—we have no money left," he said, in a low voice, as he glanced at his companions; "so that, if we do have to go back, we don't know what is to be done."

"Have you received no money for travelling expenses?" inquired Kozeltzoff.

"No," replied he, in a whisper; "they only promised to give it to us here."

"Have you the certificate?"

"I know that—the principal thing—is the certificate; but a senator in Moscow,—he's my uncle,—when I was at his house, said that they would give it to us here; otherwise, he would have given me some himself. So they will give it to us here?"

"Most certainly they will."

"I too think that they will," he said, in a tone which showed that, after having made the same identical inquiry in thirty posting-stations, and having everywhere received different answers, he no longer believed any one implicitly.

V.

"Who ordered beet-soup?" called out the slatternly mistress of the house, a fat woman of forty, as she entered the room with a bowl of soup.

The conversation ceased at once, and all who were in the room fixed their eyes on the woman.

"Ah, it was Kozeltzoff who ordered it," said the young officer. "He must be waked. Get up for your dinner," he said, approaching the sleeper on the sofa, and jogging his elbow.

A young lad of seventeen, with merry black eyes and red cheeks, sprang energetically from the sofa, and stood in the middle of the room, rubbing his eyes.

"Ah, excuse me, please," he said to the doctor, whom he had touched in rising.

Lieutenant Kozeltzoff recognized his brother immediately, and stepped up to him.

"Don't you know me?" he said with a smile.

"A-a-a-!" exclaimed the younger brother; "this is astonishing!" And he began to kiss his brother.

They kissed twice, but stopped at the third repetition as though the thought had occurred to both of them:—

"Why is it necessary to do it exactly three times?"

"Well, how delighted I am!" said the elder, looking at his brother. "Let us go out on the porch; we can have a talk."

"Come, come, I don't want any soup. You eat it, Federsohn!" he said to his comrade.

"But you wanted something to eat."

"I don't want anything."

When they emerged on the porch, the younger kept asking his brother: "Well, how are you; tell me all about it." And still he kept on saying how glad he was to see him, but he told nothing himself.

When five minutes had elapsed, during which time they had succeeded in becoming somewhat silent, the elder brother inquired why the younger had not gone into the guards, as they had all expected him to do.

He wanted to get to Sevastopol as speedily as possible, he said; for if things turned out favorably there, he could get advancement more rapidly there than in the guards. There it takes ten years to reach the grade of colonel, while here Todleben had risen in two years from lieutenant-colonel to general. Well, and if one did get killed, there was nothing to be done.

"What a fellow you are!" said his brother, smiling.

"But the principal thing, do you know, brother," said the younger, smiling and blushing as though he were preparing to say something very disgraceful, "all this is nonsense, and the principal reason why I asked it was that I was ashamed to live in Petersburg when men are dying for their country here. Yes, and I wanted to be with you," he added, with still greater shamefacedness.

"How absurd you are!" said the elder brother, pulling out his cigarette-machine, and not even glancing at him. "It's a pity, though, that we can't be together."

"Now, honestly, is it so terrible in the bastions?" inquired the younger man, abruptly.

"It is terrible at first, but you get used to it afterwards. It's nothing. You will see for yourself."

"And tell me still another thing. What do you think?—will Sevastopol be taken? I think that it will not."

"God knows!"

"But one thing is annoying. Just imagine what bad luck! A whole bundle was stolen from us on the road, and it had my shako in it, so that now I am in a dreadful predicament; and I don't know how I am to show myself."

The younger Kozeltzoff, Vladímir, greatly resembled his brother Mikháïl, but he resembled him as a budding rose-bush resembles one that is out of flower. His hair was chestnut also, but it was thick and lay in curls on his temples. On the soft white back of his neck there was a blond lock; a sign of good luck, so the nurses say. The full-blooded crimson of youth did not stand fixed on the soft, white hue of his face, but flashed up and betrayed all the movements of his mind. He had the same eyes as his brother, but they were more widely opened, and clearer, which appeared the more peculiar because they were veiled frequently by a slight moisture. A golden down was sprouting on his cheeks, and over his ruddy lips, which were often folded into a shy smile, displaying teeth of dazzling whiteness. He was a well formed and broad-shouldered fellow, in unbuttoned coat, from beneath which was visible a red shirt with collar turned back. As he stood before his brother, leaning his elbows on the railing of the porch, with cigarette in hand and innocent joy in his face and gesture, he was so agreeable and comely a youth that any one would have gazed at him with delight. He was extremely pleased with his brother, he looked at him with respect and pride, fancying him his hero; but in some ways, so far as judgments on worldly culture, ability to talk French, behavior in the society of distinguished people, dancing, and so on, he was somewhat ashamed of him, looked down on him, and even cherished a hope of improving him if such a thing were possible.

All his impressions, so far, were from Petersburg, at the house of a lady who was fond of good-looking young fellows, and who had had him spend his holidays with her, and from Moscow, at the house of a senator, where he had once danced at a great ball.

VI.

Having nearly talked their fill and having arrived at the feeling that you frequently experience, that there is little in common between you, though you love one another, the brothers were silent for a few moments.

"Pick up your things and we will set out at once," said the elder.

The younger suddenly blushed, stammered, and became confused.

"Are we to go straight to Sevastopol?" he inquired, after a momentary pause.

"Why, yes. You can't have many things, and we can manage to carry them, I think."

"Very good! we will start at once," said the younger, with a sigh, and he went inside.

But he paused in the vestibule without opening the door, dropped his head gloomily, and began to reflect.

"Straight to Sevastopol, on the instant, within range of the bombs—frightful! It's no matter, however; it must have come sometime. Now, at all events, with my brother—"

The fact was that it was only now, at the thought that, once seated in the cart, he should enter Sevastopol without dismounting from it, and that no chance occurrence could any longer detain him, that the danger which he was seeking clearly presented itself to him, and he was troubled at the very thought of its nearness. He managed to control himself in some way, and entered the room; but a quarter of an hour elapsed, and still he had not rejoined his brother, so that the latter opened the door at last, in order to call him. The younger Kozeltzoff, in the attitude of a naughty school-boy, was saying something to an officer named P. When his brother opened the door, he became utterly confused.

"Immediately. I'll come out in a minute!" he cried, waving his hand at his brother. "Wait for me there, please."

A moment later he emerged, in fact, and approached his brother, with a deep sigh.

"Just imagine! I cannot go with you, brother," he said.

"What? What nonsense is this?"

"I will tell you the whole truth, Misha! Not one of us has any money, and we are all in debt to that staff-captain whom you saw there. It is horribly mortifying!"

The elder brother frowned, and did not break the silence for a long while.

"Do you owe much?" he asked, glancing askance at his brother.

"A great deal—no, not a great deal; but I am dreadfully ashamed of it. He has paid for me for three stages, and all his sugar is gone, so that I do not know—yes, and we played at preference. I am a little in his debt there, too."

"This is bad, Volodya! Now, what would you have done if you had not met me?" said the elder, sternly, without looking at his brother.

"Why, I was thinking, brother, that I should get that travelling-money at Sevastopol, and that I would give him that. Surely, that can be done; and it will be better for me to go with him to-morrow."

The elder brother pulled out his purse, and, with fingers that shook a little, he took out two ten-ruble notes and one for three rubles.

"This is all the money I have," said he. "How much do you owe?"

Kozeltzoff did not speak the exact truth when he said that this was all the money he had. He had, besides, four gold pieces sewn into his cuff, in case of an emergency; but he had taken a vow not to touch them.

It appeared that Kozeltzoff, what with preference and sugar, was in debt to the amount of eight rubles only. The elder brother gave him this sum, merely remarking that one should not play preference when one had no money.

"What did you play for?"

The younger brother answered not a word. His brother's question seemed to him to cast a reflection on his honor. Vexation at himself, a shame at his conduct, which could give rise to such a suspicion, and the insult from his brother, of whom he was so fond, produced upon his sensitive nature so deeply painful an impression that he made no reply. Sensible that he was not in a condition to restrain the sobs which rose in his throat, he took the money without glancing at it, and went back to his comrades.

VII.

Nikolaeff, who had fortified himself at Duvanka, with two jugs of vodka, purchased from a soldier who was peddling it on the bridge, gave the reins a jerk, and the team jolted away over the stony road, shaded here and there, which led along the Belbek to Sevastopol; but the brothers, whose legs jostled each other, maintained a stubborn silence, although they were thinking of each other every instant.

"Why did he insult me?" thought the younger. "Could he not have held his tongue about that? It is exactly as though he thought that I was a thief; yes, and now he is angry, apparently, so that we have quarrelled for good. And how splendid it would have been for us to be together in Sevastopol. Two brothers, on friendly terms, both fighting the foe! one of them, the elder, though not very cultivated, yet a valiant warrior, and the other younger, but a brave fellow too. In a week's time I would have showed them that I am not such a youngster after all! I shall cease to blush, there will be manliness in my countenance, and, though my moustache is not very large now, it would grow to a good size by that time;" and he felt of the down which was making its appearance round the edges of his mouth. "Perhaps we shall arrive to-day, and get directly into the conflict, my brother and I. He must be obstinate and very brave, one of those who do not say much, but act better than others. I should like to know," he continued, "whether he is squeezing me against the side of the wagon on purpose or not. He probably is conscious that I feel awkward, and he is pretending not to notice me. We shall arrive to-day," he went on with his argument, pressing close to the side of the wagon, and fearing to move lest his brother should observe that he was uncomfortable, "and, all at once, we shall go straight to the bastion. We shall both go together, I with my equipments, and my brother with his company. All of a sudden, the French throw themselves on us. I begin to fire, and fire on them. I kill a terrible number; but they still continue to run straight at me. Now, it is impossible to fire any longer, and there is no hope for me; all at once my brother rushes out in front with his sword, and I grasp my gun, and we rush on with the soldiers. The French throw themselves on my brother. I hasten up; I kill one Frenchman, then another, and I save my brother. I am wounded in one arm; I seize my gun with the other, and continue my flight; but my brother is slain by my side by the bullets. I halt for a moment, and gaze at him so sorrowfully; then I straighten myself up and shout: 'Follow me! We will avenge him! I loved my brother more than any one in the world,' I shall say, 'and I have lost him. Let us avenge him! Let us annihilate the foe, or let us all die together there!' All shout, and fling themselves after me. Then the whole French army makes a sortie, including even Pelissier himself. We all fight; but, at last, I am wounded a second, a third time, and I fall, nearly dead. Then, all rush up to me. Gortchakoff comes up and asks what I would like. I say that I want nothing—except that I may be laid beside my brother; that I wish to die with him. They carry me, and lay me down by the side of my brother's bloody corpse. Then I shall raise myself, and merely say: 'Yes, you did not understand how to value two men who really loved their father-land; now they have both fallen,—and may God forgive you!' and I shall die.

Who knows in what measure these dreams will be realized?

"Have you ever been in a hand to hand fight?" he suddenly inquired of his brother, quite forgetting that he had not meant to speak to him.

"No, not once," answered the elder. "Our regiment has lost two thousand men, all on the works; and I, also, was wounded there. War is not carried on in the least as you fancy, Volodya."

The word "Volodya" touched the younger brother. He wanted to come to an explanation with his brother, who had not the least idea that he had offended Volodya.

"You are not angry with me, Misha?" he said, after a momentary silence.

"What about?"

"No, because—because we had such a—nothing."

"Not in the least," replied the elder, turning to him, and slapping him on the leg.

"Then forgive me, Misha, if I have wounded you."

And the younger brother turned aside, in order to hide the tears that suddenly started to his eyes.

VIII.

"Is this Sevastopol already?" asked the younger brother, as they ascended the hill.

And before them appeared the bay, with its masts of ships, its shipping, and the sea, with the hostile fleet, in the distance; the white batteries on the shore, the barracks, the aqueducts, the docks and the buildings of the town, and the white and lilac clouds of smoke rising incessantly over the yellow hills, which surrounded the town and stood out against the blue sky, in the rosy rays of the sun, which was reflected by the waves, and sinking towards the horizon of the shadowy sea.

Volodya, without a shudder, gazed upon this terrible place of which he had thought so much; on the contrary, he did so with an æsthetic enjoyment, and a heroic sense of self-satisfaction at the idea that here he was—he would be there in another half-hour, that he would behold that really charmingly original spectacle—and he stared with concentrated attention from that moment until they arrived at the north fortification, at the baggage-train of his brother's regiment, where they were to ascertain with certainty the situations of the regiment and the battery.

The officer in charge of the train lived near the so-called new town (huts built of boards by the sailors' families), in a tent, connecting with a tolerably large shed, constructed out of green oak-boughs, that were not yet entirely withered.

The brothers found the officer seated before a greasy table, upon which stood a glass of cold tea, a tray with vodka, crumbs of dry sturgeon roe, and bread, clad only in a shirt of a dirty yellow hue, and engaged in counting a huge pile of bank-bills on a large abacus.

But before describing the personality of the officer, and his conversation, it is indispensable that we should inspect with more attention the interior of his shed, and become a little acquainted, at least, with his mode of life and his occupations. The new shed, like those built for generals and regimental commanders, was large, closely wattled, and comfortably arranged, with little tables and benches, made of turf. The sides and roof were hung with three rugs, to keep the leaves from showering down, and, though extremely ugly, they were new, and certainly costly.

Upon the iron bed, which stood beneath the principal rug, with a young amazon depicted on it, lay a plush coverlet, of a brilliant crimson, a torn and dirty pillow, and a raccoon cloak. On the table stood a mirror, in a silver frame, a silver brush, frightfully dirty, a broken horn comb, full of greasy hair, a silver candlestick, a bottle of liqueur, with a huge gold and red label, a gold watch, with a portrait of Peter I., two gold pens, a small box, containing pills of some sort, a crust of bread, and some old, castaway cards, and there were bottles, both full and empty, under the bed.

This officer had charge of the commissariat of the regiment and the fodder of the horses. With him lived his great friend, the commissioner who had charge of the operations.

At the moment when the brothers entered, the latter was asleep in the booth, and the commissary officer was making up his accounts of the government money, in anticipation of the end of the month. The commissary officer had a very comely and warlike exterior. His stature was tall, his moustache huge, and he possessed a respectable amount of plumpness. The only disagreeable points about him were a certain perspiration and puffiness of the whole face, which almost concealed his small gray eyes (as though he was filled up with porter), and an excessive lack of cleanliness, from his thin, greasy hair to his big, bare feet, thrust into some sort of ermine slippers.

"Money, money!" said Kozeltzoff number one, entering the shed, and fixing his eyes, with involuntary greed, upon the pile of bank-notes. "You might lend me half of that, Vasíly Mikhaïlitch!"

The commissary officer cringed at the sight of his visitors, and, sweeping up his money, he bowed to them without rising.

"Oh, if it only belonged to me! It's government money, my dear fellow. And who is this you have with you?" said he, thrusting the money into a coffer which stood beside him, and staring at Volodya.

"This is my brother, who has just come from the military academy. We have both come to learn from you where our regiment is stationed."

"Sit down, gentlemen," said the officer, rising, and going into the shed, without paying any heed to his guests. "Won't you have something to drink? Some porter, for instance?" said he.

"Don't put yourself out, Vasíly Mikhaïlitch."

Volodya was impressed by the size of the commissary officer, by his carelessness of manner, and by the respect with which his brother addressed him.

"It must be that this is one of their very fine officers, whom every one respects. Really, he is simple, but hospitable and brave," he thought, seating himself in a timid and modest manner on the sofa.

"Where is our regiment stationed, then?" called out his elder brother into the board hut.

"What?"

He repeated his query.

"Zeifer has been here to-day. He told me that they had removed to the fifth bastion."

"Is that true?"

"If I say so, it must be true; but the deuce only knows anyway! He would think nothing of telling a lie. Won't you have some porter?" said the commissary officer, still from the tent.

"I will if you please," said Kozeltzoff.

"And will you have a drink, Osip Ignatievitch?" went on the voice in the tent, apparently addressing the sleeping commissioner. "You have slept enough; it's five o'clock."

"Why do you worry me? I am not asleep," answered a shrill, languid little voice.

"Come, get up! we find it stupid without you."

And the commissary officer came out to his guests.

"Fetch some Simferopol porter!" he shouted.

A servant entered the booth, with a haughty expression of countenance, as it seemed to Volodya, and, having jostled Volodya, he drew forth the porter from beneath the bench.

The bottle of porter was soon emptied, and the conversation had proceeded in the same style for rather a long time when the flap of the tent flew open and out stepped a short, fresh-colored man, in a blue dressing-gown with tassels, in a cap with a red rim and a cockade. At the moment of his appearance, he was smoothing his small black moustache, and, with his gaze fixed on the rugs, he replied to the greetings of the officer with a barely perceptible movement of the shoulders.

"I will drink a small glassful too!" said he, seating himself by the table. "What is this, have you come from Petersburg, young man?" he said, turning courteously to Volodya.

"Yes, sir, I am on my way to Sevastopol."

"Did you make the application yourself?"

"Yes, sir."

"What queer tastes you have, gentlemen! I do not understand it!" continued the commissioner. "It strikes me that I should be ready just now to travel on foot to Petersburg, if I could get away. By Heavens, I am tired of this cursed life!"

"What is there about it that does not suit you?" said the elder Kozeltzoff, turning to him. "You're the very last person to complain of life here!"

The commissioner cast a look upon him, and then turned away.

"This danger, these privations, it is impossible to get anything here," he continued, addressing Volodya. "And why you should take such a freak, gentlemen, I really cannot understand. If there were any advantages to be derived from it, but there is nothing of the sort. It would be a nice thing, now, wouldn't it, if you, at your age, were to be left a cripple for life!"

"Some need the money, and some serve for honor's sake!" said the elder Kozeltzoff, in a tone of vexation, joining the discussion once more.

"What's the good of honor, when there's nothing to eat!" said the commissioner with a scornful laugh, turning to the commissary, who also laughed at this. "Give us something from 'Lucia'; we will listen," he said, pointing to the music-box. "I love it."

"Well, is that Vasíly Mikhaïlitch a fine man?" Volodya asked his brother when they emerged, at dusk, from the booth, and pursued their way to Sevastopol.

"Not at all; but such a niggard that it is a perfect terror! And I can't bear the sight of that commissioner, and I shall give him a thrashing one of these days."

IX.

Volodya was not precisely out of sorts when, nearly at nightfall, they reached the great bridge over the bay, but he felt a certain heaviness at his heart. All that he had heard and seen was so little in consonance with the impressions which had recently passed away; the huge, light examination hall, with its polished floor, the kind and merry voices and laughter of his comrades, the new uniform, his beloved tsar, whom he had been accustomed to see for the last seven years, and who, when he took leave of them, had called them his children, with tears in his eyes,—and everything that he had seen so little resembled his very beautiful, rainbow-hued, magnificent dreams.

"Well, here we are at last!" said the elder brother, when they arrived at the Mikhaïlovsky battery, and dismounted from their cart. "If they let us pass the bridge, we will go directly to the Nikolaevsky barracks. You stay there until morning, and I will go to the regiment and find out where your battery is stationed, and to-morrow I will come for you."

"But why? It would be better if we both went together," said Volodya; "I will go to the bastion with you. It won't make any difference; I shall have to get used to it. If you go, then I can too."

"Better not go."

"No, if you please; I do know, at least, that...."

"My advice is, not to go; but if you choose...."

The sky was clear and dark; the stars, and the fires of the bombs in incessant movement and discharges, were gleaming brilliantly through the gloom. The large white building of the battery, and the beginning of the bridge stood out in the darkness. Literally, every second several discharges of artillery and explosions, following each other in quick succession or occurring simultaneously, shook the air with increasing thunder and distinctness. Through this roar, and as though repeating it, the melancholy dash of the waves was audible. A faint breeze was drawing in from the sea, and the air was heavy with moisture. The brothers stepped upon the bridge. A soldier struck his gun awkwardly against his arm, and shouted:—

"Who goes there?"

"A soldier."

"The orders are not to let any one pass!"

"What of that! We have business! We must pass!"

"Ask the officer."

The officer, who was drowsing as he sat on an anchor, rose up and gave the order to let them pass.

"You can go that way, but not this. Where are you driving to, all in a heap!" he cried to the transport wagons piled high with gabions, which had clustered about the entrance.

As they descended to the first pontoon, the brothers encountered soldiers who were coming thence, and talking loudly.

"If he has received his ammunition money, then he has squared his accounts in full—that's what it is!"

"Eh, brothers!" said another voice, "when you get over on the Severnaya you will see the world, by heavens! The air is entirely different."

"You may say more!" said the first speaker. "A cursed shell flew in there the other day, and it tore the legs off of two sailors, so that...."

The brothers traversed the first pontoon, while waiting for the wagon, and halted on the second, which was already flooded with water in parts. The breeze, which had seemed weak inland, was very powerful here, and came in gusts; the bridge swayed to and fro, and the waves, beating noisily against the beams, and tearing at the cables and anchors, flooded the planks. At the right the gloomily hostile sea roared and darkled, as it lay separated by an interminable level black line from the starry horizon, which was light gray in its gleam; lights flashed afar on the enemy's fleet; on the left towered the black masts of one of our vessels, and the waves could be heard as they beat against her hull; a steamer was visible, as it moved noisily and swiftly from the Severnaya.

The flash of a bomb, as it burst near it, illuminated for a moment the lofty heaps of gabions on the deck, two men who were standing on it, and the white foam and the spurts of greenish waves, as the steamer ploughed through them. On the edge of the bridge, with his legs dangling in the water, sat a man in his shirt-sleeves, who was repairing something connected with the bridge. In front, over Sevastopol, floated the same fires, and the terrible sounds grew louder and louder. A wave rolled in from the sea, flowed over the right side of the bridge, and wet Volodya's feet; two soldiers passed them, dragging their feet through the water. Something suddenly burst with a crash and lighted up the bridge ahead of them, the wagon driving over it, and a man on horseback. The splinters fell into the waves with a hiss, and sent up the water in splashes.

"Ah, Mikhaïlo Semyónitch!" said the rider, stopping, reining in his horse in front of the elder Kozeltzoff, "have you fully recovered already?"

"As you see. Whither is God taking you?"

"To the Severnaya, for cartridges; I am on my way to the adjutant of the regiment ... we expect an assault to-morrow, at any hour."

"And where is Martzoff?"

"He lost a leg yesterday; he was in the town, asleep in his room.... Perhaps you know it?"

"The regiment is in the fifth bastion, isn't it?"

"Yes; it has taken the place of the M—— regiment. Go to the field-hospital; some of our men are there, and they will show you the way."

"Well, and are my quarters on the Morskaya still intact?"

"Why, my good fellow, they were smashed to bits long ago by the bombs. You will not recognize Sevastopol now; there's not a single woman there now, nor any inns nor music; the last establishment took its departure yesterday. It has become horribly dismal there now.... Farewell!"

And the officer rode on his way at a trot.

All at once, Volodya became terribly frightened; it seemed to him as though a cannon-ball or a splinter of bomb would fly in their direction, and strike him directly on the head. This damp darkness, all these sounds, especially the angry splashing of the waves, seemed to be saying to him that he ought not to go any farther, that nothing good awaited him yonder, that he would never again set foot on the ground upon this side of the bay, that he must turn about at once, and flee somewhere or other, as far as possible from this terrible haunt of death. "But perhaps it is too late now, everything is settled," thought he, trembling partly at this thought and partly because the water had soaked through his boots and wet his feet.

Volodya heaved a deep sigh, and went a little apart from his brother.

"Lord, will they kill me—me in particular? Lord, have mercy on me!" said he, in a whisper, and he crossed himself.

"Come, Volodya, let us go on!" said the elder brother, when their little cart had driven upon the bridge. "Did you see that bomb?"

On the bridge, the brothers met wagons filled with the wounded, with gabions, and one loaded with furniture, which was driven by a woman. On the further side no one detained them.

Clinging instinctively to the walls of the Nikolaevsky battery, the brothers listened in silence to the noise of the bombs, exploding overhead, and to the roar of the fragments, showering down from above, and came to that spot in the battery where the image was. There they learned that the fifth light battery, to which Volodya had been assigned, was stationed on the Korabelnaya, and they decided that he should go, in spite of the danger, and pass the night with the elder in the fifth bastion, and that he should from there join his battery the next day. They turned into the corridor, stepping over the legs of the sleeping soldiers, who were lying all along the walls of the battery, and at last they arrived at the place where the wounded were attended to.

X.

As they entered the first room, surrounded with cots on which lay the wounded, and permeated with that frightful and disgusting hospital odor, they met two Sisters of Mercy, who were coming to meet them.

One woman, of fifty, with black eyes, and a stern expression of countenance, was carrying bandages and lint, and was giving strict orders to a young fellow, an assistant surgeon, who was following her; the other, a very pretty girl of twenty, with a pale and delicate little fair face, gazed in an amiably helpless way from beneath her white cap, held her hands in the pockets of her apron, as she walked beside the elder woman, and seemed to be afraid to quit her side.

Kozeltzoff addressed to them the question whether they knew where Martzoff was—the man whose leg had been torn off on the day before.

"He belonged to the P—— regiment, did he not?" inquired the elder. "Is he a relative of yours?"

"No, a comrade."

"Show them the way," said she, in French, to the young sister. "Here, this way," and she approached a wounded man, in company with the assistant.

"Come along; what are you staring at?" said Kozeltzoff to Volodya, who, with uplifted eyebrows and somewhat suffering expression of countenance, could not tear himself away, but continued to stare at the wounded. "Come, let us go."

Volodya went off with his brother, still continuing to gaze about him, however, and repeating unconsciously:—

"Ah, my God! Ah, my God!"

"He has probably not been here long?" inquired the sister of Kozeltzoff, pointing at Volodya, who, groaning and sighing, followed them through the corridor.

"He has but just arrived."

The pretty little sister glanced at Volodya, and suddenly burst out crying. "My God! my God! when will there be an end to all this?" she said, with the accents of despair. They entered the officer's hut. Martzoff was lying on his back, with his muscular arms, bare to the elbow, thrown over his head, and with the expression on his yellow face of a man who is clenching his teeth in order to keep from shrieking with pain. His whole leg, in its stocking, was thrust outside the coverlet, and it could be seen how he was twitching his toes convulsively inside it.

"Well, how goes it, how do you feel?" asked the sister, raising his bald head with her slender, delicate fingers, on one of which Volodya noticed a gold ring, and arranging his pillow. "Here are some of your comrades come to inquire after you."

"Badly, of course," he answered, angrily. "Let me alone! it's all right,"— the toes in his stocking moved more rapidly than ever. "How do you do? What is your name? Excuse me," he said, turning to Kozeltzoff.... "Ah, yes, I beg your pardon! one forgets everything here," he said, when the latter had mentioned his name. "You and I lived together," he added, without the slightest expression of pleasure, glancing interrogatively at Volodya.

"This is my brother, who has just arrived from Petersburg to-day."

"Hm! Here I have finished my service," he said, with a frown. "Ah, how painful it is!... The best thing would be a speedy end."

He drew up his leg, and covered his face with his hands, continuing to move his toes with redoubled swiftness.

"You must leave him," said the sister, in a whisper, while the tears stood in her eyes; "he is in a very bad state."

The brothers had already decided on the north side to go to the fifth bastion; but, on emerging from the Nikolaevsky battery, they seemed to have come to a tacit understanding not to subject themselves to unnecessary danger, and, without discussing the subject, they determined to go their ways separately.

"Only, how are you to find your way, Volodya?" said the elder. "However, Nikolaeff will conduct you to the Korabelnaya, and I will go my way alone, and will be with you to-morrow."

Nothing more was said at this last leave-taking between the brothers.

XI.

The thunder of the cannon continued with the same power as before, but Yekaterinskaya street, along which Volodya walked, followed by the taciturn Nikolaeff, was quiet and deserted. All that he could see, through the thick darkness, was the wide street with the white walls of large houses, battered in many places, and the stone sidewalk beneath his feet; now and then, he met soldiers and officers. As he passed along the left side of the street, near the Admiralty building, he perceived, by the light of a bright fire burning behind the wall, the acacias planted along the sidewalk, with green guards beneath, and the wretchedly dusty leaves of these acacias.

He could plainly hear his own steps and those of Nikolaeff, who followed him, breathing heavily. He thought of nothing; the pretty little Sister of Mercy, Martzoff's leg with the toes twitching in its stocking, the bombs, the darkness, and divers pictures of death floated hazily through his mind. All his young and sensitive soul shrank together, and was borne down by his consciousness of loneliness, and the indifference of every one to his fate in the midst of danger.

"They will kill me, I shall be tortured, I shall suffer, and no one will weep." And all this, instead of the hero's life, filled with energy and sympathy, of which he had cherished such glorious dreams. The bombs burst and shrieked nearer and ever nearer. Nikolaeff sighed more frequently, without breaking the silence. On crossing the bridge leading to the Korabelnaya, he saw something fly screaming into the bay, not far from him, which lighted up the lilac waves for an instant with a crimson glow, then disappeared, and threw on high a cloud of foam.

"See there, it was not put out!" said Nikolaeff, hoarsely.

"Yes," answered Volodya, involuntarily, and quite unexpectedly to himself, in a thin, piping voice.

They encountered litters with wounded men, then more regimental transports with gabions; they met a regiment on Korabelnaya street; men on horseback passed them. One of them was an officer, with his Cossack. He was riding at a trot, but, on catching sight of Volodya, he reined in his horse near him, looked into his face, turned and rode on, giving the horse a blow of his whip.

"Alone, alone; it is nothing to any one whether I am in existence or not," thought the lad, and he felt seriously inclined to cry.

After ascending the hill, past a high white wall, he entered a street of small ruined houses, incessantly illuminated by bombs. A drunken and dishevelled woman, who was coming out of a small door in company with a sailor, ran against him.

"If he were only a fine man," she grumbled,—"Pardon, Your Honor the officer."

The poor boy's heart sank lower and lower, and more and more frequently flashed the lightnings against the dark horizon, and the bombs screamed and burst about him with ever increasing frequency. Nikolaeff sighed, and all at once he began to speak, in what seemed to Volodya a frightened and constrained tone.

"What haste we made to get here from home. It was nothing but travelling. A pretty place to be in a hurry to get to!"

"What was to be done, if my brother was well again," replied Volodya, in hope that he might banish by conversation the frightful feeling that was taking possession of him.

"Well, what sort of health is it when he is thoroughly ill! Those who are really well had better stay in the hospital at such a time. A vast deal of joy there is about it, isn't there? You will have a leg or an arm torn off, and that's all you will get! It's not far removed from a downright sin! And here in the town it's not at all like the bastion, and that is a perfect terror. You go and you say your prayers the whole way. Eh, you beast, there you go whizzing past!" he added, directing his attention to the sound of a splinter of shell whizzing by near them. "Now, here," Nikolaeff went on, "I was ordered to show Your Honor the way. My business, of course, is to do as I am bid; but the cart has been abandoned to some wretch of a soldier, and the bundle is undone.... Go on and on; but if any of the property disappears, Nikolaeff will have to answer for it."

After proceeding a few steps further, they came out on a square. Nikolaeff held his peace, but sighed.

"Yonder is your artillery, Your Honor!" he suddenly said. "Ask the sentinel; he will show you."

And Volodya, after he had taken a few steps more, ceased to hear the sound of Nikolaeff's sighs behind him.

All at once, he felt himself entirely and finally alone. This consciousness of solitude in danger, before death, as it seemed to him, lay upon his heart like a terribly cold and heavy stone.

He halted in the middle of the square, glanced about him, to see whether he could catch sight of any one, grasped his head, and uttered his thought aloud in his terror:—"Lord! Can it be that I am a coward, a vile, disgusting, worthless coward ... can it be that I so lately dreamed of dying with joy for my father-land, my tsar? No, I am a wretched, an unfortunate, a wretched being!" And Volodya, with a genuine sentiment of despair and disenchantment with himself, inquired of the sentinel for the house of the commander of the battery, and set out in the direction indicated.

XII.

The residence of the commander of the battery, which the sentinel had pointed out to him, was a small, two-story house, with an entrance on the court-yard. In one of the windows, which was pasted over with paper, burned the feeble flame of a candle. A servant was seated on the porch, smoking his pipe; he went in and announced Volodya to the commander, and then led him in. In the room, between the two windows, and beneath a shattered mirror, stood a table, heaped with official documents, several chairs, and an iron bedstead, with a clean pallet, and a small bed-rug by its side.

Near the door stood a handsome man, with a large moustache,—a sergeant, in sabre and cloak, on the latter of which hung a cross and a Hungarian medal. Back and forth in the middle of the room paced a short staff-officer of forty, with swollen cheeks bound up, and dressed in a thin old coat.

"I have the honor to report myself, Cornet Kozeltzoff, 2d, ordered to the fifth light battery," said Volodya, uttering the phrase which he had learned by heart, as he entered the room.

The commander of the battery responded dryly to his greeting, and, without offering his hand, invited him to be seated.

Volodya dropped timidly into a chair, beside the writing-table, and began to twist in his fingers the scissors, which his hand happened to light upon. The commander of the battery put his hands behind his back, and, dropping his head, pursued his walk up and down the room, in silence, only bestowing an occasional glance at the hands which were twirling the scissors, with the aspect of a man who is trying to recall something.

The battery commander was a rather stout man, with a large bald spot on the crown of his head, a thick moustache, which drooped straight down and concealed his mouth, and pleasant brown eyes. His hands were handsome, clean, and plump; his feet small and well turned, and they stepped out in a confident and rather dandified manner, proving that the commander was not a timid man.

"Yes," he said, coming to a halt in front of the sergeant; "a measure must be added to the grain to-morrow, or our horses will be getting thin. What do you think?"

"Of course, it is possible to do so, Your Excellency! Oats are very cheap just now," replied the sergeant, twitching his fingers, which he held on the seams of his trousers, but which evidently liked to assist in the conversation. "Our forage-master, Franchuk, sent me a note yesterday, from the transports, Your Excellency, saying that we should certainly be obliged to purchase oats; they say they are cheap. Therefore, what are your orders?"

"To buy, of course. He has money, surely." And the commander resumed his tramp through the room. "And where are your things?" he suddenly inquired of Volodya, as he paused in front of him.

Poor Volodya was so overwhelmed by the thought that he was a coward, that he espied scorn for himself in every glance, in every word, as though they had been addressed to a pitiable poltroon. It seemed to him that the commander of the battery had already divined his secret, and was making sport of him. He answered, with embarrassment, that his effects were on the Grafskaya, and that his brother had promised to send them to him on the morrow.

But the lieutenant-colonel was not listening to him, and, turning to the sergeant, he inquired:—

"Where are we to put the ensign?"

"The ensign, sir?" said the sergeant, throwing Volodya into still greater confusion by the fleeting glance which he cast upon him, and which seemed to say, "What sort of an ensign is this?"—"He can be quartered downstairs, with the staff-captain, Your Excellency," he continued, after a little reflection. "The captain is at the bastion just now, and his cot is empty."

"Will that not suit you, temporarily?" said the commander.—"I think you must be tired, but we will lodge you better to-morrow."

Volodya rose and bowed.

"Will you not have some tea?" said the commander, when he had already reached the door. "The samovár can be brought in."

Volodya saluted and left the room. The lieutenant-colonel's servant conducted him downstairs, and led him into a bare, dirty chamber, in which various sorts of rubbish were lying about, and where there was an iron bedstead without either sheets or coverlet. A man in a red shirt was fast asleep on the bed, covered over with a thick cloak.

Volodya took him for a soldier.

"Piotr Nikolaïtch!" said the servant, touching the sleeper on the shoulder. "The ensign is to sleep here.... This is our yunker," he added, turning to the ensign.

"Ah, don't trouble him, please," said Volodya; but the yunker, a tall, stout, young man, with a handsome but very stupid face, rose from the bed, threw on his cloak, and, evidently not having had a good sleep, left the room.

"No matter; I'll lie down in the yard," he growled out.

<u>XIII.</u>

Left alone with his own thoughts, Volodya's first sensation was a fear of the incoherent, forlorn state of his own soul. He wanted to go to sleep, and forget all his surroundings, and himself most of all. He extinguished the candle, lay down on the bed, and, taking off his coat, he wrapped his head up in it, in order to relieve his terror of the darkness, with which he had been afflicted since his childhood. But all at once the thought occurred to him that a bomb might come and crush in the roof and kill him. He began to listen attentively; directly overhead, he heard the footsteps of the battery commander.

"Anyway, if it does come," he thought, "it will kill any one who is upstairs first, and then me; at all events, I shall not be the only one."

This thought calmed him somewhat.

"Well, and what if Sevastopol should be taken unexpectedly, in the night, and the French make their way hither? What am I to defend myself with?"

He rose once more, and began to pace the room. His terror of the actual danger outweighed his secret fear of the darkness. There was nothing heavy in the room except the samovár and a saddle. "I am a scoundrel, a coward, a miserable coward!" the thought suddenly occurred to him, and again he experienced that oppressive sensation of scorn and disgust, even for himself. Again he threw himself on the bed, and tried not to think.

Then the impressions of the day involuntarily penetrated his imagination, in consequence of the unceasing sounds, which made the glass in the solitary window rattle, and again the thought of danger recurred to him: now he saw visions of wounded men and blood, now of bombs and splinters, flying into the room, then of the pretty little Sister of Mercy, who was applying a bandage to him, a dying man, and weeping over him, then of his mother, accompanying him to the provincial town, and praying, amid burning tears, before the wonder-working images, and once more sleep appeared an impossibility to him.

But suddenly the thought of Almighty God, who can do all things, and who hears every supplication, came clearly into his mind. He knelt down, crossed himself, and folded his hands as he had been taught to do in his childhood, when he prayed. This gesture, all at once, brought back to him a consoling feeling, which he had long since forgotten.

"If I must die, if I must cease to exist, 'thy will be done, Lord,'" he thought; "let it be quickly; but if bravery is needed, and the firmness which I do not possess, give them to me; deliver me from shame and disgrace, which I cannot bear, but teach me what to do in order to fulfil thy will."

His childish, frightened, narrow soul was suddenly encouraged; it cleared up, and caught sight of broad, brilliant, and new horizons. During the brief period while this feeling lasted, he felt and thought many other things, and soon fell asleep quietly and unconcernedly, to the continuous sounds of the roar of the bombardment and the rattling of the window-panes.

Great Lord! thou alone hast heard, and thou alone knowest those ardent, despairing prayers of ignorance, of troubled repentance, those petitions for the healing of the body and the enlightenment of the mind, which have ascended to thee from that terrible precinct of death, from the general who, a moment before, was thinking of his cross of the George on his neck, and conscious in his terror of thy near presence, to the simple soldier writhing on the bare earth of the Nikolaevsky battery, and beseeching thee to bestow upon him there the reward, unconsciously presaged, for all his sufferings.

XIV.

The elder Kozeltzoff, meeting on the street a soldier belonging to his regiment, betook himself at once, in company with the man, to the fifth bastion.

"Keep under the wall, Your Honor," said the soldier.

"What for?"

"It's dangerous, Your Honor; there's one passing over," said the soldier, listening to the sound of a screaming cannon-ball, which struck the dry road, on the other side of the street.

Kozeltzoff, paying no heed to the soldier, walked bravely along the middle of the street.

These were the same streets, the same fires, even more frequent now, the sounds, the groans, the encounters with the wounded, and the same batteries, breastworks, and trenches, which had been there in the spring, when he was last in Sevastopol; but, for some reason, all this was now more melancholy, and, at the same time, more energetic, the apertures in the houses were larger, there were no longer any lights in the windows, with the exception of the Kushtchin house (the hospital), not a woman was to be met with, the earlier tone of custom and freedom from care no longer rested over all, but, instead, a certain impress of heavy expectation, of weariness and earnestness.

But here is the last trench already, and here is the voice of a soldier of the P—— regiment, who has recognized the former commander of his company, and here stands the third battalion in the gloom, clinging close to the wall, and lighted up now and then, for a moment, by the discharges, and a sound of subdued conversation, and the rattling of guns.

"Where is the commander of the regiment?" inquired Kozeltzoff.

"In the bomb-proofs with the sailors, Your Honor," replied the soldier, ready to be of service. "I will show you the way, if you like."

From trench to trench the soldier led Kozeltzoff, to the small ditch in the trench. In the ditch sat a sailor, smoking his pipe; behind him a door was visible, through whose cracks shone a light.

"Can I enter?"

"I will announce you at once," and the sailor went in through the door.

Two voices became audible on the other side of the door.

"If Prussia continues to observe neutrality," said one voice, "then Austria also...."

"What difference does Austria make," said the second, "when the Slavic lands ... well, ask him to come in."

Kozeltzoff had never been in this casemate. He was struck by its elegance. The floor was of polished wood, screens shielded the door. Two bedsteads stood against the wall, in one corner stood a large ikon of the mother of God, in a gilt frame, and before her burned a rose-colored lamp.

On one of the beds, a naval officer, fully dressed, was sleeping. On the other, by a table upon which stood two bottles of wine, partly empty, sat the men who were talking—the new regimental commander and his adjutant.

Although Kozeltzoff was far from being a coward, and was certainly not guilty of any wrongdoing so far as his superior officers were concerned, nor towards the regimental commander, yet he felt timid before the colonel, who had been his comrade not long before, so proudly did this colonel rise and listen to him.

"It is strange," thought Kozeltzoff, as he surveyed his commander, "it is only seven weeks since he took the regiment, and how visible already is his power as regimental commander, in everything about him—in his dress, his bearing, his look. Is it so very long," thought he, "since this Batrishtcheff used to carouse with us, and he wore a cheap cotton shirt, and ate by himself, never inviting any one to his quarters, his eternal meat-balls and curd-patties? But now! and that expression of cold pride in his eyes, which says to you, 'Though I am your comrade, because I am a regimental commander of the new school, yet, believe me, I am well aware that you would give half your life merely for the sake of being in my place!'"

"You have been a long time in recovering," said the colonel to Kozeltzoff, coldly, with a stare.

"I was ill, colonel! The wound has not closed well even now."

"Then there was no use in your coming," said the colonel, casting an incredulous glance at the captain's stout figure. "You are, nevertheless, in a condition to fulfil your duty?"

"Certainly I am, sir."

"Well I'm very glad of that, sir. You will take the ninth company from Ensign Zaitzoff—the one you had before; you will receive your orders immediately."

"I obey, sir."

"Take care to send me the regimental adjutant when you arrive," said the regimental commander, giving him to understand, by a slight nod, that his audience was at an end.

On emerging from the casemate, Kozeltzoff muttered something several times, and shrugged his shoulders, as though pained, embarrassed, or vexed at something, and vexed, not at the regimental commander (there was no cause for that), but at himself, and he appeared to be dissatisfied with himself and with everything about him.

XV.

Before going to his officers, Kozeltzoff went to greet his company, and to see where it was stationed.

The breastwork of gabions, the shapes of the trenches, the cannons which he passed, even the fragments of shot, bombs, over which he stumbled in his path—all this, incessantly illuminated by the light of the firing, was well known to him, all this had engraved itself in vivid colors on his memory, three months before, during the two weeks which he had spent in this very bastion, without once leaving it. Although there was much that was terrible in these reminiscences, a certain charm of past things was mingled with it, and he recognized the familiar places and objects with pleasure, as though the two weeks spent there had been agreeable ones. The company was stationed along the defensive wall toward the sixth bastion.

Kozeltzoff entered the long casemate, utterly unprotected at the entrance side, in which they had told him that the ninth company was stationed. There was, literally, no room to set his foot in the casemate, so filled was it, from the very entrance, with soldiers. On one side burned a crooked tallow candle, which a recumbent soldier was holding to illuminate the book which another one was spelling out slowly. Around the candle, in the reeking half-light, heads were visible, eagerly raised in strained attention to the reader. The little book in question was a primer. As Kozeltzoff entered the casemate, he heard the following:

"Pray-er af-ter lear-ning. I thank Thee, Crea-tor ..."

"Snuff that candle!" said a voice. "That's a splendid book." "My ... God ..." went on the reader.

When Kozeltzoff asked for the sergeant, the reader stopped, the soldiers began to move about, coughed, and blew their noses, as they always do after enforced silence. The sergeant rose near the group about the reader, buttoning up his coat as he did so, and stepping over and on the feet of those who had no room to withdraw them, and came forward to his officer.

"How are you, brother? Do all these belong to our company?"

"I wish you health! Welcome on your return, Your Honor!" replied the sergeant, with a cheerful and friendly look at Kozeltzoff. "Has Your Honor recovered your health? Well, God be praised. It has been very dull for us without you."

It was immediately apparent that Kozeltzoff was beloved in the company.

In the depths of the casemate, voices could be heard. Their old commander, who had been wounded, Mikhaïl Semyónitch Kozeltzoff, had arrived, and so forth; some even approached, and the drummer congratulated him.

"How are you, Obantchuk?" said Kozeltzoff. "Are you all right? Good-day, children!" he said, raising his voice.

"We wish you health!" sounded through the casemate.

"How are you getting on, children?"

"Badly, Your Honor. The French are getting the better of us.—Fighting from behind the fortifications is bad work, and that's all there is about it! and they won't come out into the open field."

"Perhaps luck is with me, and God will grant that they shall come out into the field, children!" said Kozeltzoff. "It won't be the first time that you and I have taken a hand together: we'll beat them again."

"We'll be glad to try it, Your Honor!" exclaimed several voices.

"And how about them—are they really bold?"

"Frightfully bold!" said the drummer, not loudly, but so that his words were audible, turning to another soldier, as though justifying before him the words of the commander, and persuading him that there was nothing boastful or improbable in these words.

From the soldiers, Kozeltzoff proceeded to the defensive barracks and his brother officers.

XVI.

In the large room of the barracks there was a great number of men; naval, artillery, and infantry officers. Some were sleeping, others were conversing, seated on the shot-chests and gun-carriages of the cannons of the fortifications; others still, who formed a very numerous and noisy group behind the arch, were seated upon two felt rugs, which had been spread on the floor, and were drinking porter and playing cards.

"Ah! Kozeltzoff, Kozeltzoff! Capital! it's a good thing that he has come!

He's a brave fellow!... How's your wound?" rang out from various quarters. Here also it was evident that they loved him and were rejoiced at his coming.

After shaking hands with his friends, Kozeltzoff joined the noisy group of officers engaged in playing cards. There were some of his acquaintances among them. A slender, handsome, dark-complexioned man, with a long, sharp nose and a huge moustache, which began on his cheeks, was dealing the cards with his thin, white, taper fingers, on one of which there was a heavy gold seal ring. He was dealing straight on, and carelessly, being evidently excited by something,—and merely desirous of making a show of heedlessness. On his right, and beside him, lay a gray-haired major, supporting himself on his elbow, and playing for half a ruble with affected coolness, and settling up immediately. On his left squatted an officer with a red, perspiring face, who was laughing and jesting in a constrained way. When his cards won, he moved one hand about incessantly in his empty trousers pocket. He was playing high, and evidently no longer for ready money, which displeased the handsome, dark-complexioned man. A thin and pallid officer with a bald head, and a huge nose and mouth, was walking about the room, holding a large package of bank-notes in his hand, staking ready money on the bank, and winning.

Kozeltzoff took a drink of vodka, and sat down by the players.

"Take a hand, Mikhaïl Semyónitch!" said the dealer to him; "you have brought lots of money, I suppose."

"Where should I get any money! On the contrary, I got rid of the last I had in town."

"The idea! Some one certainly must have fleeced you in Simpferopol."

"I really have but very little," said Kozeltzoff, but he was evidently desirous that they should not believe him; then he unbuttoned his coat, and took the old cards in his hand.

"I don't care if I do try; there's no knowing what the Evil One will do! queer things do come about at times. But I must have a drink, to get up my courage."

And within a very short space of time he had drunk another glass of vodka and several of porter, and had lost his last three rubles.

A hundred and fifty rubles were written down against the little, perspiring officer.

"No, he will not bring them," said he, carelessly, drawing a fresh card.

"Try to send it," said the dealer to him, pausing a moment in his occupation of laying out the cards, and glancing at him.

"Permit me to send it to-morrow," repeated the perspiring officer, rising, and moving his hand about vigorously in his empty pocket.

"Hm!" growled the dealer, and, throwing the cards angrily to the right and left, he completed the deal. "But this won't do," said he, when he had dealt the cards. "I'm going to stop. It won't do, Zakhár Ivánitch," he added, "we have been playing for ready money and not on credit."

"What, do you doubt me? That's strange, truly!"

"From whom is one to get anything?" muttered the major, who had won about eight rubles. "I have lost over twenty rubles, but when I have won—I get nothing."

"How am I to pay," said the dealer, "when there is no money on the table?"

"I won't listen to you!" shouted the major, jumping up, "I am playing with you, but not with him."

All at once the perspiring officer flew into a rage.

"I tell you that I will pay to-morrow; how dare you say such impertinent things to me?"

"I shall say what I please! This is not the way to do—that's the truth!" shouted the major.

"That will do, Feódor Feodoritch!" all chimed in, holding back the major.

108

But let us draw a veil over this scene. To-morrow, to-day, it may be, each one of these men will go cheerfully and proudly to meet his death, and he will die with firmness and composure; but the one consolation of life in these conditions, which terrify even the coldest imagination in the absence of all that is human, and the hopelessness of any escape from them, the one consolation is forgetfulness, the annihilation of consciousness. At the bottom of the soul of each lies that noble spark, which makes of him a hero; but this spark wearies of burning clearly—when the fateful moment comes it flashes up into a flame, and illuminates great deeds.

XVII.

On the following day, the bombardment proceeded with the same vigor. At eleven o'clock in the morning, Volodya Kozeltzoff was seated in a circle of battery officers, and, having already succeeded to some extent in habituating himself to them, he was surveying the new faces, taking observations, making inquiries, and telling stories.

The discreet conversation of the artillery officers, which made some pretensions to learning, pleased him and inspired him with respect. Volodya's shy, innocent, and handsome appearance disposed the officers in his favor.

The eldest officer in the battery, the captain, a short, sandy-complexioned man, with his hair arranged in a topknot, and smooth on the temples, educated in the old traditions of the artillery, a squire of dames, and a would-be learned man, questioned Volodya as to his acquirements in artillery and new inventions, jested caressingly over his youth and his pretty little face, and treated him, in general, as a father treats a son, which was extremely agreeable to Volodya.

Sub-Lieutenant Dyadenko, a young officer, who talked with a Little Russian accent, had a tattered cloak and dishevelled hair, although he talked very loudly, and constantly seized opportunities to dispute acrimoniously over some topic, and was very abrupt in his movements, pleased Volodya, who, beneath this rough exterior, could not help detecting in him a very fine and extremely good man. Dyadenko was incessantly offering his services to Volodya, and pointing out to him that not one of the guns in Sevastopol was properly placed, according to rule.

Lieutenant Tchernovitzky, with his brows elevated on high, though he was more courteous than any of the rest, and dressed in a coat that was tolerably clean, but not new, and carefully patched, and though he displayed a gold watch-chain on a satin waistcoat, did not please Volodya. He kept inquiring what the Emperor and the minister of war were doing, and related to him, with unnatural triumph, the deeds of valor which had been performed in Sevastopol, complained of the small number of true patriots, and displayed a great deal of learning, and sense, and noble feeling in general; but, for some reason, all this seemed unpleasant and unnatural to Volodya. The principal thing which he noticed was that the other officers hardly spoke to Tchernovitzky.

Yunker Vlang, whom he had waked up on the preceding evening, was also there. He said nothing, but, seated modestly in a corner, laughed when anything amusing occurred, refreshed their memories when they forgot anything, handed the vodka, and made cigarettes for all the officers. Whether it was the modest, courteous manners of Volodya, who treated him exactly as he did the officers, and did not torment him as though he were a little boy, or his agreeable personal appearance which captivated Vlanga, as the soldiers called him, declining his name, for some reason or other, in the feminine gender, at all events, he never took his big, kind eyes from the face of the new officer. He divined and anticipated all his wishes, and remained uninterruptedly in a sort of lover-like ecstasy, which, of course, the officers perceived, and made fun of.

Before dinner, the staff-captain was relieved from the battery, and joined their company. Staff-Captain Kraut was a light-complexioned, handsome, dashing officer, with a heavy, reddish moustache, and side-whiskers; he spoke Russian capitally, but too elegantly and correctly for a Russian. In the service and in his life, he had been the same as in his language; he served very well, was a capital comrade, and the most faithful of men in money matters; but simply as a man something was lacking in him, precisely because everything about him was so excellent. Like all Russian-Germans, by a strange contradiction with the ideal German, he was "praktisch" to the highest degree.

"Here he is, our hero makes his appearance!" said the captain, as Kraut, flourishing his arms and jingling his spurs, entered the room. "Which will you have, Friedrich Krestyanitch, tea or vodka?"

"I have already ordered my tea to be served," he answered, "but I may take a little drop of vodka also, for the refreshing of the soul. Very glad to make your acquaintance; I beg that you will love us, and lend us your favor," he said to Volodya, who rose and bowed to him. "Staff-Captain Kraut.... The gun-sergeant on the bastion informed me that you arrived last night."

"Much obliged for your bed; I passed the night in it."

"I hope you found it comfortable? One of the legs is broken; but no one can stand on ceremony—in time of siege—you must prop it up."

"Well, now, did you have a fortunate time on your watch?" asked Dyadenko.

"Yes, all right; only Skvortzoff was hit, and we mended one of the gun-carriages last night. The cheek was smashed to atoms."

He rose from his seat, and began to walk up and down; it was plain that he was wholly under the influence of that agreeable sensation which a man experiences who has just escaped a danger.

"Well, Dmitri Gavrilitch," he said, tapping the captain on the knee, "how are you getting on, my dear fellow? How about your promotion?—no word yet?"

"Nothing yet."

"No, and there will be nothing," interpolated Dyadenko: "I proved that to you before."

"Why won't there?"

"Because the story was not properly written down."

"Oh, you quarrelsome fellow, you quarrelsome fellow!" said Kraut, smiling gayly; "a regular obstinate Little Russian! Now, just to provoke you, he'll turn out your lieutenant."

"No, he won't."

"Vlang! fetch me my pipe, and fill it," said he, turning to the yunker, who at once hastened up obligingly with the pipe.

Kraut made them all lively; he told about the bombardment, he inquired what had been going on in his absence, and entered into conversation with every one.

XVIII.

"Well, how are things? Have you already got settled among us?" Kraut asked Volodya.... "Excuse me, what is your name and patronymic? that's the custom with us in the artillery, you know. Have you got hold of a saddle-horse?"

"No," said Volodya; "I do not know what to do. I told the captain that I had no horse, and no money, either, until I get some for forage and travelling expenses. I want to ask the battery commander for a horse in the meantime, but I am afraid that he will refuse me."

"Apollon Sergiéitch, do you mean?" he produced with his lips a sound indicative of the strongest doubt, and glanced at the captain; "not likely."

"What's that? If he does refuse, there'll be no harm done," said the captain. "There are horses, to tell the truth, which are not needed, but still one might try; I will inquire to-day."

"What! Don't you know him?" Dyadenko interpolated. "He might refuse anything, but there is no reason for refusing this. Do you want to bet on it?..."

"Well, of course, everybody knows already that you always contradict."

"I contradict because I know. He is niggardly about other things, but he will give the horse because it is no advantage to him to refuse."

"No advantage, indeed, when it costs him eight rubles here for oats!" said Kraut. "Is there no advantage in not keeping an extra horse?"

"Ask Skvoretz yourself, Vladímir Semyónitch!" said Vlang, returning with Kraut's pipe. "It's a capital horse."

"The one you tumbled into the ditch with, on the festival of the forty martyrs, in March? Hey! Vlang?" remarked the staff-captain.

"No, and why should you say that it costs eight rubles for oats," pursued Dyadenko, "when his own inquiries show him that it is ten and a half; of course, he has no object in it."

"Just as though he would have nothing left! So when you get to be battery commander, you won't let any horses go into the town?"

"When I get to be battery commander, my dear fellow, my horses will get four measures of oats to eat, and I shall not accumulate an income, never fear!"

"If we live, we shall see," said the staff-captain; "and you will act just so, and so will he when he commands a battery," he added, pointing at Volodya.

"Why do you think, Friedrich Krestyanitch, that he would turn it to his profit?" broke in Tchernovitzky. "Perhaps he has property of his own; then why should he turn it to profit?"

"No, sir, I ... excuse me, captain," said Volodya, reddening up to his ears, "that strikes me as insulting."

"Oh ho, ho! What a madcap he is!" said Kraut.

"That has nothing to do with it; I only think that if the money were not mine, I should not take it."

"Now, I'll tell you something right here, young man," began the staff-captain in a more serious tone, "you are to understand that when you command a battery, if you manage things well, that's sufficient; the commander of a battery does not meddle with provisioning the soldiers; that is the way it has been from time immemorial in the artillery. If you are a bad manager, you will have nothing left. Now, these are the expenditures in conformity with your position: for shoeing your horse,—one (he closed one finger); for the apothecary,—two (he closed another finger); for office work,—three (he shut a third); for extra horses, which cost five hundred rubles, my dear fellow,— that's four; you must change the soldiers' collars, you will use a great deal of coal, you must keep open table for your officers. If you are a battery-commander, you must live decently; you need a carriage, and a fur coat, and this thing and that thing, and a dozen more ... but what's the use of enumerating them all!"

"But this is the principal thing, Vladímir Semyónitch," interpolated the captain, who had held his peace all this time; "imagine yourself to be a man who, like myself, for instance, has served twenty years, first for two hundred, then for three hundred rubles pay; why should he not be given at least a bit of bread, against his old age?"

"Eh! yes, there you have it!" spoke up the staff-captain again, "don't be in a hurry to pronounce judgment, but live on and serve your time."

Volodya was horribly ashamed and sorry for having spoken so thoughtlessly, and he muttered something and continued to listen in silence, when Dyadenko undertook, with the greatest zeal, to dispute it and to prove the contrary.

The dispute was interrupted by the arrival of the colonel's servant, who summoned them to dinner.

"Tell Apollon Sergiéitch that he must give us some wine to-day," said Tchernovitzky, to the captain, as he buttoned up his uniform.—"Why is he so stingy with it? He will be killed, and no one will get the good of it."

"Tell him yourself."

"Not a bit of it. You are my superior officer. Rank must be regarded in all things."

XIX.

The table had been moved out from the wall, and spread with a soiled table-cloth, in the same room in which Volodya had presented himself to the colonel on the preceding evening. The battery commander now offered him his hand, and questioned him about Petersburg and his journey.

"Well, gentlemen, I beg the favor of a glass with any of you who drink vodka. The ensigns do not drink," he added, with a smile.

On the whole, the battery commander did not appear nearly so stern today as he had on the preceding evening; on the contrary, he had the appearance of a kindly, hospitable host, and an elder comrade among the officers. But, in spite of this, all the officers, from the old captain down to Ensign Dyadenko, by their very manner of speaking and looking the commander straight in the eye, as they approached, one after the other, to drink their vodka, exhibited great respect for him.

The dinner consisted of a large wooden bowl of cabbage-soup, in which floated fat chunks of beef, and a huge quantity of pepper and laurel-leaves, mustard, and Polish meat-balls in a cabbage leaf, turnover patties of chopped meat and dough, and with butter, which was not perfectly fresh. There were no napkins, the spoons were of pewter and wood, there were only two glasses, and on the table stood a decanter of water with a broken neck; but the dinner was not dull; conversation never halted.

At first, their talk turned on the battle of Inkerman, in which the battery had taken part, as to the causes of failure, of which each one gave his own impressions and ideas, and held his tongue as soon as the battery commander himself began to speak; then the conversation naturally changed to the insufficiency of calibre of the light guns, and upon the new lightened cannons, in which connection Volodya had an opportunity to display his knowledge of artillery.

But their talk did not dwell upon the present terrible position of Sevastopol, as though each of them had meditated too much on that subject to allude to it again. In the same way, to Volodya's great amazement and disappointment, not a word was said about the duties of the service which he was to fulfil, just as though he had come to Sevastopol merely for the purpose of telling about the new cannon and dining with the commander of the battery.

While they were at dinner, a bomb fell not far from the house in which they were seated. The walls and the floor trembled, as though in an earthquake, and the window was obscured with the smoke of the powder.

"You did not see anything of this sort in Petersburg, I fancy; but these surprises often take place here," said the battery commander.

"Look out, Vlang, and see where it burst."

Vlang looked, and reported that it had burst on the square, and then there was nothing more said about the bomb.

Just before the end of the dinner, an old man, the clerk of the battery, entered the room, with three sealed envelopes, and handed them to the commander.

"This is very important; a messenger has this moment brought these from the chief of the artillery."

All the officers gazed, with impatient curiosity, at the commander's practised fingers as they broke the seal of the envelope and drew forth the very important paper. "What can it be?" each one asked himself.

It might be that they were to march out of Sevastopol for a rest, it might be an order for the whole battery to betake themselves to the bastions.

"Again!" said the commander, flinging the paper angrily on the table.

"What's it about, Apollon Sergiéitch?" inquired the eldest officer.

"An officer and crew are required for a mortar battery over yonder, and I have only four officers, and there is not a full gun-crew in the line," growled the commander: "and here more are demanded of me. But some one must go, gentlemen," he said, after a brief pause: "the order requires him to be at the barrier at seven o'clock.... Send the sergeant! Who is to go, gentlemen? decide," he repeated.

"Well, here's one who has never been yet," said Tchernovitzky, pointing to Volodya. The commander of the battery made no reply.

"Yes, I should like to go," said Volodya, as he felt the cold sweat start out on his back and neck.

"No; why should you? There's no occasion!" broke in the captain. "Of course, no one will refuse, but neither is it proper to ask any one; but if Apollon Sergiéitch will permit us, we will draw lots, as we did once before."

All agreed to this. Kraut cut some paper into bits, folded them up, and dropped them into a cap. The captain jested, and even plucked up the audacity, on this occasion, to ask the colonel for wine, to keep up their courage, he said. Dyadenko sat in gloomy silence, Volodya smiled at something or other, Tchernovitzky declared that it would infallibly fall to him, Kraut was perfectly composed.

Volodya was allowed to draw first; he took one slip, which was rather long, but it immediately occurred to him to change it; he took another, which was smaller and thinner, unfolded it, and read on it, "I go."

"It has fallen to me," he said, with a sigh.

"Well, God be with you. You will get your baptism of fire at once," said the commander of the battery, gazing at the perturbed countenance of the ensign with a kindly smile; "but you must get there as speedily as possible. And, to make it more cheerful for you, Vlang shall go with you as gun-sergeant."

XX.

Vlang was exceedingly well pleased with the duty assigned to him, and ran hastily to make his preparations, and, when he was dressed, he went to the assistance of Volodya, and tried to persuade the latter to take his cot and fur coat with him, and some old "Annals of the Country," and a spirit-lamp coffee-pot, and other useless things. The captain advised Volodya to read up his "Manual,"[L] first, about mortar-firing, and immediately to copy the tables out of it.

Volodya set about this at once, and, to his amazement and delight, he perceived that, though he was still somewhat troubled with a sensation of fear of danger, and still more lest he should turn out a coward, yet it was far from being to that degree to which it had affected him on the preceding evening.

The reason for this lay partly in the daylight and in active occupation, and partly, principally, also, in the fact that fear and all powerful emotions cannot long continue with the same intensity. In a word, he had already succeeded in recovering from his terror.

At seven o'clock, just as the sun had begun to hide itself behind the Nikolaevsky barracks, the sergeant came to him, and announced that the men were ready and waiting for him.

"I have given the list to Vlanga. You will please to ask him for it, Your Honor!" said he.

Twenty artillery-men, with side-arms, but without loading-tools, were standing at the corner of the house. Volodya and the yunker stepped up to them.

"Shall I make them a little speech, or shall I simply say, 'Good day, children!' or shall I say nothing at all?" thought he. "And why should I not say, 'Good day, children!' Why, I ought to say that much!" And he shouted boldly, in his ringing voice:—

"Good day, children!"

The soldiers responded cheerfully. The fresh, young voice sounded pleasant in the ears of all. Volodya marched vigorously at their head, in front of the soldiers, and, although his heart beat as if he had run several versts at the top of his speed, his step was light and his countenance cheerful.

On arriving at the Malakoff mound, and climbing the slope, he perceived that Vlang, who had not lagged a single pace behind him, and who had appeared such a valiant fellow at home in the house, kept constantly swerving to one side, and ducking his head, as though all the cannon-balls and bombs, which whizzed by very frequently in that locality, were flying straight at him. Some of the soldiers did the same, and the faces of the majority of them betrayed, if not fear, at least anxiety. This circumstance put the finishing touch to Volodya's composure and encouraged him finally.

"So here I am also on the Malakoff mound, which I imagined to be a thousand times more terrible! And I can walk along without ducking my head before the bombs, and am far less terrified than the rest! So I am not a coward, after all?" he thought with delight, and even with a somewhat enthusiastic self-sufficiency.

But this feeling was soon shaken by a spectacle upon which he stumbled in the twilight, on the Kornilovsky battery, in his search for the commander of the bastion. Four sailors standing near the breastworks were holding the bloody body of a man, without shoes or coat, by its arms and legs, and staggering as they tried to fling it over the ramparts.

(On the second day of the bombardment, it had been found impossible, in some localities, to carry off the corpses from the bastions, and so they were flung into the trench, in order that they might not impede action in the batteries.)

Volodya stood petrified for a moment, as he saw the corpse waver on the summit of the breastworks, and then roll down into the ditch; but, luckily for him, the commander of the bastion met him there, communicated his orders, and furnished him with a guide to the battery and to the bomb-proofs designated for his service. We will not enumerate the remaining dangers and disenchantments which our hero underwent that evening: how, instead of the firing, such as he had seen on the Volkoff field, according to the rules of accuracy and precision, which he had expected to find here, he found two cracked mortars, one of which had been crushed by a cannon-ball in the muzzle, while the other stood upon the splinters of a ruined platform; how he could not obtain any workmen until the following morning in order to repair the platform; how not a single charge was of the weight prescribed in the "Manual;" how two soldiers of his command were wounded, and how he was twenty times within a hair's-breadth of death.

Fortunately, there had been assigned for his assistant a gun-captain of gigantic size, a sailor, who had served on the mortars since the beginning of the siege, and who convinced him of the practicability of using them, conducted him all over the bastion, with a lantern, during the night, exactly as though it had been his own kitchen-garden, and who promised to put everything in proper shape on the morrow.

The bomb-proof to which his guide conducted him was excavated in the rocky soil, and consisted of a long hole, two cubic fathoms in extent, covered with oaken planks an arshin in thickness. Here he took up his post, with all his soldiers. Vlang was the first, when he caught sight of the little door, twenty-eight inches high, of the bomb-proof, to rush headlong into it, in front of them all, and, after nearly cracking his skull on the stone floor, he huddled down in a corner, from which he did not again emerge.

And Volodya, when all the soldiers had placed themselves along the wall on the floor, and some had lighted their pipes, set up his bed in one corner, lighted a candle, and lay upon his cot, smoking a cigarette.

Shots were incessantly heard, over the bomb-proof, but they were not very loud, with the exception of those from one cannon, which stood close by and shook the bomb-proof with its thunder. In the bomb-proof itself all was still; the soldiers, who were a little shy, as yet, of the new officer, only exchanged a few words, now and then, as they requested each other to move out of the way or to furnish a light for a pipe. A rat scratched somewhere among the stones, or Vlang, who had not yet recovered himself, and who still gazed wildly about him, uttered a sudden vigorous sigh.

Volodya, as he lay on his bed, in his quiet corner, surrounded by the men, and illuminated only by a single candle, experienced that sensation of well-being which he had known as a child, when, in the course of a game of hide-and-seek, he used to crawl into a cupboard or under his mother's skirts, and listen, not daring to draw his breath, and afraid of the dark, and yet conscious of enjoying himself. He felt a little oppressed, but cheerful.

XXI.

After the lapse of about ten minutes, the soldiers began to change about and to converse together. The most important personages among them—the two gun-sergeants—placed themselves nearest the officer's light and bed;—one was old and gray-haired, with every possible medal and cross except the George;—the other was young, a militia-man, who smoked cigarettes, which he was rolling. The drummer, as usual, assumed the duty of waiting on the officer. The bombardiers and cavalrymen sat next, and then farther away, in the shadow of the entrance, the underlings took up their post. They too began to talk among themselves. It was caused by the hasty entrance of a man into the casemate.

"How now, brother! couldn't you stay in the street? Didn't the girls sing merrily?" said a voice.

"They sing such marvellous songs as were never heard in the village," said the man who had fled into the casemate, with a laugh.

"But Vasin does not love bombs—ah, no, he does not love them!" said one from the aristocratic corner.

"The idea! It's quite another matter when it's necessary," drawled the voice of Vasin, who made all the others keep silent when he spoke: "since the 24th, the firing has been going on desperately; and what is there wrong about it? You'll get killed for nothing, and your superiors won't so much as say 'Thank you!' for it."

At these words of Vasin, all burst into a laugh.

"There's Melnikoff, that fellow who will sit outside the door," said some one.

"Well, send him here, that Melnikoff," added the old gunner; "they will kill him, for a fact, and that to no purpose."

"Who is this Melnikoff?" asked Volodya.

"Why, Your Honor, he's a stupid soldier of ours. He doesn't seem to be afraid of anything, and now he keeps walking about outside. Please to take a look at him; he looks like a bear."

"He knows a spell," said the slow voice of Vasin, from the corner.

Melnikoff entered the bomb-proof. He was fat (which is extremely rare among soldiers), and a sandy-complexioned, handsome man, with a huge, bulging forehead and prominent, light blue eyes.

"Are you afraid of the bombs?" Volodya asked him.

"What is there about the bombs to be afraid of!" replied Melnikoff, shrugging his shoulders and scratching his head, "I know that I shall not be killed by a bomb."

"So you would like to go on living here?"

"Why, of course, I would. It's jolly here!" he said, with a sudden outburst of laughter.

"Oh, then you must be detailed for the sortie! I'll tell the general so, if you like?" said Volodya, although he was not acquainted with a single general there.

"Why shouldn't I like! I do!"

And Melnikoff disappeared behind the others.

"Let's have a game of noski,[M] children! Who has cards?" rang out his brisk voice.

And, in fact, it was not long before a game was started in the back corner, and blows on the nose, laughter, and calling of trumps were heard.

Volodya drank some tea from the samovár, which the drummer served for him, treated the gunners, jested, chatted with them, being desirous of winning popularity, and felt very well content with the respect which was shown him. The soldiers, too, perceiving that the gentleman put on no airs, began to talk together.

One declared that the siege of Sevastopol would soon come to an end, because a trustworthy man from the fleet had said that the emperor's brother Constantine was coming to our relief with the 'Merican fleet, and there would soon be an agreement that there should be no firing for two weeks, and that a rest should be allowed, and if any one did fire a shot, every discharge would have to be paid for at the rate of seventy-five kopeks each.

Vasin, who, as Volodya had already noticed, was a little fellow, with large, kindly eyes, and side-whiskers, related, amid a general silence at first, and afterwards amid general laughter, how, when he had gone home on leave, they had been glad at first to see him, but afterwards his father had begun to send him off to work, and the lieutenant of the foresters' corps sent his drozhki for his wife.

All this amused Volodya greatly. He not only did not experience the least fear or inconvenience from the closeness and heavy air in the bomb-proof, but he felt in a remarkably cheerful and agreeable frame of mind.

Many of the soldiers were already snoring. Vlang had also stretched himself out on the floor, and the old gun-sergeant, having spread out his cloak, was crossing himself and muttering his prayers, preparatory to sleep, when Volodya took a fancy to step out of the bomb-proof, and see what was going on outside.

"Take your legs out of the way!" cried one soldier to another, as soon as he rose, and the legs were pressed aside to make way for him.

Vlang, who appeared to be asleep, suddenly raised his head, and seized Volodya by the skirt of his coat.

"Come, don't go! how can you!" he began, in a tearfully imploring tone. "You don't know about things yet; they are firing at us out there all the time; it is better here."

But, in spite of Vlang's entreaties, Volodya made his way out of the bomb-proof, and seated himself on the threshold, where Melnikoff was already sitting.

The air was pure and fresh, particularly after the bomb-proof—the night was clear and still. Through the roar of the discharges could be heard the sounds of cart-wheels, bringing gabions, and the voices of the men who were at work on the magazine. Above their heads was the lofty, starry sky, across which flashed the fiery streaks caused by the bombs; an arshin away, on the left, a tiny opening led to another bomb-proof, through which the feet and backs of the soldiers who lived there were visible, and through which their voices were audible; in front, the elevation produced by the powder-vault could be seen, and athwart it flitted the bent figures of men, and upon it, at the very summit, amid the bullets and the bombs which whistled past the spot incessantly, stood a tall form in a black paletot, with his hands in his pockets, and feet treading down the earth, which other men were fetching in sacks. Often a bomb would fly over, and burst close to the cave. The soldiers engaged in bringing the earth bent over and ran aside; but the black figure never moved; went on quietly stamping down the dirt with his feet, and remained on the spot in the same attitude as before.

"Who is that black man?" inquired Volodya of Melnikoff.

"I don't know; I will go and see."

"Don't go! it is not necessary."

But Melnikoff, without heeding him, walked up to the black figure, and stood beside him for a tolerably long time, as calm and immovable as the man himself.

"That is the man who has charge of the magazine, Your Honor!" he said, on his return. "It has been pierced by a bomb, so the infantry-men are fetching more earth."

Now and then, a bomb seemed to fly straight at the door of the bomb-proof. On such occasions, Volodya shrank into the corner, and then peered forth again, gazing upwards, to see whether another was not coming from some direction. Although Vlang, from the interior of the bomb-proof, repeatedly besought Volodya to come back, the latter sat on the threshold for three hours, and experienced a sort of satisfaction in thus tempting fate and in watching the flight of the bombs. Towards the end of the evening, he had learned from what point most of the firing proceeded, and where the shots struck.

XXII.

On the following day, the 27th, after a ten-hours sleep, Volodya, fresh and active, stepped out on the threshold of the casement; Vlang also started to crawl out with him, but, at the first sound of a bullet, he flung himself backwards through the opening of the bomb-proof, bumping his head as he did so, amid the general merriment of the soldiers, the majority of whom had also come out into the open air. Vlang, the old gun-sergeant, and a few others were the only ones who rarely went out into the trenches; it was impossible to restrain the rest; they all scattered about in the fresh morning air, escaping from the fetid air of the bomb-proof, and, in spite of the fact that the bombardment was as vigorous as on the preceding evening, they disposed themselves around the door, and some even on the breastworks. Melnikoff had been strolling about among the batteries since daybreak, and staring up with perfect coolness.

Near the entrance sat two old soldiers and one young, curly-haired fellow, a Jew, who had been detailed from the infantry. This soldier picked up one of the bullets which were lying about, and, having smoothed it against a stone with a potsherd, with his knife he carved from it a cross, after the style of the order of St. George; the others looked on at his work as they talked. The cross really turned out to be quite handsome.

"Now, if we stay here much longer," said one of them, "then, when peace is made, the time of service will be up for all of us."

"Nothing of the sort; I have at least four years service yet before my time is up, and I have been in Sevastopol these five months."

"It is not counted towards the discharge, do you understand," said another.

At that moment, a cannon-ball shrieked over the heads of the speakers, and struck only an arshin away from Melnikoff, who was approaching them from the trenches.

"That came near killing Melnikoff," said one man.

"I shall not be killed," said Melnikoff.

"Here's the cross for you, for your bravery," said the young soldier, who had made the cross, handing it to Melnikoff.

"No, brother, a month here counts for a year, of course—that was the order," the conversation continued.

"Think what you please, but when peace is declared, there will be an imperial review at Orshava, and if we don't get our discharge, we shall be allowed to go on indefinite leave."

At that moment, a shrieking little bullet flew past the speakers' heads, and struck a stone.

"You'll get a full discharge before evening—see if you don't," said one of the soldiers.

They all laughed.

Not only before evening, but before the expiration of two hours, two of them received their full discharge, and five were wounded; but the rest jested on as before.

By morning, the two mortars had actually been brought into such a condition that it was possible to fire them. At ten o'clock, in accordance with the orders which he had received from the commander of the bastion, Volodya called out his command, and marched to the battery with it.

In the men, as soon as they proceeded to action, there was not a drop of that sentiment of fear perceptible which had been expressed on the preceding evening. Vlang alone could not control himself; he dodged and ducked just as before, and Vasin lost some of his composure, and fussed and fidgeted and changed his place incessantly.

But Volodya was in an extraordinary state of enthusiasm; the thought of danger did not even occur to him. Delight that he was fulfilling his duty, that he was not only not a coward, but even a valiant fellow, the feeling that he was in command, and the presence of twenty men, who, as he was aware, were surveying him with curiosity, made a thoroughly brave man of him. He was even vain of his valor, put on airs before his soldiers, climbed up on the banquette, and unbuttoned his coat expressly that he might render himself the more distinctly visible.

The commander of the bastion, who was going the rounds of his establishment as he expressed it, at the moment, accustomed as he had become during his eight-months experience to all sorts of bravery, could not refrain from admiring this handsome lad, in the unbuttoned coat, beneath which a red shirt was visible, encircling his soft white neck, with his animated face and eyes, as he clapped his hands and shouted: "First! Second!" and ran gayly along the ramparts, in order to see where his bomb would fall.

At half-past eleven the firing ceased on both sides, and at precisely twelve o'clock the storming of the Malakoff mound, of the second, third, and fifth bastions began.

<u>XXIII.</u>

On this side of the bay, between Inkerman and the northern fortifications, on the telegraph hill, about midday, stood two naval men; one was an officer, who was engaged in observing Sevastopol through a telescope, and the other had just arrived at the signal-station with his orderly.

The sun stood high and brilliant above the bay, and played with the ships which floated upon it, and with the moving sails and boats, with a warm and cheerful glow. The light breeze hardly moved the leaves of the dry oak-shrubs which stood about the signal-pole, puffed out the sails of the boats, and ruffled the waves.

Sevastopol, with her unfinished church, her columns, her line of shore, her boulevard showing green against the hill, and her elegant library building, with her tiny azure inlets, filled with masts, with the picturesque arches of her aqueducts, and the clouds of blue smoke, lighted up now and then by red flashes of flame from the firing; the same beautiful, proud, festive Sevastopol, hemmed in on one side by yellow, smoke-crowned hills, on the other by the bright blue sea, which glittered in the sun, was visible the same as ever, on the other side of the bay.

Over the horizon-line of the sea, along which floated a long wreath of black smoke from some steamer, crept long white clouds, portending a gale. Along the entire line of the fortifications, especially over the hills on the left, rose columns of thick, dense, white smoke; suddenly, abruptly, and incessantly illuminated by flashes, lightnings, which shone even amid the light of high noon, and which constantly increased in volume, assuming divers forms, as they swept upwards, and tinged the heavens. These puffs of smoke flashing now here, now there, took their birth on the hills, in the batteries of the enemy, in the city, and high against the sky. The sound of the discharges never ceased, but shook the air with their mingled roar.

At twelve o'clock, the puffs of smoke began to occur less and less frequently, and the atmosphere quivered less with the roar.

"But the second bastion is no longer replying at all," said the officer of hussars, who sat there on horseback; "it is utterly destroyed! Horrible!"

"Yes, and the Malakoff only sends one shot to their three," replied the officer who was looking through his glass. "It enrages me to have them silent. They are firing straight on the Kornilovsky battery, and it is not answering at all."

"But you see that they always cease the bombardment at twelve o'clock, just as I said. It is the same to-day. Let us go and get some breakfast ... they are already waiting for us ... there's nothing to see."

"Stop, don't interfere," said the officer with the glass, gazing at Sevastopol with peculiar eagerness.

"What's going on there? What is it?"

"There is a movement in the trenches, and heavy columns are marching."

"Yes, that is evident," said the other. "The columns are under way. We must give the signal."

"See, see! They have emerged from the trenches."

In truth, it was visible to the naked eye that dark masses were moving down the hill, across the narrow valley, from the French batteries to the bastions. In front of these specks, dark streaks were visible, which were already close to our lines. White puffs of smoke of discharges burst out at various points on the bastions, as though the firing were running along the line.

The breeze bore to them the sounds of musketry-shots, exchanged briskly, like rain upon the window-pane. The black streaks moved on, nearer and nearer, into the very smoke. The sounds of firing grew louder and louder, and mingled in a lengthened, resounding roar.

The smoke, rising more and more frequently, spread rapidly along the line, flowed together in one lilac-hued cloud, which dispersed and joined again, and through which, here and there, flitted flames and black points—and all sounds were commingled in one reverberating crash.

"An assault," said the officer, with a pale face, as he handed the glass to the naval officer.

Orderlies galloped along the road, officers on horseback, the commander-in-chief in a calash, and his suite passed by. Profound emotion and expectation were visible on all countenances.

"It cannot be that they have taken it!" said the mounted officer.

"By Heavens, there's the standard! Look, look!" said the other, sighing and abandoning the glass. "The French standard on the Malakoff!"

"It cannot be!"

XXIV.

The elder Kozeltzoff, who had succeeded in winning back his money and losing it all again that night, including even the gold pieces which were sewed into his cuffs, had fallen, just before daybreak, into a heavy, unhealthy, but profound slumber, in the fortified barracks of the fifth battalion, when the fateful cry, repeated by various voices, rang out:—

"The alarm!"

"Why are you sleeping, Mikhaïl Semyónitch! There's an assault!" a voice shouted to him.

"That is probably some school-boy," he said, opening his eyes, but putting no faith in it.

But all at once he caught sight of an officer running aimlessly from one corner to the other, with such a pale face that he understood it all. The thought that he might be taken for a coward, who did not wish to go out to his company at a critical moment, struck him with terrible force. He ran to

129

his corps at the top of his speed. Firing had ceased from the heavy guns; but the crash of musketry was at its height. The bullets whistled, not singly like rifle-balls, but in swarms, like a flock of birds in autumn, flying past overhead. The entire spot on which his battalion had stood the night before was veiled in smoke, and the shouts and cries of the enemy were audible. Soldiers, both wounded and unwounded, met him in throngs. After running thirty paces further, he caught sight of his company, which was hugging the wall.

"They have captured Schwartz," said a young officer. "All is lost!"

"Nonsense!" said he, angrily, grasping his blunt little iron sword, and he began to shout:—

"Forward, children! Hurrah!"

His voice was strong and ringing; it roused even Kozeltzoff himself. He ran forward along the traverse; fifty soldiers rushed after him, shouting as they went. From the traverse he ran out upon an open square. The bullets fell literally like hail. Two struck him,—but where, and what they did, whether they bruised or wounded him, he had not the time to decide.

In front, he could already see blue uniforms and red trousers, and could hear shouts which were not Russian; one Frenchman was standing on the breastworks, waving his cap, and shouting something. Kozeltzoff was convinced that he was about to be killed; this gave him courage.

He ran on and on. Some soldiers overtook him; other soldiers appeared at one side, also running. The blue uniforms remained at the same distance from him, fleeing back from him to their own trenches; but beneath his feet were the dead and wounded. When he had run to the outermost ditch, everything became confused before Kozeltzoff's eyes, and he was conscious of a pain in the breast.

Half an hour later, he was lying on a stretcher, near the Nikolaevsky barracks, and knew that he was wounded, though he felt hardly any pain; all he wanted was something cooling to drink, and to be allowed to lie still in peace.

A plump little doctor, with black side-whiskers, approached him, and unbuttoned his coat. Kozeltzoff stared over his chin at what the doctor was doing to his wound, and at the doctor's face, but he felt no pain. The doctor covered his wound with his shirt, wiped his fingers on the skirts of his coat, and, without a word or glance at the wounded man, went off to some one else.

Kozeltzoff's eyes mechanically took note of what was going on before him, and, recalling the fact that he had been in the fifth bastion, he thought, with an extraordinary feeling of self-satisfaction, that he had fulfilled his duty well, and that, for the first time in all his service, he had behaved as handsomely as it was possible for any one, and had nothing with which to reproach himself. The doctor, after bandaging the other officer's wound, pointed to Kozeltzoff, and said something to a priest, with a huge reddish beard, and a cross, who was standing near by.

"What! am I dying?" Kozeltzoff asked the priest, when the latter approached him.

The priest, without making any reply, recited a prayer and handed the cross to the wounded man.

Death had no terrors for Kozeltzoff. He grasped the cross with his weak hands, pressed it to his lips, and burst into tears.

"Well, were the French repulsed?" he inquired of the priest, in firm tones.

"The victory has remained with us at every point," replied the priest, in order to comfort the wounded man, concealing from him the fact that the French standard had already been unfurled on the Malakoff mound.

"Thank God!" said the wounded man, without feeling the tears which were trickling down his cheeks.

The thought of his brother occurred to his mind for a single instant. "May God grant him the same good-fortune," he said to himself.

XXV.

But the same fate did not await Volodya. He was listening to a tale which Vasin was in the act of relating to him, when there was a cry,—"The

French are coming!" The blood fled for a moment to Volodya's heart, and he felt his cheeks turn cold and pale. For one second he remained motionless, but, on glancing about him, he perceived that the soldiers were buttoning up their coats with tolerable equanimity, and crawling out, one after the other. One even, probably Melnikoff, remarked, in a jesting way:—

"Go out and offer them the bread and salt of hospitality, children!"

Volodya, in company with Vlang, who never separated from him by so much as a step, crawled out of the bomb-proof, and ran to the battery.

There was no artillery firing whatever in progress on either side. It was not so much the sight of the soldiers' composure which aroused his courage as the pitiful and undisguised cowardice of Vlang. "Is it possible for me to be like him?" he said to himself, and he ran on gayly up to the breastworks, near which his mortars stood. It was clearly apparent to him that the French were making straight for him through an open space, and that masses of them, with their bayonets glittering in the sun, were moving in the nearest trenches.

One, a short, broad-shouldered fellow, in zouave uniform, and armed with a sword, ran on in front and leaped the ditch.

"Fire grape-shot!" shouted Volodya, hastening from the banquette; but the soldiers had already made their preparations without waiting for his orders, and the metallic sound of the grape-shot which they discharged shrieked over his head, first from one and then from the other mortar.

"First! second!" commanded Volodya, running from one mortar to the other, and utterly oblivious of danger.

On one side, and near at hand, the crash of musketry from our men under shelter, and anxious cries, were heard.

All at once a startling cry of despair, repeated by several voices, was heard on the left: "They are surrounding us! They are surrounding us!"

Volodya looked round at this shout. Twenty Frenchmen made their appearance in the rear. One of them, a handsome man with a black beard, was in front of all; but, after running up to within ten paces of the battery, he halted, and fired straight at Volodya, and then ran towards him once more.

For a second, Volodya stood as though turned to stone, and did not believe his eyes. When he recovered himself and glanced about him, there were blue uniforms in front of him on the ramparts; two Frenchmen were even spiking a cannon not ten paces distant from him.

There was no one near him, with the exception of Melnikoff, who had been killed by a bullet beside him, and Vlang, who, with a handspike clutched in his hand, had rushed forwards, with an expression of wrath on his face, and with eyes lowered.

"Follow me, Vladímir Semyónitch! Follow me!" shouted the desperate voice of Vlang, as he brandished his handspike over the French, who were pouring in from the rear. The yunker's ferocious countenance startled them. He struck the one who was in advance, on the head; the others involuntarily paused, and Vlang continued to glare about him, and to shout in despairing accents: "Follow me, Vladímir Semyónitch! Why do you stand there? Run!" and ran towards the trenches in which lay our infantry, firing at the French. After leaping into the trench, he came out again to see what his adored ensign was doing. Something in a coat was lying prostrate where Volodya had been standing, and the whole place was filled with Frenchmen, who were firing at our men.

XXVI.

Vlang found his battery on the second line of defence. Out of the twenty soldiers who had been in the mortar battery, only eight survived.

At nine o'clock in the evening, Vlang set out with the battery on a steamer loaded down with soldiers, cannon, horses, and wounded men, for Severnaya.

There was no firing anywhere. The stars shone brilliantly in the sky, as on the preceding night; but a strong wind tossed the sea. On the first and second bastions, lightnings flashed along the earth; explosions rent the atmosphere, and illuminated strange black objects in their vicinity, and the stones which flew through the air.

Something was burning near the docks, and the red glare was reflected in the water. The bridge, covered with people, was lighted up by the fire from the Nikolaevsky battery. A vast flame seemed to hang over the water, from the distant promontory of the Alexandrovsky battery, and illuminated the clouds of smoke beneath, as it rose above them; and the same tranquil, insolent, distant lights as on the preceding evening gleamed over the sea, from the hostile fleet.

The fresh breeze raised billows in the bay. By the red light of the conflagrations, the masts of our sunken ships, which were settling deeper and deeper into the water, were visible. Not a sound of conversation was heard on deck; there was nothing but the regular swish of the parted waves, and the steam, the neighing and pawing of the horses, the words of command from the captain, and the groans of the wounded. Vlang, who had had nothing to eat all day, drew a bit of bread from his pocket, and began to chew it; but all at once he recalled Volodya, and burst into such loud weeping that the soldiers who were near him heard it.

"See how our Vlanga[N] is eating his bread and crying too," said Vasin.

"Wonderful!" said another.

"And see, they have fired our barracks," he continued, with a sigh. "And how many of our brothers perished there; and the French got it for nothing!"

"At all events, we have got out of it alive—thank God for that!" said Vasin.

"But it's provoking, all the same!"

"What is there provoking about it? Do you suppose they are enjoying themselves there? Not exactly! You wait, our men will take it away from them again. And however many of our brethren perish, as God is holy, if the emperor commands, they will win it back. Can ours leave it to them thus? Never! There you have the bare walls; but they have destroyed all the breastworks. Even if they have planted their standard on the hill, they won't be able to make their way into the town."

"Just wait, we'll have a hearty reckoning with you yet, only give us time," he concluded, addressing himself to the French.

"Of course we will!" said another, with conviction.

Along the whole line of bastions of Sevastopol, which had for so many months seethed with remarkably vigorous life, which had for so many months seen dying heroes relieved one after another by death, and which had for so many months awakened the terror, the hatred, and finally the admiration of the enemy,—on the bastions of Sevastopol, there was no longer a single man. All was dead, wild, horrible,—but not silent.

Destruction was still in progress. On the earth, furrowed and strewn with the recent explosions, lay bent gun-carriages, crushing down the bodies of Russians and of the foe; heavy iron cannons silenced forever, bombs and cannon-balls hurled with horrible force into pits, and half-buried in the soil, then more corpses, pits, splinters of beams, bomb-proofs, and still more silent bodies in gray and blue coats. All these were still frequently shaken and lighted up by the crimson glow of the explosions, which continued to shock the air.

The foe perceived that something incomprehensible was going on in that menacing Sevastopol. Those explosions and the death-like silence on the bastions made them shudder; but they dared not yet believe, being still under the influence of the calm and forcible resistance of the day, that their invincible enemy had disappeared, and they awaited motionless and in silence the end of that gloomy night.

The army of Sevastopol, like the gloomy, surging sea, quivering throughout its entire mass, wavering, ploughing across the bay, on the bridge, and at the north fortifications, moved slowly through the impenetrable darkness of the night; away from the place where it had left so many of its brave brethren, from the place all steeped in its blood, from the place which it had defended for eleven months against a foe twice as powerful as itself, and which it was now ordered to abandon without a battle.

The first impression produced on every Russian by this command was inconceivably sad. The second feeling was a fear of pursuit. The men felt that they were defenceless as soon as they abandoned the places on which they were accustomed to fight, and they huddled together uneasily in the dark, at the entrance to the bridge, which was swaying about in the heavy breeze.

The infantry pressed forward, with a clash of bayonets, and a thronging of regiments, equipages, and arms; cavalry officers made their way about with orders, the inhabitants and the military servants accompanying the baggage wept and besought to be permitted to cross, while the artillery, in haste to get off, forced their way to the bay with a thunder of wheels.

In spite of the diversions created by the varied and anxious demands on their attention, the instinct of self-preservation and the desire to escape as speedily as possible from that dread place of death were present in every soul. This instinct existed also in a soldier mortally wounded, who lay among the five hundred other wounded, upon the stone pavement of the Pavlovsky quay, and prayed God to send death; and in the militia-man, who with his last remaining strength pressed into the compact throng, in order to make way for a general who rode by, and in the general in charge of the transportation, who was engaged in restraining the haste of the soldiers, and in the sailor, who had become entangled in the moving battalion, and who, crushed by the surging throng, had lost his breath, and in the wounded officer, who was being borne along in a litter by four soldiers, who, stopped by the crowd, had placed him on the ground by the Nikolaevsky battery, and in the artillery-man, who had served his gun for sixteen years, and who, at his superior's command, to him incomprehensible, to throw overboard the guns, had, with the aid of his comrades, sent them over the steep bank into the bay; and in the men of the fleet, who had just closed the port-holes of the ships, and had rowed lustily away in their boats. On stepping upon the further end of the bridge, nearly every soldier pulled off his cap and crossed himself.

But behind this instinct there was another, oppressive and far deeper, existing along with it; this was a feeling which resembled repentance, shame, and hatred. Almost every soldier, as he gazed on abandoned Sevastopol, from the northern shore, sighed with inexpressible bitterness of heart, and menaced the foe.

FOOTNOTES:

[I] In many regiments the officers call a soldier, half in scorn, half caressingly, Moskva (Moscovite), or prisyaga (an oath).

[J] This effect cannot be reproduced in English.

[K] "My good sir," a familiarly respectful mode of address.

[L] "Manual for Artillery Officers," by Bezak.

[M] A game in which the loser is rapped on the nose with the cards.

[N] The feminine form, as previously referred to.

THREE DAYS IN THE VILLAGE, AND OTHER SKETCHES

THREE DAYS IN THE VILLAGE

FIRST DAY-TRAMPS

Something entirely new, unseen and unheard-of formerly, has lately shown itself in our country districts. To our village, consisting of eighty homesteads, from half a dozen to a dozen cold, hungry, tattered tramps come every day, wanting a night's lodging.

These people, ragged, half-naked, barefoot, often ill, and extremely dirty, come into the village and go to the village policeman. That they should not die in the street of hunger and exposure, he quarters them on the inhabitants of the village, regarding only the peasants as "inhabitants." He does not take them to the squire, who besides his own ten rooms has ten other apartments: office, coachman's room, laundry, servants' and upper-servants' hall and so on; nor does he take them to the priest or deacon or shopkeeper, in whose houses, though not large, there is still some spare room; but he takes them to the peasants, whose whole family, wife, daughters-in-law, unmarried daughters, and big and little children, all live in one room—sixteen, nineteen, or twenty-three feet long. And the master of the hut takes the cold, hungry, stinking, ragged, dirty man, and not merely gives him a night's lodging, but feeds him as well.

"When you sit down to table yourself," an old peasant householder told me, "it's impossible not to invite him too, or your own soul accepts nothing. So one feeds him and gives him a drink of tea."

Those are the nightly visitors. But during the day, not two or three, but ten or more such visitors call at each hut, and again it is: "Why, it is impossible...," etc.

And for almost every tramp the housewife cuts a slice of bread, thinner or thicker according to the man's appearance—though she knows her rye will not last till next harvest.

"If you were to give to all who come, a loaf [the big peasant loaf of black bread] would not last a day," some housewives said to me. "So sometimes one hardens one's heart and refuses!"

And this goes on every day, all over Russia. An enormous yearly-increasing army of beggars, cripples, administrative exiles, helpless old men, and above all unemployed workmen, lives—that is to say, shelters itself from cold and wet—and is actually fed by the hardest-worked and poorest class, the country peasants.

We have Workhouses,[1] Foundlings' Hospitals, Boards of Public Relief, and all sorts of philanthropic organisations in our towns; and in all those institutions, in buildings with electric light, parquet floors, neat servants, and various well-paid attendants, thousands of helpless people of all sorts are sheltered. But however many such there may be, they are but a drop in the ocean of the enormous (unnumbered, but certainly enormous) population which now tramps destitute over Russia, and is sheltered and fed apart from any institutions, solely by the village peasants whose own Christian feelings induce them to bear this heavy and gigantic tax.

Just think what people who are not peasants would say, if—even once a week—such a shivering, starving, dirty, lousy tramp were placed in each of their bedrooms! But the peasants not only house them, but feed them and give them tea, because "one's own soul accepts nothing unless one has them to table."

In the more remote parts of Sarátof, Tambóf, and other Provinces, the peasants do not wait for the policeman to bring these tramps, but always receive them and feed them of their own accord.

And, as is the case with all really good deeds, the peasants do this without knowing that they are doing a good deed; and yet it is not merely a good deed "for one's soul," but is of enormous importance for the whole of Russian society. It is of such importance for Russian society because, but for this peasant population and the Christian feeling that lives so strongly in it, it is difficult to imagine what the fate would be, not only of these hundreds of thousands of unfortunate, houseless tramps, but of all the well-to-do—and especially of the wealthy who have their houses in the country.

It is only necessary to see the state of privation and suffering to which these homeless tramps have come or have been brought, and to imagine the mental condition they must be in, and to realise that it is only this help rendered to them by the peasants that restrains them from committing violence, which would be quite natural in their position, upon those who possess in superfluity all the things these unfortunates lack to keep themselves alive.

So that it is not the philanthropic organisations, not the Government with its police and all its juridical institutions, that protects us, the well-to-do, from being attacked by those who wander, cold, hungry, and homeless, after having sunk—or, for the most part, having been brought—to the lowest depths of poverty and despair; but we are protected, as well as fed and supported, by that same basic strength of the Russian nation—the peasantry.

Yes! Were it not that there is among Russia's vast peasant population a deep religious consciousness of the brotherhood of all men, not only would these homeless people, having reached the last stages of despair, have long since destroyed the houses of the rich, in spite of any police force (there are and must be so few of them in country districts), but they would even have killed all who stood in their way. So that we ought not to be horrified or surprised when we hear or read of people being robbed, or killed that they may be robbed, but we should understand and remember that if such things happen as seldom as they do, we owe this to the unselfish help rendered by the peasants to this unfortunate tramping population.

Every day from ten to fifteen people come to our house to beg. Some among them are regular beggars, who for some reason have chosen that means of livelihood, and having clothed and shod themselves as best they might, and having made sacks to hold what they collect, have started out to tramp the country. Among them some are blind, and some have lost a leg or an arm; and sometimes, though rarely, there are women and children among them. But these are only a small part. The majority of the beggars that come now are passers-by, without a beggar's sack, mostly young, and not crippled. They are all in a most pitiable state, barefoot, half-naked, emaciated, and shivering with cold. You ask them, "Where are you going?" The answer is always the same: "To look for work"; or, "Have been looking for work, but found none, and am making my way home. There's no work; they are shutting down everywhere." Many of these people are returning from exile.

A few days ago I was barely awake when our servant, Ilyá Vasílyevitch, told me:

"There are five tramps waiting near the porch."

"Take some money there is on the table, and give it them," said I.

Ilyá Vasílyevitch took it, and, as is the custom, gave each of them five copecks [five farthings]. About an hour passed. I went out into the porch. A dreadfully tattered little man with a sickly face, swollen eyelids, restless eyes, and boots all falling to pieces, began bowing, and held out a certificate to me.

"Have you received something?"

"Your Excellency, what am I to do with five copecks?... Your Excellency, put yourself in my place! Please, your Excellency, look ... please see!" and he shows me his clothing. "Where am I to go to, your Excellency?" (it is "Excellency" after every word, though his face expresses hatred). "What am I to do? Where am I to go?"

I tell him that I give to all alike. He continues to entreat, and demands that I should read his certificate. I refuse. He kneels down. I ask him to leave me.

"Very well! That means, it seems, that I must put an end to myself! That's all that's left me to do.... Give me something, if only a trifle!"

I give him twenty copecks, and he goes away, evidently angry.

There are a great many such peculiarly insistent beggars, who feel they

142

have a right to demand their share from the rich. They are literate for the most part, and some of them are even well-read persons on whom the Revolution has had an effect. These men, unlike the ordinary, old-fashioned beggars, look on the rich, not as on people who wish to save their souls by distributing alms, but as on highwaymen and robbers who suck the blood of the working classes. It often happens that a beggar of this sort does no work himself and carefully avoids work, and yet considers himself, in the name of the workers, not merely justified, but bound, to hate the robbers of the people—that is to say, the rich—and to hate them from the depths of his heart; and if, instead of demanding from them, he begs, that is only a pretence.

There are a great number of these men, many of them drunkards, of whom one feels inclined to say, "It's their own fault"; but there are also a great many tramps of quite a different type: meek, humble, and very pathetic, and it is terrible to think of their position.

Here is a tall, good-looking man, with nothing on over his short, tattered jacket. His boots are bad and trodden down. He has a good, intelligent face. He takes off his cap and begs in the ordinary way. I give him something, and he thanks me. I ask him where he comes from and where he is going to.

"From Petersburg, home to our village in Toúla Government."

I ask him, "Why on foot?"

"It's a long story," he answers, shrugging his shoulders.

I ask him to tell it me. He relates it with evident truthfulness.

"I had a good place in an office in Petersburg, and received thirty roubles [three guineas] a month. Lived very comfortably. I have read your books War and Peace and Anna Karénina," says he, again smiling a particularly pleasant smile. "Then my folks at home got the idea of migrating to Siberia, to the Province of Tomsk." They wrote to him asking whether he would agree to sell his share of land in the old place. He agreed. His people left, but the land allotted them in Siberia turned out worthless. They spent all they had, and came back. Being now landless, they are living in hired lodgings in their former village, and work for wages. It happened, just at the same time, that he lost his place in Petersburg. It was not his doing. The firm he was with became bankrupt, and dismissed its employees. "And just then, to tell the truth, I came across a seamstress." He smiled again. "She quite entangled me.... I used to help my people, and now see what a smart chap I have become!... Ah well, God is not without mercy; maybe I'll manage somehow!"

He was evidently an intelligent, strong, active fellow, and only a series of misfortunes had brought him to his present condition.

Take another: his legs swathed in strips of rag; girdled with a rope; his clothing quite threadbare and full of small holes, evidently not torn, but worn-out to the last degree; his face, with its high cheek-bones, pleasant, intelligent, and sober. I give him the customary five copecks, and he thanks me and we start a conversation. He has been an administrative exile in Vyátka. It was bad enough there, but it is worse here. He is going to Ryazán, where he used to live. I ask him what he has been. "A newspaper man. I took the papers round."

"For what were you exiled?"

"For selling forbidden literature."

We began talking about the Revolution. I told him my opinion, that the evil was all in ourselves; and that such an enormous power as that of the Government cannot be destroyed by force. "Evil outside ourselves will only be destroyed when we have destroyed it within us," said I.

"That is so, but not for a long time."

"It depends on us."

"I have read your book on Revolution."

"It is not mine, but I agree with it."

"I wished to ask you for some of your books."

"I should be very pleased.... Only I'm afraid they may get you into trouble. I'll give you the most harmless."

"Oh, I don't care! I am no longer afraid of anything.... Prison is better for me than this! I am not afraid of prison.... I even long for it sometimes," he said sadly.

"What a pity it is that so much strength is wasted uselessly!" said I. "How people like you destroy your own lives!... Well, and what do you mean to do now?"

"I?" he said, looking intently into my face.

At first, while we talked about past events and general topics, he had answered me boldly and cheerfully; but as soon as our conversation referred to himself personally and he noticed my sympathy, he turned away, hid his eyes with his sleeve, and I noticed that the back of his head was shaking.

And how many such people there are!

They are pitiable and pathetic, and they, too, stand on the threshold beyond which a state of despair begins that makes even a kindly man ready to go all lengths.

"Stable as our civilisation may seem to us," says Henry George, "disintegrating forces are already developing within it. Not in deserts and forests, but in city slums and on the highways, the barbarians are being bred who will do for our civilisation what the Huns and Vandals did for the civilisation of former ages."

Yes! What Henry George foretold some twenty years ago, is happening now before our eyes, and in Russia most glaringly—thanks to the amazing blindness of our Government, which carefully undermines the foundations on which alone any and every social order stands or can stand.

We have the Vandals foretold by Henry George quite ready among us in Russia. And, strange as it may seem to say so, these Vandals, these doomed men, are specially dreadful here among our deeply religious population. These Vandals are specially dreadful here, because we have not the restraining principles of convention, propriety, and public opinion, that are so strongly developed among the European nations. We have either real, deep, religious feeling, or—as in Sténka Rázin and Pougatchéf—a total absence of any restraining principle: and, dreadful to say, this army of Sténkas and Pougatchéfs is growing greater and greater, thanks to the Pougatchéf-like conduct of our Government in these later days, with its horrors of police violence, insane banishments, imprisonments, exiles, fortresses, and daily executions.

Such actions release the Sténka Rázins from the last remnants of moral restraint. "If the learned gentlefolk act like that, God Himself permits us to do so," say and think they.

I often receive letters from that class of men, chiefly exiles. They know I have written something about not resisting evil by violence, and for the greater part they retort ungrammatically, though with great fervour, that what the Government and the rich are doing to the poor, can and must be answered only in one way: "Revenge, revenge, revenge!"

Yes! The blindness of our Government is amazing. It does not and will not see that all it does to disarm its enemies merely increases their number and energy. Yes! These people are terrible, terrible for the Government and for the rich, and for those who live among the rich.

But besides the feeling of terror these people inspire, there is also another feeling, much more imperative than that of fear, and one we cannot help experiencing towards those who, by a series of accidents, have fallen into this terrible condition of vagrancy. That feeling is one of shame and sympathy.

And it is not fear, so much as shame and pity, that should oblige us, who are not in that condition, to respond in one way or other to this new and terrible phenomenon in Russian life.[2]

SECOND DAY—THE LIVING AND THE DYING

As I sat at my work, Ilyá Vasílyevitch entered softly and, evidently reluctant to disturb me at my work, told me that some wayfarers and a woman had been waiting a long time to see me.

"Here," I said, "please take this, and give it them."

"The woman has come about some business."

I told him to ask her to wait a while, and continued my work. By the time I came out, I had quite forgotten about her, till I saw a young peasant woman with a long, thin face, and clad very poorly and too lightly for the weather, appear from behind a corner of the house.

"What do you want? What is the matter?"

"I've come to see you, your Honour."

"Yes ... what about? What is the matter?"

"To see you, your Honour."

"Well, what is it?"

"He's been taken wrongfully.... I'm left with three children."

"Who's been taken, and where to?"

"My husband ... sent off to Krapívny."

"Why? What for?"

"For a soldier, you know. But it's wrong—because, you see, he's the breadwinner! We can't get on without him.... Be a father to us, sir!"

"But how is it? Is he the only man in the family?"

"Just so ... the only man!"

"Then how is it they have taken him, if he's the only man?"

"Who can tell why they've done it?... Here am I, left alone with the children! There's nothing for me but to die.... Only I'm sorry for the children! My last hope is in your kindness, because, you see, it was not right!"

I wrote down the name of her village, and her name and surname, and told her I would see about it and let her know.

"Help me, if it's only ever so little!... The children are hungry, and, God's my witness, I haven't so much as a crust. The baby is worst of all ... there's no milk in my breasts. If only the Lord would take him!"

"Haven't you a cow?" I asked.

"A cow? Oh, no!... Why, we're all starving!" said she, crying, and trembling all over in her tattered coat.

I let her go, and prepared for my customary walk. It turned out that the doctor, who lives with us, was going to visit a patient in the village the soldier's wife had come from, and another patient in the village where the District Police Station is situated, so I joined him, and we drove off together.

I went into the Police Station, while the doctor attended to his business in that village.

The District Elder was not in, nor the clerk, but only the clerk's assistant—a clever lad whom I knew. I asked him about the woman's husband, and why, being the only man in the family, he had been taken as a conscript.

The clerk's assistant looked up the particulars, and replied that the woman's husband was not the only man in the family: he had a brother.

"Then why did she say he was the only one?"

"She lied! They always do," replied he, with a smile.

I made some inquiries about other matters I had to attend to, and then the doctor returned from visiting his patient, and we drove towards the village in which the soldier's wife lived. But before we were out of the first village, a girl of about twelve came quickly across the road towards us.

"I suppose you're wanted?" I said to the doctor.

"No, it's your Honour I want," said the girl to me.

"What is it?"

"I've come to your Honour, as mother is dead, and we are left orphans—five of us. Help us!... Think of our needs!"

"Where do you come from?"

The girl pointed to a brick house, not badly built.

"From here ... that is our house. Come and see for yourself!"

I got out of the sledge, and went towards the house. A woman came out and asked me in. She was the orphans' aunt. I entered a large, clean room; all the children were there, four of them: besides the eldest girl—two boys, a girl, and another boy of about two. Their aunt told me all about the family's circumstances. Two years ago the father had been killed in a mine. The widow tried to get compensation, but failed. She was left with four children; the fifth was born after her husband's death. She struggled on alone as best she could, hiring a labourer at first to work her land. But without her husband things went worse and worse. First they had to sell their cow, then the horse, and at last only two sheep were left. Still they managed to live somehow; but two months ago the woman herself fell ill and died, leaving five children, the eldest twelve years old.

"They must get along as best they can. I try to help them, but can't do much. I can't think what's to become of them! I wish they'd die!... If one could only get them into some Orphanage—or at least some of them!"

The eldest girl evidently understood and took in the whole of my conversation with her aunt.

"If at least one could get little Nicky placed somewhere! It's awful; one can't leave him for a moment," said she, pointing to the sturdy little two-year old urchin, who with his little sister was merrily laughing at something or other, and evidently did not at all share his aunt's wish.

I promised to take steps to get one or more of the children into an

Orphanage. The eldest girl thanked me, and asked when she should come for an answer. The eyes of all the children, even of Nicky, were fixed on me, as on some fairy being capable of doing anything for them.

Before I had reached the sledge, after leaving the house, I met an old man. He bowed, and at once began speaking about these same orphans.

"What misery!" he said; "it's pitiful to see them. And the eldest little girlie, how she looks after them—just like a mother! Wonderful how the Lord helps her! It's a mercy the neighbours don't forsake them, or they'd simply die of hunger, the dear little things!... They are the sort of people it does no harm to help," he added, evidently advising me to do so.

I took leave of the old man, the aunt, and the little girl, and drove with the doctor to the woman who had been to see me that morning.

At the first house we came to, I inquired where she lived. It happened to be the house of a widow I know very well; she lives on the alms she begs, and she has a particularly importunate and pertinacious way of extorting them. As usual, she at once began to beg. She said she was just now in special need of help to enable her to rear a calf.

"She's eating me and the old woman out of house and home. Come in and see her."

"And how is the old woman?"

"What about the old woman?... She's hanging on...."

I promised to come and see, not so much the calf as the old woman, and again inquired where the soldier's wife lived. The widow pointed to the next hut but one, and hastened to add that no doubt they were poor, but her brother-in-law "does drink dreadfully!"

Following her instructions, I went to the next house but one.

Miserable as are the huts of all the poor in our villages, it is long since I saw one so dilapidated as that. Not only the whole roof, but the walls were so crooked that the windows were aslant.

Inside, it was no better than outside. The brick oven took up one-third of the black, dirty little hut, which to my surprise was full of people. I thought I should find the widow alone with her children; but here was a sister-in-law (a young woman with children) and an old mother-in-law. The soldier's wife herself had just returned from her visit to me, and was warming herself on the top of the oven. While she was getting down, her mother-in-law began telling me of their life. Her two sons had lived together at first, and they all managed to feed themselves.

"But who remain together nowadays? All separate," the garrulous old woman went on. "The wives began quarrelling, so the brothers separated, and life became still harder. We had little land, and only managed to live by their wage-labour; and now they have taken Peter as a soldier! So where is she to turn to with her children? She's living with us now, but we can't manage to feed them all! We can't think what we are to do. They say he may be got back."

The soldier's wife, having climbed down from the oven, continued to implore me to take steps to get her husband back. I told her it was impossible, and asked what property her husband had left behind with his brother, to keep her and the children. There was none. He had handed over his land to his brother, that he might feed her and the children. They had had three sheep; but two had been sold to pay the expenses of getting her husband off, and there was only some old rubbish left, she said, besides a sheep and two fowls. That was all she had. Her mother-in-law confirmed her words.

I asked the soldier's wife where she had come from. She came from Sergíevskoe. Sergíevskoe is a large, well-to-do village some thirty miles off. I asked if her parents were alive. She said they were alive, and living comfortably.

"Why should you not go to them?" I asked.

"I thought of that myself, but am afraid they won't have the four of us."

"Perhaps they will. Why not write to them? Shall I write for you?"

The woman agreed, and I noted down her parents' address.

While I was talking to the woman, the eldest child—a fat-bellied girl—

came up to her mother, and, pulling at her sleeve, began asking for something, probably food. The woman went on talking to me, and paid no attention to the girl, who again pulled and muttered something.

"There's no getting rid of you!" exclaimed the woman, and with a swing of her arm struck her on the head. The girl burst into a howl.

Having finished my business there, I left the hut and went back to the widow.

She was outside her house, waiting for me, and again asked me to come and look at her calf. I went in, and in the passage there really was a calf. The widow asked me to look at it. I did so, feeling that she was so engrossed in her calf that she could not imagine that anyone could help being interested in seeing it.

Having looked at the calf, I stepped inside, and asked:

"Where is the old woman?"

"The old woman?" the widow repeated, evidently surprised that after having seen the calf, I could still be interested in the old woman. "Why, on the top of the oven! Where else should she be?"

I went up to the oven, and greeted the old woman.

"Oh! ... oh!" answered a hoarse, feeble voice. "Who is it?"

I told her, and asked how she was getting on.

"What's my life worth?"

"Are you in pain?"

"Everything aches! Oh! ... oh!"

"The doctor is here with me; shall I call him in?"

"Doctor!... Oh! ... oh! What do I want with your doctor?... My doctor is up there.... Oh! ... oh!"

"She's old, you know," said the widow.

"Not older than I am," replied I.

"Not older? Much older! People say she is ninety," said the widow. "All her hair has come out. I cut it all off the other day."

"Why did you do that?"

"Why, it had nearly all come out, so I cut it off!"

"Oh! ... oh!" moaned the old woman; "oh! God has forgotten me! He does not take my soul. If the Lord won't take it, it can't go of itself! Oh! ... oh! It must be for my sins! ... I've nothing to moisten my throat.... If only I had a drop of tea to drink before I die.... Oh! ... oh!"

The doctor entered the hut, and I said goodbye and went out into the street.

We got into the sledge, and drove to a small neighbouring village to see the doctor's last patient, who had sent for him the day before. We went into the hut together.

The room was small, but clean; in the middle of it a cradle hung from the ceiling, and a woman stood rocking it energetically. At the table sat a girl of about eight, who gazed at us with surprised and frightened eyes.

"Where is he?" the doctor asked.

"On the oven," replied the woman, not ceasing to rock the cradle.

The doctor climbed up, and, leaning over the patient, did something to him.

I drew nearer, and asked about the sick man's condition.

The doctor gave me no answer. I climbed up, too, and gazing through the darkness gradually began to discern the hairy head of the man on the oven-top. Heavy, stifling air hung about the sick man, who lay on his back. The doctor was holding his left hand to feel the pulse.

"Is he very bad?" I asked.

Without answering me, the doctor turned to the woman.

"Light a lamp," he said.

She called the girl, told her to rock the cradle, and went and lit a lamp and handed it to the doctor. I got down, so as not to be in his way. He took the lamp, and continued to examine the patient.

The little girl, staring at us, did not rock the cradle strongly enough, and the baby began to cry piercingly and piteously. The mother, having handed the lamp to the doctor, pushed the girl angrily aside and again began to rock the cradle.

I returned to the doctor, and again asked how the patient was. The doctor, still occupied with the patient, softly whispered one word.

I did not hear, and asked again.

"The death-agony," he repeated, purposely using a non-Russian word, and got down and placed the lamp on the table.

The baby did not cease crying in a piteous and angry voice.

"What's that? Is he dead?" said the woman, as if she had understood the foreign word the doctor had used.

"Not yet, but there is no hope!" replied he.

"Then I must send for the priest," said the woman in a dissatisfied voice, rocking the screaming baby more and more violently.

"If only my husband was at home!... But now, who can I send? They've all gone to the forest for firewood."

"I can do nothing more here," said the doctor; and we went away.

I heard afterwards that the woman found someone to send for the priest, who had just time to administer the Sacrament to the dying man.

We drove home in silence, both, I think, experiencing the same feeling.

"What was the matter with him?" I asked at length.

"Inflammation of the lungs. I did not expect it to end so quickly. He had a very strong constitution, but the conditions were deadly. With 105 degrees of fever, he went and sat outside the hut, where there were only 20 degrees."

Again we drove on in silence for a long time.

"I noticed no bedding or pillow on the oven," said I.

"Nothing!" replied the doctor. And, evidently knowing what I was thinking about, he went on:

"Yesterday I was at Kroutoe to see a woman who has had a baby. To examine her properly, as was necessary, she should have been placed so that she could lie stretched out full length; but there was no place in the whole hut where that could be done."

Again we were silent, and again we probably both had the same thoughts. We reached home in silence. At the porch stood a fine pair of horses, harnessed tandem to a carpet-upholstered sledge. The handsome coachman was dressed in a sheepskin coat, and wore a thick fur cap. They belonged to my son, who had driven over from his estate.

And here we are sitting at the dinner-table, laid for ten persons. One of the places is empty. It is my little granddaughter's. She is not quite well to-day, and is having her dinner in her room with her nurse. A specially hygienic dinner has been prepared for her: beef-tea and sago.

At our big dinner of four courses, with two kinds of wine, served by two footmen, and eaten at a table decorated with flowers, this is the kind of talk that goes on:

"Where do these splendid roses come from?" asks my son.

My wife tells him that a lady, who will not divulge her name, sends them from Petersburg.

"Roses like these cost three shillings each," says my son, and goes on to relate how at some concert or play such roses were showered on a performer till they covered the stage. The conversation passes on to music, and then to a man who is a very good judge and patron of music.

"By the by, how is he?"

"Oh, he is always ailing. He is again going to Italy. He always spends the winter there, and his health improves wonderfully."

"But the journey is very trying and tedious."

"Oh no! Not if one takes the express—it is only thirty-nine hours."

"All the same, it is very dull."

"Wait a bit! We shall fly before long!"

THIRD DAY-TAXES

Besides my ordinary visitors and applicants, there are to-day some special ones. The first is a childless old peasant who is ending his life in great poverty. The second is a poor woman with a crowd of children. The third is, I believe, a well-to-do peasant.

All three have come from our village, and all have come about the same business. The taxes are being collected before the New Year, and the old man's samovár, the woman's only sheep, and one of the well-to-do peasant's cows, have been noted down for seizure in case of non-payment. They all ask me to defend them or assist them, or to do both.

The well-to-do peasant, a tall, handsome, elderly man, is the first to speak. He tells me that the Village Elder came, noted down the cow, and demands twenty-seven roubles. This levy is for the obligatory Grain Reserve Fund, and ought not, the peasant thinks, to be collected at this time of year. I know nothing about it, and tell him that I will inquire in the District Government Office, and will let him know whether the payment of the tax can be postponed or not.

The second to speak is the old man whose samovár has been noted. The small, thin, weakly, poorly clad man relates, with pathetic grief and bewilderment, how they came, took his samovár, and demanded three roubles and seventy copecks of him, which he has not got and can't get.

I ask him what the tax is for.

"Some kind of Government tax.... Who can tell what it is? Where am I and my old woman to get the money? As it is, we hardly manage to live!... What kind of laws are these? Have pity on our old age, and help us somehow!"

I promise to inquire, and to do what I can, and I turn to the woman. She is thin and worn-out. I know her, and know that her husband is a drunkard, and that she has five children.

"They have seized my sheep! They come and say: 'Pay the money!' 'My husband is away, working,' I say. 'Pay up!' say they. But where am I to find it? I only had one sheep, and they are taking it!" And she begins to cry.

I promise to find out, and to help her if I can. First, I go to the Village Elder, to find out what the taxes are, and why they are collecting them so rigorously.

In the village street, two other petitioners stop me. Their husbands are away at work. One asks me to buy some of her home-woven linen, and offers it for two roubles. "Because they have seized my hens! I had just reared them, and live by selling the eggs. Do buy it; it is good linen! I would not let it go for three roubles if I were not in great need!"

I send her away, promising to consider matters when I return—perhaps I may be able to arrange about the tax.

Before I reach the Elder's house, a woman comes to meet me: a quick-eyed, black-eyed ex-pupil of mine—Ólga, now already an old woman. She is in the same plight: they have seized her calf.

I come to the Elder. He is a strong, intelligent-looking peasant, with a grizzly beard. He comes out into the street to me. I ask him what taxes are being collected, and why so rigorously. He replies that he has had very strict orders to get in all arrears before the New Year.

"Have you had orders to confiscate samovárs and cattle?"

"Of course!" replies the Village Elder, shrugging his shoulders. "The taxes must be paid.... Take Abakoúmof now, for instance," said he, referring to the well-to-do peasant whose cow had been taken in payment of some Grain Reserve Fund. "His son is an isvóstchik: they have three horses. Why shouldn't he pay? He's always trying to get out of it."

"Well, suppose it so in his case," say I; "but how about those who are really poor?" And I name the old man whose samovár they are taking.

"Yes; they really are poor, and have nothing to pay with. But just as if such things get considered up there!"

158

I name the woman whose sheep was taken. The Elder is sorry for her too, but, as if excusing himself, explains that he must obey orders.

I inquire how long he has been an Elder, and what pay he gets.

"How much do I get?" he says, replying not to the question I ask, but to the question in my mind, which he guesses namely, why he takes part in such proceedings. "Well, I do want to resign! We get thirty roubles a month, but are obliged to do things that are wrong."

"Well, and will they really confiscate the samovárs and sheep and fowls?" I ask.

"Why, of course! We are bound to take them, and the District Government will arrange for their sale."

"And will the things be sold?"

"The folk will manage to pay up somehow."

I go to the woman who came to me about her sheep. Her hut is tiny, and in the passage outside is her only sheep, which is to go to support the Imperial Budget. Seeing me, she, a nervous woman worn out by want and overwork, begins to talk excitedly and rapidly, as peasant women do.

"See how I live! They're taking my last sheep, and I myself and these brats are barely alive!" She points up at the bunks and the oven-top, where her children are. "Come down!... Now then, don't be frightened!... There now, how's one to keep oneself and them naked brats?"

The brats, almost literally naked, with nothing on but tattered shirts—not even any trousers—climb down from the oven and surround their mother.

The same day I go to the District Office, to make inquiries about this way of exacting taxation, which is new to me.

The District Elder is not in. He will be back soon. In the Office several persons are standing behind the grating, also waiting to see him.

I ask them who they are, and what they have come about. Two of them have come to get passports, in order to be able to go out to work at a distance. They have brought money to pay for the passports. Another has come to get a copy of the District Court's decision rejecting his petition that the homestead—where he has lived and worked for twenty-three years, and which has belonged to his uncle, who adopted him,—now that his uncle and aunt are dead, should not be taken from him by his uncle's granddaughter. She, being the direct heiress, and taking advantage of the law of the 9th November, is selling the freehold of the land and homestead on which the petitioner lived. His petition has been rejected, but he cannot believe that this is the law, and wants to appeal to some higher Court—though he does not know what Court. I explain that there is such a law, and this provokes disapproval, amounting to perplexity and incredulity, among all those who are present.

Hardly have I finished talking with this man, when a tall peasant with a stern, severe face asks me for an explanation of his affairs. The business he has come about is this: he and his fellow villagers have, from time immemorial, been getting iron ore from their land; and now a decree has been published prohibiting this. "Not dig on one's own land? What laws are these? We only live by digging the iron! We have been trying for more than a month, and can't get anything settled. We don't know what to think of it; they'll ruin us completely, and that will be the end of the matter!"

I can say nothing comforting to this man, and turn to the Elder—who has just come back—to inquire about the vigorous measures which are being taken to exact payment of arrears of taxation in our village. I ask under what clauses of the Act the taxes are being levied. The Elder tells me that there are seven different kinds of rates and taxes, the arrears of all of which are now being collected from the peasants: (1) the Imperial Taxes, (2) the Local Government Taxes, (3) the Insurance Taxes, (4) the arrears of Former Grain Reserve Funds, (5) New Grain Reserve Funds in lieu of contributions in kind, (6) Communal and District Taxes, and (7) Village Taxes.

The District Elder tells me, as the Village Elder had done, that the taxes were being collected with special rigour by order of the higher authorities. He admits that it is no easy task to collect the taxes from the poor, but he shows less sympathy than the Village Elder did. He does not venture to censure the authorities; and, above all, he has hardly any doubt of the usefulness of his office, or of the rightness of taking part in such activity.

"One can't, after all, encourage...."

Soon after, I had occasion to talk about these things with a Zémsky Natchálnik.[3] He had very little compassion for the hard lot of the poverty-stricken folk whom he scarcely ever saw, and just as little doubt of the morality and lawfulness of his activity. In his conversation with me he admitted that, on the whole, it would be pleasanter not to serve at all; but he considered himself a useful functionary, because other men in his place would do even worse things. "And once one is living in the country, why not take the salary, small as it is, of a Zémsky Natchálnik?"

The views of a Governor on the collection of taxes necessary to meet the needs of those who are occupied in arranging for the nation's welfare, were entirely free from any considerations as to samovárs, sheep, homespun linen, or calves taken from the poorest inhabitants of the villages; and he had not the slightest doubt as to the usefulness of his activity.

And finally, the Ministers and those who are busy managing the liquor traffic, those who are occupied in teaching men to kill one another, and those who are engaged in condemning people to exile, to prison, to penal servitude, or to the gallows—all the Ministers and their assistants are quite convinced that samovárs and sheep and linen and calves taken from beggars, are put to their best use in producing vódka (which poisons the people), weapons for killing men, the erection of gaols and lock-ups, and, among other things, in paying to them and to their assistants the salaries they require to furnish drawing-rooms, to buy dresses for their wives, and for journeys and amusements which they undertake as relaxations after fulfilling their arduous labours for the welfare of the coarse and ungrateful masses.

CONCLUSION–A DREAM

A few nights ago I dreamt so significant a dream that several times during the following day I asked myself, "What has happened to-day that is so specially important?" And then I remembered that the specially important thing was what I had seen, or rather heard, in my dream.

It was a speech that struck me greatly, spoken by one who, as often happens in dreams, was a combination of two men: my old friend, now dead, Vladímir Orlóf, with grey curls on each side of his bald head, and Nicholas Andréyevitch, a copyist who lived with my brother.

The speech was evoked by the conversation of a rich lady, the hostess, with a landowner who was visiting her house. The lady had recounted how the peasants on a neighbouring estate had burnt the landlord's house and several sheds which sheltered century-old cherry trees and duchesse pears. Her visitor, the landowner, related how the peasants had cut down some oaks in his forest, and had even carted away a stack of hay.

"Neither arson nor robbery is considered a crime nowadays. The immorality of our people is terrible: they have all become thieves!" said someone.

And in answer to those words, that man, combined of two, spoke as follows:

"The peasants have stolen oaks and hay, and are thieves, and the most immoral class," he began, addressing no one in particular. "Now, in the Caucasus, a chieftain used to raid the Aouls and carry off all the horses of the inhabitants. But one of them found means to get back from the chieftain's herds at least one of the horses that had been stolen from him. Was that man a thief, because he got back one of the many horses stolen from him? And is it not the same with the trees, the grass, the hay, and all the rest of the things you say the peasants have stolen from you? The earth is the Lord's, and common to all; and if the peasants have taken what was grown on the common land of which they have been deprived, they have not stolen, but have only resumed possession of a small part of what has been stolen from them.

"I know you consider land to be the property of the landlord, and therefore call the restoration to themselves of its produce by the peasants—robbery; but, you know, that is not true! The land never was, and never can be, anyone's property. If a man has more of it than he requires, while others have none, then he who possesses the surplus land possesses not land but men; and men cannot be the property of other men.

"Because a dozen mischievous lads have burnt some cherry tree sheds, and have cut down some trees, you say the peasants are thieves, and the most immoral class!...

"How can your tongue frame such words! They have stolen ten oaks from you. Stolen! 'To prison with them!'

"Why, if they had taken not your oaks alone but everything that is in this house, they would only have taken what is theirs: made by them and their brothers, but certainly not by you! 'Stolen oaks!' But for ages you have been stealing from them, not oaks but their lives, and the lives of their children, their womenfolk and their old men—who withered away before their time—only because they were deprived of the land God gave to them in common with all men, and they were obliged to work for you.

"Only think of the life those millions of men have lived and are living, and of how you live! Only consider what they do, supplying you with all the comforts of life, and of what you do for them, depriving them of everything—even of the possibility of supporting themselves and their families! All you live on—everything in this room, everything in this house, and in all your splendid cities, all your palaces, all your mad, literally mad, luxuries—has been made, and is still continually being made, by them.

"And they know this. They know that these parks of yours, and your race-horses, motor cars, palaces, dainty dishes and finery, and all the nastiness and stupidity you call 'science' and 'art'—are purchased with the lives of their brothers and sisters. They know and cannot help knowing this. Then think what feelings these people would have towards you, if they were like you!

"One would suppose that, knowing all you inflict on them, they could not but hate you from the bottom of their souls, and could not help wishing to revenge themselves on you. And you know there are tens of millions of them, and only some thousands of you. But what do they do?... Why, instead of crushing you as useless and harmful reptiles, they continue to repay your evil with good, and live their laborious and reasonable, though hard life, patiently biding the day when you will become conscious of your sin and will amend your ways. But instead of that, what do you do? From the height of your refined, self-confident immorality, you deign to stoop to those 'depraved, coarse people.' You enlighten them, and play the benefactor to them; that is to say, with the means supplied to you by their labour, you inoculate them with your depravity, and blame, correct, and best of all 'punish' them, as unreasoning or vicious infants bite the breasts that feed them.

"Yes, look at yourselves, and consider what you are and what they are! Realise that they alone live, while you, with your Doúmas, Ministries, Synods, Academies, Universities, Conservatoires, Law Courts, armies, and all such stupidities and nastinesses, are but playing at life, and spoiling it for yourselves and others. They, the people, are alive. They are the tree, and you are harmful growths—fungi on the plant. Realise, then, all your insignificance and their grandeur! Understand your sin, and try to repent, and at all costs set the people free...."

"How well he speaks!" thought I. "Can it be a dream?"

And as I thought that, I awoke.

This dream set me again thinking about the land question: a question of which those who live constantly in the country, among a poverty-stricken agricultural peasant population, cannot help thinking. I know I have often written about it; but under the influence of that dream, even at the risk of repeating myself, I once more felt the need to express myself. Carthago delenda est. As long as people's attitude towards private property in land remains unchanged, the cruelty, madness and evil of this form of the enslavement of some men by others, cannot be pointed out too frequently.

People say that land is property, and they say this because the Government recognises private property in land. But fifty years ago the Government upheld private property in human beings; yet a time came when it was admitted that human beings cannot be private property, and the Government ceased to hold them to be property. So it will be with property in land. The Government now upholds that property, and protects it by its power; but a day will come when the Government will cease to acknowledge this kind of property, and will abolish it. The Government will have to abolish it, because private property in land is just such an injustice as property in men—serfdom—used to be. The difference lies only in the fact that serfdom was a direct, definite slavery, while land-slavery is indirect and indefinite. Then Peter was John's slave, whereas now Peter is the slave of some person unknown, but certainly of him who owns the land Peter requires in order to feed himself and his family. And not only is land-slavery as unjust and cruel a slavery as serfdom used to be, it is even harder on the slaves, and more criminal on the part of the slave-holders. For under serfdom—if not from sympathy, then at least from self-interest—the owner was obliged to see to it that his serf did not wither away and die of want, but to the best of his ability and understanding he looked after his slaves' morality. Now the landowner cares nothing if his landless slave withers away or becomes demoralised; for he knows that however many men die or become depraved at his work, he will always be able to find workmen.

The injustice and cruelty of the new, present-day slavery—land-slavery—is so evident, and the condition of the slaves is everywhere so hard, that one would have expected this new slavery to have been recognised by this time as out of date, just as serfdom was admittedly out of date half a century ago; and it should, one would have thought, have been abolished, as serfdom was abolished.

"But," it is said, "property in land cannot be abolished, for it would be impossible to divide equally among all the labourers and non-labourers the advantages given by land of different qualities."

But that is not true. To abolish property in land, no distribution of land is necessary.

Just as, when serfdom was abolished, no distribution of the people

165

liberated was necessary, but all that was needed was the abolition of the law that upheld serfdom, so with the abolition of private property in land: no distribution of land is needed, but only the abolition of the law sanctioning private property in land. And as when serfdom was abolished, the serfs of their own accord settled down as best suited them, so when private property in land is abolished, people will find a way of sharing the land among themselves so that all may have equal advantage from it. How this will be arranged, whether by Henry George's Single-Tax system, or in some other way, we cannot foresee. But it is certain that the Government need only cease to uphold by force the obviously unjust and oppressive rights of property in land, and the people, released from those restrictions, will always find means of apportioning the land by common consent, in such a way that everyone will have an equal share of the benefits the use of the land confers.

It is only necessary for the majority of land-owners—that is, slave-owners—to understand (as they did in the matter of serfdom) that property in land is as hard on the present-day slaves, and as great an iniquity on the part of the slave-owners, as serfdom was; and, having understood that, it is only necessary for them to impress on the Government the necessity of repealing the laws sanctioning property in land—that is, land-slavery. One would have thought that, as in the 'fifties, the best members of society (chiefly the serf-owning nobles themselves), having understood the criminality of their position, explained to the Government the necessity for abolishing their evidently out-of-date and immoral rights, and serfdom was abolished, so it should be now with regard to private property in land, which is land-slavery.

But strange to say, the present slave-owners, the landed proprietors, not only fail to see the criminality of their position, and do not impress on the Government the necessity of abolishing land-slavery, but on the contrary they consciously and unconsciously, by all manner of means, blind themselves and their slaves to the criminality of their position.

The reasons of this are: first, that serfdom in the 'fifties, being the plain, downright enslavement of man by man, ran too clearly counter to religious and moral feeling; while land-slavery is not a direct, immediate slavery, but is a form of slavery more hidden from the slaves, and especially from the slave-owners, by complicated governmental, social and economic institutions. And the second reason is that, while in the days of serfdom only one class were slave-owners, all classes, except the most numerous one—consisting of peasants who have too little land: labourers and working men—are slave-owners now. Nowadays nobles, merchants, officials, manufacturers, professors, teachers, authors, musicians, painters, rich peasants, rich men's servants, well-paid artisans, electricians, mechanics, etc., are all slave-owners of the peasants who have insufficient land, and of the unskilled workmen who—apparently as a result of most varied causes, but in reality as a result of one cause alone (the appropriation of land by the landed proprietors)—are obliged to give their labour and even their lives to those who possess the advantages land affords. These two reasons—that the new slavery is less evident than the old, and that the new slave-owners are much more numerous than the old ones—account for the fact that the slave-owners of our day do not see, and do not admit, the cruelty and criminality of their position, and do not free themselves from it.

The slave-owners of our day not only do not admit that their position is criminal, and do not try to escape from it, but are quite sure that property in land is a necessary institution, essential to the social order, and that the wretched condition of the working classes—which they cannot help noticing—results from most varied causes, but certainly not from the recognition of some people's right to own land as private property.

This opinion of land-owning, and of the causes of the wretched condition of the labourers, is so well established in all the leading countries of the Christian world—France, England, Germany, America, etc.—that with very rare exceptions it never occurs to their public men to look in the right direction for the cause of the wretched condition of the workers.

That is so in Europe and America; but one would have expected that for us Russians, with our hundred million peasant population who deny the principle of private ownership in land, and with our enormous tracts of land, and with the almost religious desire of our people for agricultural life, an answer very different to the general European answer to questions as to the causes of the distress among the workers, and as to the means of bettering their position, would naturally present itself.

One would think that we Russians might understand that if we really are concerned about, and desire to improve, the position of the people and to free them from the aggravating and demoralising fetters with which they are bound, the means to do this are indicated both by common-sense and by the voice of the people, and are simply—the abolition of private property in land, that is to say, the abolition of land-slavery.

But, strange to relate, in Russian society, occupied with questions of the improvement of the condition or the working classes, there is no suggestion of this one, natural, simple and self-evident means of improving their condition. We Russians, though our peasants' outlook on the land question is probably centuries ahead of the rest of Europe, can devise nothing better for the improvement of our people's condition than to establish among ourselves, on the European model, Doúmas, Councils, Ministries, Courts, Zémstvos, Universities, Extension Lectures, Academies, elementary schools, fleets, submarines, air-ships, and many other of the queerest things quite foreign to and unnecessary for the people, and we do not do the one thing that is demanded by religion, morality, and common-sense, as well as by the whole of the peasantry.

Nor is this all. While arranging the fate of our people, who do not and never did acknowledge land-ownership, we, imitating Europe, try in all sorts of cunning ways, and by deception, bribery, and even force, to accustom them to the idea of property in land—that is to say, we try to deprave them and to destroy their consciousness of the truth they have held for ages, and which sooner or later will certainly be acknowledged by the whole human race: the truth that all who live on the earth cannot but have an equal right to its use.

These efforts to inoculate the people with the idea of landed property that is so foreign to them, are unceasingly made, with great perseverance and zeal by the Government, and consciously or for the most part unconsciously, from an instinct of self-preservation, by all the slave-holders of our time. And the slave-holders of our time are not the land-owners alone, but are all those who, as a result of the people being deprived of the land, enjoy power over them.

Most strenuous efforts are made to deprave the people; but, thank God! it may be safely said that till now all those efforts have only had an effect on the smallest and worst part of Russia's peasant population. The many-millioned majority of Russian workmen who hold but little land and live—not the depraved, parasitic life of the slave-owners, but their own reasonable, hard-working lives—do not yield to those efforts; because for them the solution of the land question is not one of personal advantage, as it is regarded by all the different slave-owners of to-day. For the enormous majority of peasants, the solution of that problem is not arrived at by mutually contradictory economic theories that spring up to-day and to-morrow are forgotten, but is found in the one truth, which is realised by them, and always has been and is realised by all reasonable men the world over,—the truth that all men are brothers and have therefore all an equal right to all the blessings of the world and, among the rest, to the most necessary of all rights—namely, the equal right of all to the use of the land.

Living in this truth, an enormous majority of the peasants attach no importance to all the wretched measures adopted by the Government about this or that alteration of the laws of land-ownership, for they know that there is only one solution to the land question—the total abolition of private property in land, and of land-slavery. And, knowing this, they quietly await their day, which sooner or later must come.

SINGING IN THE VILLAGE

Voices and an accordion sounded as if close by, though through the mist nobody could be seen. It was a work-day morning, and I was surprised to hear music.

"Oh, it's the recruits' leave-taking," thought I, remembering that I had heard something a few days before about five men being drawn from our village. Involuntarily attracted by the merry song, I went in the direction whence it proceeded.

As I approached the singers, the sound of song and accordion suddenly stopped. The singers, that is the lads who were leave-taking, entered the double-fronted brick cottage belonging to the father of one of them. Before the door stood a small group of women, girls, and children.

While I was finding out whose sons were going, and why they had entered that cottage, the lads themselves, accompanied by their mothers and sisters, came out at the door. There were five of them: four bachelors and one married man. Our village is near the town where nearly all these conscripts had worked. They were dressed town-fashion, evidently wearing their best clothes: peajackets, new caps, and high, showy boots. Conspicuous among them was a young fellow, well built though not tall, with a sweet, merry, expressive face, a small beard and moustache just beginning to sprout, and bright hazel eyes. As he came out, he at once took a big, expensive-looking accordion that was hanging over his shoulders and, having bowed to me, started playing the merry tune of "Bárynya," running his fingers nimbly over the keys and keeping exact time, as he moved with rhythmic step jauntily down the road.

Beside him walked a thick-set, fair-haired lad, also of medium height. He looked gaily from side to side, and sang second with spirit, in harmony with the first singer. He was the married one. These two walked ahead of the other three, who were also well dressed, and not remarkable in any way except that one of them was tall.

Together with the crowd I followed the lads. All their songs were merry, and no expression of grief was heard while the procession was going along; but as soon as we came to the next house at which the lads were to be treated, the lamentations of the women began. It was difficult to make out what they were saying; only a word here and there could be distinguished: "death ... father and mother ... native land ..."; and after every verse, the woman who led the chanting took a deep breath, and burst out into long-drawn moans, followed by hysterical laughter. The women were the mothers and sisters of the conscripts. Beside the lamentations of these relatives, one heard the admonitions of their friends.

"Now then, Matryóna, that's enough! You must be tired out," I heard one woman say, consoling another who was lamenting.

The lads entered the cottage. I remained outside, talking with a peasant acquaintance, Vasíly Oréhof, a former pupil of mine. His son, one of the five, was the married man who had been singing second as he went along.

"Well," I said, "it is a pity!"

"What's to be done? Pity or not, one has to serve."

And he told me of his domestic affairs. He had three sons: the eldest was living at home, the second was now being taken, and a third (who, like the second, had gone away to work) was contributing dutifully to the support of the home. The one who was leaving had evidently not sent home much.

"He has married a townswoman. His wife is not fit for our work. He is a lopped-off branch and thinks only of keeping himself. To be sure it's a pity, but it can't be helped!"

While we were talking, the lads came out into the street, and the lamentations, shrieks, laughter, and adjurations recommenced. After standing about for some five minutes, the procession moved on with songs and accordion accompaniment. One could not help marvelling at the energy and spirit of the player, as he beat time accurately, stamped his foot, stopped short, and then after a pause again took up the melody most merrily, exactly on the right beat, while he gazed around with his kind, hazel eyes. Evidently he had a real and great talent for music.

I looked at him, and (so at least it seemed to me) he felt abashed when he met my eyes, and with a twitch of his brows he turned away, and again burst out with even more spirit than before. When we reached the fifth and last of the cottages, the lads entered, and I followed them. All five of them were made to sit round a table covered with a cloth, on which were bread and vódka. The host, the man I had been talking to, who was now to take leave of his married son, poured out the vódka and handed it round. The lads hardly drank at all (at most a quarter of a glass) or even handed it back after just raising it to their lips. The hostess cut some bread, and served slices round to eat with the vódka.

While I was looking at the lads, a woman, dressed in clothes that seemed to me strange and incongruous, got down from the top of the oven, close to where I sat. She wore a light green dress (silk, I think) with fashionable trimmings, and high-heeled boots. Her fair hair was arranged in quite the modern style, like a large round cap, and she wore big, ring-shaped, gold earrings. Her face was neither sad nor cheerful, but looked as if she were offended.

After getting down, she went out into the passage, clattering with the heels of her new boots and paying no heed to the lads. All about this woman—her clothing, the offended expression of her face, and above all her earrings—was so foreign to the surroundings that I could not understand how she had come to be on the top of Vasíly Oréhof's oven. I asked a woman sitting near me who she was.

"Vasíly's daughter-in-law; she has been a housemaid," was the answer.

The host began offering vódka a third time, but the lads refused, rose, said grace, thanked the hosts, and went out.

In the street, the lamentations recommenced at once. The first to raise her voice was a very old woman with a bent back. She lamented in such a peculiarly piteous voice, and wailed so, that the women kept soothing the sobbing, staggering old creature, and supported her by her elbows.

"Who is she?" I inquired.

"Why, it's his granny; Vasíly's mother, that is."

The old woman burst into hysterical laughter and fell into the arms of the women who supported her, and just then the procession started again, and again the accordion and the merry voices struck up their tune. At the end of the village the procession was overtaken by the carts which were to carry the conscripts to the District Office. The weeping and wailing stopped. The accordion-player, getting more and more elated, bending his head to one side and resting on one foot, turned out the toes of the other and stamped with it, while his fingers produced brilliant fioritures, and exactly at the right instant the bold, high, merry tones of his song, and the second of Vasíly's son, again chimed in. Old and young, and especially the children who surrounded the crowd, and I with them, fixed their eyes admiringly on the singer.

"He is clever, the rascal!" said one of the peasants.

"'Sorrow weeps, and sorrow sings!'" replied another.

At that moment one of the young fellows whom we were seeing off— the tall one—came up with long, energetic strides, and stooped to speak to the one who played the accordion.

"What a fine fellow," I thought; "they will put him in the Guards." I did not know who he was or what house he belonged to.

"Whose son is that one? That gallant fellow?" I asked a little old man, pointing to the fine lad.

The old man raised his cap and bowed to me, but did not hear my question.

"What did you say?" asked he.

I had not recognised him, but as soon as he spoke I knew him at once. He is a hard-working, good peasant who, as often happens, seems specially marked out for misfortune: first, two horses were stolen from him, then his house burnt down, and then his wife died. I had not seen Prokófey for a long time, and remembered him as a bright red-haired man of medium height; whereas he was now not red, but quite grey-haired, and small.

"Ah, Prokófey, it's you!" I said. "I was asking whose son that fine fellow is—that one who has just spoken to Alexander?"

"That one?" Prokófey replied, pointing with a motion of his head to the tall lad. He shook his head and mumbled something I did not understand.

"I'm asking whose son the lad is?" I repeated, and turned to look at Prokófey.

His face was puckered, and his jaw trembled.

"He's mine!" he muttered, and, turning away and hiding his face in his hand, began to whimper like a child.

And only then, after the two words, "He's mine!" spoken by Prokófey, did I realise, not only in my mind but in my whole being, the horror of what was taking place before my eyes that memorable misty morning. All the disjointed, incomprehensible, strange things I had seen suddenly acquired a simple, clear, and terrible significance. I became painfully ashamed of having looked on as at an interesting spectacle. I stopped, conscious of having acted ill, and I turned to go home.

And to think that these things are at the present moment being done to tens of thousands of men all over Russia, and have been done, and will long continue to be done, to the meek, wise, and saintly Russian people, who are so cruelly and treacherously deceived!

TRAVELLER AND PEASANT

[The interior of a peasant hut. An old Traveller is sitting on a bench, reading a book. A Peasant, the master of the hut, just home from his work, sits down to supper and asks the Traveller to share it. The Traveller declines. The Peasant eats, and when he has finished, rises, says grace, and sits down beside the old man.]

PEASANT. What brings you?...

TRAVELLER [taking off his spectacles and putting down his book]. There is no train till to-morrow. The station is crowded, so I asked your missis to let me stay the night with you, and she allowed it.

PEASANT. That's all right, you can stay.

TRAVELLER. Thank you!... Well, and how are you living nowadays?

PEASANT. Living? What's our life like?... As bad as can be!

TRAVELLER. How's that?

PEASANT. Why, because we've nothing to live on! Our life is so hard that if we wanted a worse one, we couldn't get it.... You see, there are nine of us in family; all want to eat, and I have only got in four bushels of corn. Try and live on that! Whether one likes it or not, one has to go and work for wages ... and when you look for a job, wages are down!... The rich do what they like with us. The people increase, but the land doesn't, and taxes keep piling up! There's rent, and the district tax, and the land tax, and the tax for bridges, and insurance, and police, and for the corn store ... too many to count! And there are the priests and the landlords.... They all ride on our backs, except those who are too lazy!

TRAVELLER. I thought the peasants were doing well nowadays.

PEASANT. So well, that we go hungry for days at a time!

TRAVELLER. The reason I thought so, was that they have taken to squandering so much money.

PEASANT. Squandering what money? How strange you talk!... Here are people starving to death, and you talk of squandering money!

TRAVELLER. But how is it? The papers say that 700 million roubles (and a million is a thousand thousands)—700 million were spent by the peasants on vódka last year.

PEASANT. Are we the only ones that drink? Just look at the priests.... Don't they swill first-rate? And the gentlefolk aren't behind-hand!

TRAVELLER. Still, that's only a small part. The greater part stills falls to the peasants.

PEASANT. What of that? Are we not to drink at all?

TRAVELLER. No; what I mean is that if 700 millions were squandered on vódka in one year it shows that life can't be so very hard.... 700 millions! It's no joke ... one can hardly imagine it!

PEASANT. But how can one do without it? We didn't start the custom, and it's not for us to stop it.... There are the Church feasts, and weddings, and memorial feasts, and bargains to be wetted with a drink.... Whether one likes it or not, one can't get on without it. It's the custom!

TRAVELLER. But there are people who never drink, and yet they manage to live! After all, there's not much good in it.

PEASANT. No good at all! Only evil!

TRAVELLER. Then one ought not to drink.

PEASANT. Well, anyhow, drink or no drink, we've nothing to live on! We've not enough land. If we had land we could at least live ... but there's none to be had.

TRAVELLER. No land to be had? Why, isn't there plenty of land? Wherever one looks, one sees land!

PEASANT. There's land, right enough, but it's not ours. Your elbow's not far from your mouth, but just you try to bite it!

TRAVELLER. Not yours! Whose is it, then?

PEASANT. Whose?... Whose, indeed! There's that fat-bellied devil over there ... he's seized 5000 acres. He has no family, but he's never satisfied, while we've had to give up keeping fowls—there's nowhere for them to run about! It's nearly time for us to stop keeping cattle, too ... we've no fodder for them; and if a calf, or maybe a horse, happens to stray into his field, we have to pay fines and give him our last farthing.

TRAVELLER. What does he want all that land for?

PEASANT. What does he want the land for? Why, of course, he sows and reaps and sells, and puts the money in the bank.

TRAVELLER. How can he plough a stretch like that, and get his harvest in?

PEASANT. You talk as if you were a child!... What's he got money for, if not to hire labourers?... It's they that do the ploughing and reaping.

TRAVELLER. These labourers are some of you peasants, I expect?

PEASANT. Some are from these parts, and some from elsewhere.

TRAVELLER. Anyway, they are peasants?

PEASANT. Of course they are!... the same as ourselves. Who but a peasant ever works? Of course they are peasants.

TRAVELLER. And if the peasants did not go and work for him...?

PEASANT. Go or stay, he wouldn't let us have it. If the land were to lie idle, he'd not part with it! Like the dog in the manger, that doesn't eat the hay himself and won't let others eat it!

TRAVELLER. But how can he keep his land? I suppose it stretches over some three or four miles? How can he watch it all?

PEASANT. How queer you talk! He himself lies on his back, and fattens his paunch; but he keeps watchmen!

TRAVELLER. And those watchmen, I dare say, are also peasants?

PEASANT. What else could they be? Of course they are!

TRAVELLER. So that the peasants work the rich man's land for him, and guard it for him from themselves?

PEASANT. But how can one help it?

TRAVELLER. Simply by not going to work for him, and not being his watchmen! Then the land would be free. The land is God's, and the people are God's; let him who needs it, plough and sow and gather in the harvest!

PEASANT. That is to say, you think we ought to strike? To meet that, my friend, they have the soldiers. They'd send their soldiers ... one, two, fire!... some would get shot, and others taken up. Soldiers give short shrift!

TRAVELLER. But is it not also the likes of you that are soldiers? Why should they shoot at their own fellows?

PEASANT. How can they help it? That's what the oath is for.

TRAVELLER. The oath? What oath?

PEASANT. Don't you understand? Aren't you a Russian?... The oath is—well, it's the oath!

TRAVELLER. It means swearing, doesn't it?

PEASANT. Well, of course! They swear by the Cross and by the Gospels, to lay down their life for their country.

TRAVELLER. Well, I think that should not be done.

PEASANT. What should not be done?

TRAVELLER. Taking the oath.

PEASANT. Not done? Why, the law demands it!

TRAVELLER. No, it is not in the Law. In the Law of Christ, it is plainly forbidden. He said: "Swear not at all."

PEASANT. Come now! What about the priests?

TRAVELLER [takes a book, looks for the place, and reads]: "It was said by them of old time, Thou shalt not forswear thyself, but I say unto you, Swear not at all.... But let your speech be, Yea, yea; nay, nay: and whatsoever is more than these is of the evil one" (Matthew v. 33). So, according to Christ's Law, you must not swear.

PEASANT. If there were no oath, there would be no soldiers.

TRAVELLER. Well, and what good are the soldiers?

PEASANT. What good?... But supposing other Tsars were to come and attack our Tsar ... what then?

TRAVELLER. If the Tsars quarrel, let them fight it out themselves.

PEASANT. Come! How could that be possible?

TRAVELLER. It's very simple. He that believes in God, no matter what you may tell him, will never kill a man.

PEASANT. Then why did the priest read out in church that war was declared, and the Reserves were to be ready?

TRAVELLER. I know nothing about that; but I know that in the Commandments, in the Sixth, it says quite plainly: "Thou shalt do no murder." You see, it is forbidden for a man to kill a man.

PEASANT. That means, at home! At the wars, how could you help it? They're enemies!

TRAVELLER. According to Christ's Gospel, there is no such thing as an enemy. You are told to love everybody.

[Opens the Bible and looks for place.

PEASANT. Well, read it!

TRAVELLER. "Ye have heard that it was said by them of old time, Thou shalt not kill; and whosoever shall kill shall be in danger of the judgment.... Ye have heard that it was said, Thou shalt love thy neighbour, and hate thine enemy: but I say unto you, Love your enemies, and pray for them that persecute you" (Matthew v. 21, 43-44).

[A long pause.

PEASANT. Well, but what about taxes? Ought we to refuse to pay them too?

TRAVELLER. That's as you think best. If your own children are hungry, naturally you should first feed them.

PEASANT. So you think soldiers are not wanted at all?

TRAVELLER. What good do they do? Millions and millions are collected from you and your folk for them—it's no joke to clothe and feed such a host! There are nearly a million of those idlers, and they're only useful to keep the land from you; and it is on you they will fire.

[The PEASANT sighs, and shakes his head.

PEASANT. That's true enough! If everybody were to do it at once ... but if one or two make a stand, they'll be shot or sent to Siberia, and that will be the end of the matter.

TRAVELLER. And yet there are men, even now—young men—who by themselves stand up for the Law of God, and refuse to serve. They say: "According to Christ's Law, I dare not be a murderer! Do as you please, but I won't take a rifle in my hands!"

PEASANT. Well, and what happens?

TRAVELLER. They are put in prison; they remain there, poor fellows, three years, or four.... But I've heard that it's not so bad for them, for the authorities themselves respect them. And some are even let out as unfit for service—bad health! Though he is sometimes a strapping, broad-shouldered fellow, he's "not fit," because they're afraid of taking a man of that kind, for fear he should tell others that soldiering is against God's Law. So they let him go.

PEASANT. Really?

TRAVELLER. Yes, sometimes it happens that they are let off; but it also

180

happens that they die there. Still, soldiers die too, and even get maimed in service—lose a leg, or an arm....

PEASANT. Oh, you're a clever fellow! It would be a good thing, only it won't work out like that.

TRAVELLER. Why not?

PEASANT. That's why.

TRAVELLER. What's that?

PEASANT. That the authorities have power given them.

TRAVELLER. They only have power, because you obey them. Do not obey the authorities, and they won't have any power!

PEASANT. [shakes his head]. You do talk queer! How can one do without the authorities? It is quite impossible to do without some authority.

TRAVELLER. Of course it is! Only whom will you take for authority—the policeman, or God? Whom will you obey—the policeman, or God?

PEASANT. That goes without saying! No one is greater than God. To live for God is the chief thing.

TRAVELLER. Well, if you mean to live for God, you must obey God and not man. And if you live according to God, you will not drive people off the land: you will not be a policeman, a village elder, a tax-collector, a watchman, or above all, a soldier.... You will not promise to kill men.

PEASANT. And how about those long-maned fellows—the priests? They must see that things are being done not according to God's Law. Then why don't they teach how it ought to be?

TRAVELLER. I don't know anything about that. Let them go their way, and you go yours.

PEASANT. They are long-maned devils!

TRAVELLER. It's not right to judge others like that! We must each remember our own faults.

PEASANT. Yes, that's right enough. [Long pause. The PEASANT shakes his head, and smiles.] What it comes to is this: that if we all were to tackle it at once, the land would be ours at one go, and there would be no more taxes.

TRAVELLER. No, friend, that's not what I mean. I don't mean that if we live according to God's will, the land will be ours, and there will be no more taxes. I mean that our life is evil, only because we ourselves do evil. If one lived according to God's will, life would not be evil. What our life would be like if we lived according to God's will, God alone knows; but certainly life would not be evil. We drink, scold, fight, go to law, envy, and hate men; we do not accept God's Law; we judge others; call one fat-paunched and another long-maned; but if any one offers us money, we are ready to do anything for it: go as watchmen, policemen, or soldiers, to help ruin others, and to kill our own brothers. We ourselves live like devils, and yet we complain of others!

PEASANT. That's so! But it is hard, oh, how hard! Sometimes it's more than one can bear.

TRAVELLER. But, for our souls' sakes, we must bear it.

PEASANT. That's quite right.... We live badly, because we forget God.

TRAVELLER. Yes, that's it! That's why life is evil. Take the Revolutionaries; they say: "Let's kill this or that squire, or these fat-paunched rich folk (it's all because of them); and then our life will be happy." So they kill, and go on killing, and it profits them nothing. It's the same with the authorities: "Give us time!" they say, "and we'll hang, and do to death in the prisons, a thousand or a couple of thousand people, and then life will become good...." But it only gets worse and worse!

PEASANT. Yes, that's just it! How can judging and punishing do any good? It must be done according to God's Law.

TRAVELLER. Yes, that is just it. You must serve either God or the devil. If it's to be the devil, go and drink, scold, fight, hate, covet, don't obey God's Law, but man's laws, and life will be evil. If it is God, obey Him alone. Don't rob or kill, and don't even condemn, and do not hate any one. Do not plunge into evil actions, and then there will be no evil life.

PEASANT [sighs]. You speak well, daddy, very well—only we are taught so little! Oh, if we were taught more like that, things would be quite different! But people come from the town, and chatter about their way of bettering things: they chatter fine, but there's nothing in it.... Thank you, daddy, your words are good!... Well, where will you sleep? On the oven, yes?... The missis will make up a bed for you.

A TALK WITH A WAYFARER

I have come out early. My soul feels light and joyful. It is a wonderful morning. The sun is only just appearing from behind the trees. The dew glitters on them and on the grass. Everything is lovely; everyone is lovable. It is so beautiful that, as the saying has it, "One does not want to die." And, really, I do not want to die. I would willingly live a little longer in this world with such beauty around me and such joy in my heart. That, however, is not my affair, but the Master's....

I approach the village. Before the first house I see a man standing, motionless, sideways to me. He is evidently waiting for somebody or something, and waiting as only working people know how to wait, without impatience or vexation. I draw nearer: he is a bearded, strong, healthy peasant, with shaggy, slightly grey hair, and a simple, worker's face. He is smoking not a "cigar" twisted out of paper, but a short pipe. We greet one another.

"Where does old Alexéy live?" I ask.

"I don't know, friend; we are strangers here."

Not "I am a stranger," but "we are strangers." A Russian is hardly ever alone. If he is doing something wrong, he may perhaps say "I"; otherwise it is always "we" the family, "we" the artél, "we" the Commune.

"Strangers? Where do you come from?"

"We are from Kaloúga."

I point to his pipe. "And how much do you spend a year on smoking? Three or more roubles, I daresay!"

"Three? That would hardly be enough."

"Why not give it up?"

"How can one give it up when one's accustomed to it?"

"I also used to smoke, but have given it up ... and I feel so well—so free!"

"Well of course ... but it's dull without it."

"Give it up, and the dulness will go! Smoking is no good, you know!"

"No good at all."

"If it's no good, you should not do it. Seeing you smoke, others will do the same ... especially the young folk. They'll say, 'If the old folk smoke, God himself bids us do it!'"

"That's true enough."

"And your son, seeing you smoke, will do it too."

"Of course, my son too...."

"Well then, give it up!"

"I would, only it's so dull without it.... It's chiefly from dulness. When one feels dull, one has a smoke. That's where the mischief lies.... It's dull! At times it's so dull ... so dull ... so dull!" drawled he.

"The best remedy for that is to think of one's soul."

He threw a glance at me, and at once the expression of his face quite changed: instead of his former kindly, humorous, lively and talkative expression, he became attentive and serious.

"'Think of the soul ... of the soul,' you say?" he asked, gazing questioningly into my eyes.

"Yes! When you think of the soul, you give up all foolish things."

His face lit up affectionately.

"You are right, daddy! You say truly. To think of the soul is the great thing. The soul's the chief thing...." He paused. "Thank you, daddy, it is quite true"; and he pointed to his pipe. "What is it?... Good-for-nothing rubbish! The soul's the chief thing!" repeated he. "What you say is true," and his face grew still kindlier and more serious.

I wished to continue the conversation, but a lump rose in my throat (I have grown very weak in the matter of tears), and I could not speak. With a joyful, tender feeling I took leave of him, swallowing my tears, and I went away.

Yes, how can one help being joyful, living amid such people? How can one help expecting from such people all that is most excellent?

FROM THE DIARY

I am again staying with my friend, Tchertkóff, in the Moscow Government, and am visiting him now for the same reason that once caused us to meet on the border of the Orlóf Government, and that brought me to the Moscow Government a year ago. The reason is that Tchertkóff is allowed to live anywhere in the whole world, except in Toúla Government. So I travel to different ends of it to see him.

Before eight o'clock I go out for my usual walk. It is a hot day. At first I go along the hard clay road, past the acacia bushes already preparing to crack their pods and shed their seeds; then past the yellowing rye-field, with its still fresh and lovely cornflowers, and come out into a black fallow field, now almost all ploughed up. To the right an old man, in rough peasant-boots, ploughs with a sohá[4] and a poor, skinny horse; and I hear an angry old voice shout: "Gee-up!" and, from time to time, "Now, you devil!" and again, "Gee-up, devil!" I want to speak with him; but when I pass his furrow, he is at the other end of the field. I go on. There is another ploughman further on. This one I shall probably meet when he reaches the road. If so, I'll speak to him, if there is a chance. And we do meet just as he reaches the road.

He ploughs with a proper plough, harnessed to a big roan horse, and is a well-built young lad, well clad, and wearing good boots; and he answers my greeting of "God aid you!" pleasantly.

The plough does not cut into the hard, beaten track that crosses the field, and he lifts it over and halts.

"You find the plough better than a sohá?"

"Why, certainly ... much easier!"

"Have you had it long?"

"Not long—and it nearly got stolen...."

"But you got it back?"

"Yes! One of our own villagers had it."

"Well, and did you have the law of him?"

"Why, naturally!"

"But why prosecute, if you got the plough back?"

"Why, you see, he's a thief!"

"What then? The man will go to prison, and learn to steal worse!"

He looks at me seriously and attentively, evidently neither agreeing nor contradicting this, to him, new idea.

He has a fresh, healthy, intelligent face, with hair just appearing on his chin and upper lip, and with intelligent grey eyes.

He leaves the plough, evidently wishing to have a rest, and inclined for a talk. I take the plough-handles, and touch the perspiring, well-fed, full-grown mare. She presses her weight into her collar, and I take a few steps. But I do not manage the plough, the share jumps out of the furrow, and I stop the horse.

"No, you can't do it."

"I have only spoilt your furrow."

"That doesn't matter—I'll put it right!"

He backs his horse, to plough the part I have missed, but does not go on ploughing.

"It is hot in the sun.... Let's go and sit under the bushes," says he, pointing to a little wood just across the field.

We go into the shade of the young birches. He sits down on the ground, and I stop in front of him.

"What village are you from?"

"From Botvínino."

188

"Is that far?"

"There it is, shimmering on the hill," says he, pointing.

"Why are you ploughing so far from home?"

"This is not my land: it belongs to a peasant here. I have hired myself out to him."

"Hired yourself out for the whole summer?"

"No—to plough this ground twice, and sow it, all properly."

"Has he much land, then?"

"Yes, he sows about fifteen bushels of seed."

"Does he! And is that horse your own? It's a good horse."

"Yes, it's not a bad mare," he answers, with quiet pride.

The mare really is, in build, size, and condition, such as a peasant rarely possesses.

"I expect you are in service somewhere, and do carting?"

"No, I live at home. I'm my own master!"

"What, so young?"

"Yes! I was left fatherless at seven. My brother works at a Moscow factory. At first my sister helped; she also worked at a factory. But since I was fourteen I've had no help in all my affairs, and have worked and earned," says he, with calm consciousness of his dignity.

"Are you married?"

"No."

"Then, who does your housework?"

"Why, mother!"

"And you have a cow?"

"Two cows."

"Have you, really?... And how old are you?" I ask.

"Eighteen," he replies, with a slight smile, understanding that it interests me to see that so young a fellow has been able to manage so well. This, evidently, pleases him.

"How young you still are!" I say. "And will you have to go as a soldier?"

"Of course ... be conscripted!" says he, with the calm expression with which people speak of old age, death, and in general of things it is useless to argue about, because they are unavoidable.

As always happens now when one speaks to peasants, our talk touches on the land, and, describing his life, he says he has not enough land, and that if he did not do wage-labour, sometimes with and sometimes without his horse, he would not have anything to live on. But he says this with merry, pleased and proud self-satisfaction; and again remarks that he was left alone, master of the house, when he was fourteen, and has earned everything himself.

"And do you drink vódka?"

He evidently does not like to say that he does, and still does not wish to tell a lie.

"I do," he says, softly, shrugging his shoulders.

"And can you read and write?"

"Very well."

"And haven't you read books about strong drink?"

"No, I haven't."

"Well, but wouldn't it be better not to drink at all?"

"Of course. Little good comes of it."

"Then why not give it up?"

He is silent, evidently understanding, and thinking it over.

190

"It can be done, you know," say I, "and what a good thing it would be!... The day before yesterday I went to Ívino. When I reached one of the houses, the master came out to greet me, calling me by name. It turned out that we had met twelve years before.... It was Koúzin—do you know him?"

"Of course I do! Sergéy Timoféevitch, you mean?"

I tell him how we started a Temperance Society twelve years ago with Koúzin, who, though he used to drink, has quite given it up, and now tells me he is very glad to be rid of so nasty a habit; and, one sees, is living well, with his house and everything well managed, and who, had he not given up drinking, would have had none of these things.

"Yes, that is so!"

"Well then, you know, you should do the same. You are such a nice, good lad.... What do you need vódka for, when you say yourself there is no good in it?... You, too, should give it up!... It would be such a good thing!"

He remains silent, and looks at me intently. I prepare to go, and hold out my hand to him.

"Truly, give it up from now! It would be such a good thing!"

With his strong hand he firmly presses mine, evidently regarding my gesture as challenging him to promise.

"Very well then ... it can be done!" says he, quite unexpectedly, and in a joyous and resolute tone.

"Do you really promise?" say I, surprised.

"Well, of course! I promise," he says, nodding his head and smiling slightly.

The quiet tone of his voice, and his serious, attentive face, show that he is not joking, but that he is really making a promise he means to keep.

Old age or illness, or both together, has made me very ready to cry when I am touched with joy. The simple words of that kindly, firm, strong man, so evidently ready for all that is good, and standing so alone, touch me so that sobs rise to my throat, and I step aside, unable to utter a word.

After going a few steps, I regain control of myself, and turn to him and say (I have already asked his name):

"Mind, Alexander! ... the proverb says, 'Be slow to promise, but having promised, keep it!'"

"Yes, that's so. It will be safe."

I have seldom experienced a more joyful feeling than I had when I left him.

I have omitted to say that during our talk I had offered to give him some leaflets on drink and some booklets. [A man in a neighbouring village posted up one of those same leaflets on the wall outside his house lately, but it was pulled down and destroyed by the policeman.] He thanked me, and said he would come and fetch them in the dinner-hour.

He did not come in the dinner-hour, and I, sinner that I am, suspected that our whole conversation was not so important to him as it seemed to me, and that he did not want the books, and that, in general, I had attributed to him what was not in him. But he came in the evening, all perspiring from his work and from the walk. After finishing his work, he had ridden home, put up the plough, attended to his horse, and had now come a quarter of a mile to fetch the books.

I was sitting, with some visitors, on a splendid veranda, looking out on to flower-beds with ornamental vases on flower-set mounds—in short, in luxurious surroundings such as one is always ashamed of when one enters into human relations with working people.

I went out to him, and at once asked, "Have you not changed your mind? Will you really keep your promise?"

And again, with the same kindly smile, he replied, "Of course!... I have already told mother. She's glad, and thanks you."

I saw a bit of paper behind his ear.

"You smoke?"

"I do," he said, evidently expecting that I should begin persuading him to leave that off too. But I did not try to.

He remained silent; and then, by some strange connection of thoughts (I think he saw the interest I felt in his life, and wished to tell me of the important event awaiting him in the autumn) he said:

"But I did not tell you.... I am already betrothed...."

And he smiled, looking questioningly into my eyes. "It's to be in the autumn!"

"Really! That's a good thing! Where is she from?"

He told me.

"Has she a dowry?"

"No; what dowry should she have? But she's a good girl."

The idea came to me to put to him the question which always interests me when I come in contact with good young people of our day.

"Tell me," said I, "and forgive my asking—but please tell the truth: either do not answer at all, or tell the whole truth...."

He looked at me quietly and attentively.

"Why should I not tell you?"

"Have you ever sinned with a woman?"

Without a moment's hesitation, he replied simply:

"God preserve me! There's been nothing of the sort!"

"That's good, very good!" said I. "I am glad for you."

There was nothing more to say just then.

"Well then, I will fetch you the books, and God's help be with you!"

And we took leave of one another.

Yes, what a splendid, fertile soil on which to sow, and what a dreadful sin it is to cast upon it the seeds of falsehood, violence, drunkenness and profligacy!

FOOTNOTES:

[1] Not in the English sense, for there is no Poor-Law system entitling the destitute to demand maintenance.

[2] One of the most depressing features of L. N. Tolstoy's environment is the large number of unemployed and beggars from the adjacent highway. They wait outside the house for hours every day for the coming of Leo Nikolayevich. The consciousness of his inability to render them substantial aid weighs heavily upon him, as does also the fact that, owing to insurmountable obstacles, he cannot even feed them, and allow them to sleep in the house in which he himself lives. These unfortunates surround Leo Nikolayevich at the steps, and besiege him with their importunate requests, just at the time when he seeks the fresh air and is most in need of mental rest and solitude after long-continued and strenuous mental labour. In view of this fact, the idea has occurred to some of Leo Nikolayevich's friends, of establishing in the village of Yásnaya Polyána a lodging- and eating-house for tramps, the use of which by the latter would save L. N. unnecessary trouble. The establishment of such premises—L. N. has viewed the idea very favourably—would at least afford some temporary relief to the wandering poor who are in dire need. At the same time the peasantry of Yásnaya Polyána would be relieved of the too heavy burden of supporting the passing unemployed described by Tolstoy in his article. Lastly, it would afford Tolstoy, in his declining years, considerable mental relief, which it would seem that he has more than deserved by his incessant labours on behalf of distressed mankind. Perhaps among those who read the present sketches some will be found who, prompted by the impulses animating the author, may desire to render some material help towards the practical realisation of the projected undertaking.

Contributions may be sent to the following address: V. Tchertkoff, Editor of the Free Age Press, Christchurch, Hants, Eng.

[3] A Zémsky Natchálnik is a salaried official placed in authority in a district. He is often selected from among the local gentry, and wields very considerable authority.

[4] A primitive plough used by the peasants.

About Author

In the 1870s Tolstoy experienced a profound moral crisis, followed by what he regarded as an equally profound spiritual awakening, as outlined in his non-fiction work A Confession (1882). His literal interpretation of the ethical teachings of Jesus, centering on the Sermon on the Mount, caused him to become a fervent Christian anarchist and pacifist. Tolstoy's ideas on nonviolent resistance, expressed in such works as The Kingdom of God Is Within You (1894), were to have a profound impact on such pivotal 20th-century figures as Mahatma Gandhi and Martin Luther King Jr. Tolstoy also became a dedicated advocate of Georgism, the economic philosophy of Henry George, which he incorporated into his writing, particularly Resurrection (1899).

Origins

The Tolstoys were a well-known family of old Russian nobility who traced their ancestry to a mythical nobleman named Indris described by Pyotr Tolstoy as arriving "from Nemec, from the lands of Caesar" to Chernigov in 1353 along with his two sons Litvinos (or Litvonis) and Zimonten (or Zigmont) and a druzhina of 3000 people. While the word "Nemec" has been long used to describe Germans only, at that time it was applied to any foreigner who didn't speak Russian (from the word nemoy meaning mute). Indris was then converted to Eastern Orthodoxy under the name of Leonty and his sons – as Konstantin and Feodor, respectively. Konstantin's grandson Andrei Kharitonovich was nicknamed Tolstiy (translated as fat) by Vasily II of Moscow after he moved from Chernigov to Moscow.

Because of the pagan names and the fact that Chernigov at the time was ruled by Demetrius I Starshy some researches concluded that they were Lithuanians who arrived from the Grand Duchy of Lithuania, then part of the State of the Teutonic Order. At the same time, no mention of Indris was ever found in the 14th – 16th-century documents, while the Chernigov Chronicles used by Pyotr Tolstoy as a reference were lost. The first documented members of the Tolstoy family also lived during the 17th century, thus Pyotr

Tolstoy himself is generally considered the founder of the noble house, being granted the title of count by Peter the Great.

Life and career

Tolstoy was born at Yasnaya Polyana, a family estate 12 kilometres (7.5 mi) southwest of Tula, Russia, and 200 kilometers (120 mi) south of Moscow. He was the fourth of five children of Count Nikolai Ilyich Tolstoy (1794–1837), a veteran of the Patriotic War of 1812, and Countess Mariya Tolstaya (née Volkonskaya; 1790–1830). After his mother died when he was two and his father when he was nine, Tolstoy and his siblings were brought up by relatives. In 1844, he began studying law and oriental languages at Kazan University, where teachers described him as "both unable and unwilling to learn." Tolstoy left the university in the middle of his studies, returned to Yasnaya Polyana and then spent much of his time in Moscow, Tula and Saint Petersburg, leading a lax and leisurely lifestyle. He began writing during this period, including his first novel Childhood, a fictitious account of his own youth, which was published in 1852. In 1851, after running up heavy gambling debts, he went with his older brother to the Caucasus and joined the army. Tolstoy served as a young artillery officer during the Crimean War and was in Sevastopol during the 11-month-long siege of Sevastopol in 1854–55, including the Battle of the Chernaya. During the war he was recognised for his bravery and courage and promoted to lieutenant. He was appalled by the number of deaths involved in warfare, and left the army after the end of the Crimean War.

His conversion from a dissolute and privileged society author to the non-violent and spiritual anarchist of his latter days was brought about by his experience in the army as well as two trips around Europe in 1857 and 1860–61. Others who followed the same path were Alexander Herzen, Mikhail Bakunin and Peter Kropotkin. During his 1857 visit, Tolstoy witnessed a public execution in Paris, a traumatic experience that would mark the rest of his life. Writing in a letter to his friend Vasily Botkin: "The truth is that the State is a conspiracy designed not only to exploit, but above all to corrupt its citizens ... Henceforth, I shall never serve any government anywhere." Tolstoy's concept of non-violence or Ahimsa was bolstered when he read a

German version of the Tirukkural. He later instilled the concept in Mahatma Gandhi through his A Letter to a Hindu when young Gandhi corresponded with him seeking his advice.

His European trip in 1860–61 shaped both his political and literary development when he met Victor Hugo, whose literary talents Tolstoy praised after reading Hugo's newly finished Les Misérables. The similar evocation of battle scenes in Hugo's novel and Tolstoy's War and Peace indicates this influence. Tolstoy's political philosophy was also influenced by a March 1861 visit to French anarchist Pierre-Joseph Proudhon, then living in exile under an assumed name in Brussels. Apart from reviewing Proudhon's forthcoming publication, La Guerre et la Paix (War and Peace in French), whose title Tolstoy would borrow for his masterpiece, the two men discussed education, as Tolstoy wrote in his educational notebooks: "If I recount this conversation with Proudhon, it is to show that, in my personal experience, he was the only man who understood the significance of education and of the printing press in our time."

Fired by enthusiasm, Tolstoy returned to Yasnaya Polyana and founded 13 schools for the children of Russia's peasants, who had just been emancipated from serfdom in 1861. Tolstoy described the school's principles in his 1862 essay "The School at Yasnaya Polyana". Tolstoy's educational experiments were short-lived, partly due to harassment by the Tsarist secret police. However, as a direct forerunner to A.S. Neill's Summerhill School, the school at Yasnaya Polyana can justifiably be claimed the first example of a coherent theory of democratic education.

Towards the end of his career, Tolstoy was selected to receive the first Nobel Prize in Literature in 1901, but turned down the honor in October of the same year, worrying that the prize money would bring unwanted complications to his life.

Personal life

The death of his brother Nikolay in 1860 had an impact on Tolstoy, and led him to a desire to marry. On 23 September 1862, Tolstoy married Sophia Andreevna Behrs, who was 16 years his junior and the daughter of a court physician. She was called Sonya, the Russian diminutive of Sofia, by her family and friends. They had 13 children, eight of whom survived childhood:

Count Sergei Lvovich Tolstoy (1863–1947), composer and ethnomusicologist

Countess Tatyana Lvovna Tolstaya (1864–1950), wife of Mikhail Sergeevich Sukhotin

Count Ilya Lvovich Tolstoy (1866–1933), writer

Count Lev Lvovich Tolstoy (1869–1945), writer and sculptor

Countess Maria Lvovna Tolstaya (1871–1906), wife of Nikolai Leonidovich Obolensky

Count Peter Lvovich Tolstoy (1872–1873), died in infancy

Count Nikolai Lvovich Tolstoy (1874–1875), died in infancy

Countess Varvara Lvovna Tolstaya (1875–1875), died in infancy

Count Andrei Lvovich Tolstoy (1877–1916), served in the Russo-Japanese War

Count Michael Lvovich Tolstoy (1879–1944)

Count Alexei Lvovich Tolstoy (1881–1886)

Countess Alexandra Lvovna Tolstaya (1884–1979)

Count Ivan Lvovich Tolstoy (1888–1895)

The marriage was marked from the outset by sexual passion and emotional insensitivity when Tolstoy, on the eve of their marriage, gave her his diaries detailing his extensive sexual past and the fact that one of the serfs on his estate had borne him a son. Even so, their early married life was happy and allowed Tolstoy much freedom and the support system to compose War and Peace and Anna Karenina with Sonya acting as his secretary, editor, and financial manager. Sonya was copying and handwriting his epic works time after time. Tolstoy would continue editing War and Peace and had to have clean final drafts to be delivered to the publisher.

However, their later life together has been described by A.N. Wilson as one of the unhappiest in literary history. Tolstoy's relationship with his wife deteriorated as his beliefs became increasingly radical. This saw him seeking to reject his inherited and earned wealth, including the renunciation of the copyrights on his earlier works.

Some of the members of the Tolstoy family left Russia in the aftermath of the 1905 Russian Revolution and the subsequent establishment of the Soviet Union, and many of Leo Tolstoy's relatives and descendants today live in Sweden, Germany, the United Kingdom, France and the United States. Among them are Swedish jazz singer Viktoria Tolstoy and the Swedish landowner Christopher Paus, whose family owns the major estate Herresta outside Stockholm.

One of his great-great-grandsons, Vladimir Tolstoy (born 1962), is a director of the Yasnaya Polyana museum since 1994 and an adviser to the President of Russia on cultural affairs since 2012. Ilya Tolstoy's great-grandson, Pyotr Tolstoy, is a well-known Russian journalist and TV presenter as well as a State Duma deputy since 2016. His cousin Fyokla Tolstaya (born Anna Tolstaya in 1971), daughter of the acclaimed Soviet Slavist Nikita Tolstoy (ru) (1923–1996), is also a Russian journalist, TV and radio host.

Novels and fictional works

Tolstoy is considered one of the giants of Russian literature; his works include the novels War and Peace and Anna Karenina and novellas such as Hadji Murad and The Death of Ivan Ilyich.

Tolstoy's earliest works, the autobiographical novels Childhood, Boyhood, and Youth (1852–1856), tell of a rich landowner's son and his slow realization of the chasm between himself and his peasants. Though he later rejected them as sentimental, a great deal of Tolstoy's own life is revealed. They retain their relevance as accounts of the universal story of growing up.

Tolstoy served as a second lieutenant in an artillery regiment during the Crimean War, recounted in his Sevastopol Sketches. His experiences in battle helped stir his subsequent pacifism and gave him material for realistic depiction of the horrors of war in his later work.

His fiction consistently attempts to convey realistically the Russian society in which he lived. The Cossacks (1863) describes the Cossack life and people through a story of a Russian aristocrat in love with a Cossack girl. Anna Karenina (1877) tells parallel stories of an adulterous woman trapped by the conventions and falsities of society and of a philosophical landowner (much like Tolstoy), who works alongside the peasants in the fields and seeks to reform their lives. Tolstoy not only drew from his own life experiences but also created characters in his own image, such as Pierre Bezukhov and Prince Andrei in War and Peace, Levin in Anna Karenina and to some extent, Prince Nekhlyudov in Resurrection.

War and Peace is generally thought to be one of the greatest novels ever written, remarkable for its dramatic breadth and unity. Its vast canvas includes 580 characters, many historical with others fictional. The story moves from family life to the headquarters of Napoleon, from the court of Alexander I of Russia to the battlefields of Austerlitz and Borodino. Tolstoy's original idea for the novel was to investigate the causes of the Decembrist revolt, to which it refers only in the last chapters, from which can be deduced that Andrei Bolkonsky's son will become one of the Decembrists. The novel explores Tolstoy's theory of history, and in particular the insignificance of individuals such as Napoleon and Alexander. Somewhat surprisingly, Tolstoy did not consider War and Peace to be a novel (nor did he consider many of the great Russian fictions written at that time to be novels). This view becomes less surprising if one considers that Tolstoy was a novelist of the realist school who considered the novel to be a framework for the examination of social and political issues in nineteenth-century life. War and Peace (which is to Tolstoy really an epic in prose) therefore did not qualify. Tolstoy thought that Anna Karenina was his first true novel.

After Anna Karenina, Tolstoy concentrated on Christian themes, and his later novels such as The Death of Ivan Ilyich (1886) and What Is to Be Done? develop a radical anarcho-pacifist Christian philosophy which led to his excommunication from the Russian Orthodox Church in 1901. For all the praise showered on Anna Karenina and War and Peace, Tolstoy rejected the two works later in his life as something not as true of reality.

In his novel Resurrection, Tolstoy attempts to expose the injustice of man-made laws and the hypocrisy of institutionalized church. Tolstoy also explores and explains the economic philosophy of Georgism, of which he had become a very strong advocate towards the end of his life.

Tolstoy also tried himself in poetry with several soldier songs written during his military service and fairy tales in verse such as Volga-bogatyr and Oaf stylized as national folk songs. They were written between 1871 and 1874 for his Russian Book for Reading, a collection of short stories in four volumes (total of 629 stories in various genres) published along with the New Azbuka textbook and addressed to schoolchildren. Nevertheless, he was skeptical about poetry as a genre. As he famously said, "Writing poetry is like ploughing and dancing at the same time". According to Valentin Bulgakov, he criticised poets, including Alexander Pushkin, for their "false" epithets used "simply to make it rhyme".

Critical appraisal by other authors

Tolstoy's contemporaries paid him lofty tributes. Fyodor Dostoyevsky, who died thirty years before Tolstoy's death, thought him the greatest of all living novelists. Gustave Flaubert, on reading a translation of War and Peace, exclaimed, "What an artist and what a psychologist!" Anton Chekhov, who often visited Tolstoy at his country estate, wrote, "When literature possesses a Tolstoy, it is easy and pleasant to be a writer; even when you know you have achieved nothing yourself and are still achieving nothing, this is not as terrible as it might otherwise be, because Tolstoy achieves for everyone. What he does serves to justify all the hopes and aspirations invested in literature." The 19th-century British poet and critic Matthew Arnold opined that "A novel by Tolstoy is not a work of art but a piece of life."

Later novelists continued to appreciate Tolstoy's art, but sometimes also expressed criticism. Arthur Conan Doyle wrote "I am attracted by his earnestness and by his power of detail, but I am repelled by his looseness of construction and by his unreasonable and impracticable mysticism." Virginia

Woolf declared him "the greatest of all novelists." James Joyce noted that "He is never dull, never stupid, never tired, never pedantic, never theatrical!" Thomas Mann wrote of Tolstoy's seemingly guileless artistry: "Seldom did art work so much like nature." Vladimir Nabokov heaped superlatives upon The Death of Ivan Ilyich and Anna Karenina; he questioned, however, the reputation of War and Peace, and sharply criticized Resurrection and The Kreutzer Sonata.

Religious and political beliefs

After reading Schopenhauer's The World as Will and Representation, Tolstoy gradually became converted to the ascetic morality upheld in that work as the proper spiritual path for the upper classes: "Do you know what this summer has meant for me? Constant raptures over Schopenhauer and a whole series of spiritual delights which I've never experienced before. ... no student has ever studied so much on his course, and learned so much, as I have this summer"

In Chapter VI of A Confession, Tolstoy quoted the final paragraph of Schopenhauer's work. It explained how the nothingness that results from complete denial of self is only a relative nothingness, and is not to be feared. The novelist was struck by the description of Christian, Buddhist, and Hindu ascetic renunciation as being the path to holiness. After reading passages such as the following, which abound in Schopenhauer's ethical chapters, the Russian nobleman chose poverty and formal denial of the will:

But this very necessity of involuntary suffering (by poor people) for eternal salvation is also expressed by that utterance of the Savior (Matthew 19:24): "It is easier for a camel to go through the eye of a needle, than for a rich man to enter into the kingdom of God." Therefore, those who were greatly in earnest about their eternal salvation, chose voluntary poverty when fate had denied this to them and they had been born in wealth. Thus Buddha Sakyamuni was born a prince, but voluntarily took to the mendicant's staff; and Francis of Assisi, the founder of the mendicant orders who, as a youngster at a ball, where the daughters of all the notabilities were sitting together, was asked: "Now Francis, will you not soon make your choice from these beauties?"

and who replied: "I have made a far more beautiful choice!" "Whom?" "La povertà (poverty)": whereupon he abandoned every thing shortly afterwards and wandered through the land as a mendicant.

In 1884, Tolstoy wrote a book called What I Believe, in which he openly confessed his Christian beliefs. He affirmed his belief in Jesus Christ's teachings and was particularly influenced by the Sermon on the Mount, and the injunction to turn the other cheek, which he understood as a "commandment of non-resistance to evil by force" and a doctrine of pacifism and nonviolence. In his work The Kingdom of God Is Within You, he explains that he considered mistaken the Church's doctrine because they had made a "perversion" of Christ's teachings. Tolstoy also received letters from American Quakers who introduced him to the non-violence writings of Quaker Christians such as George Fox, William Penn and Jonathan Dymond. Tolstoy believed being a Christian required him to be a pacifist; the consequences of being a pacifist, and the apparently inevitable waging of war by government, are the reason why he is considered a philosophical anarchist.

Later, various versions of "Tolstoy's Bible" would be published, indicating the passages Tolstoy most relied on, specifically, the reported words of Jesus himself.

Tolstoy believed that a true Christian could find lasting happiness by striving for inner self-perfection through following the Great Commandment of loving one's neighbor and God rather than looking outward to the Church or state for guidance. His belief in nonresistance when faced by conflict is another distinct attribute of his philosophy based on Christ's teachings. By directly influencing Mahatma Gandhi with this idea through his work The Kingdom of God Is Within You (full text of English translation available on Wikisource), Tolstoy's profound influence on the nonviolent resistance movement reverberates to this day. He believed that the aristocracy were a burden on the poor, and that the only solution to how we live together is through anarchism.

He also opposed private property in land ownership and the institution of marriage and valued the ideals of chastity and sexual abstinence (discussed in Father Sergius and his preface to The Kreutzer Sonata), ideals also held by the young Gandhi. Tolstoy's later work derives a passion and verve from the depth of his austere moral views. The sequence of the temptation of Sergius in Father Sergius, for example, is among his later triumphs. Gorky relates how Tolstoy once read this passage before himself and Chekhov and that Tolstoy was moved to tears by the end of the reading. Other later passages of rare power include the personal crises that were faced by the protagonists of The Death of Ivan Ilyich, and of Master and Man, where the main character in the former or the reader in the latter are made aware of the foolishness of the protagonists' lives.

Tolstoy had a profound influence on the development of Christian anarchist thought. The Tolstoyans were a small Christian anarchist group formed by Tolstoy's companion, Vladimir Chertkov (1854–1936), to spread Tolstoy's religious teachings. Philosopher Peter Kropotkin wrote of Tolstoy in the article on anarchism in the 1911 Encyclopædia Britannica:

> Without naming himself an anarchist, Leo Tolstoy, like his predecessors in the popular religious movements of the 15th and 16th centuries, Chojecki, Denk and many others, took the anarchist position as regards the state and property rights, deducing his conclusions from the general spirit of the teachings of Jesus and from the necessary dictates of reason. With all the might of his talent, Tolstoy made (especially in The Kingdom of God Is Within You) a powerful criticism of the church, the state and law altogether, and especially of the present property laws. He describes the state as the domination of the wicked ones, supported by brutal force. Robbers, he says, are far less dangerous than a well-organized government. He makes a searching criticism of the prejudices which are current now concerning the benefits conferred upon men by the church, the state, and the existing distribution of property, and from the teachings of Jesus he deduces the rule of non-resistance and the absolute condemnation of all wars. His religious arguments are, however, so well combined with arguments borrowed from a dispassionate observation of the present evils, that the anarchist portions of his works appeal to the religious and the non-religious reader alike.

During the Boxer Rebellion in China, Tolstoy praised the Boxers. He was harshly critical of the atrocities committed by the Russians, Germans, Americans, Japanese, and other western troops. He accused them of engaging in slaughter when he heard about the lootings, rapes, and murders, in what he saw as Christian brutality. Tolstoy also named the two monarchs most responsible for the atrocities; Nicholas II of Russia and Wilhelm II of Germany. Tolstoy, a famous sinophile, also read the works of Chinese thinker and philosopher, Confucius. Tolstoy corresponded with the Chinese intellectual Gu Hongming and recommended that China remain an agrarian nation and warned against reform like what Japan implemented.

The Eight-Nation Alliance intervention in the Boxer Rebellion was denounced by Tolstoy as were the Philippine–American War and the Second Boer War between the British Empire and the two independent Boer republics. The words "terrible for its injustice and cruelty" were used to describe the Czarist intervention in China by Tolstoy. Confucius's works were studied by Tolstoy. The attack on China in the Boxer Rebellion was railed against by Tolstoy. The war against China was criticized by Leonid Andreev and Gorkey. To the Chinese people, an epistle, was written by Tolstoy as part of the criticism of the war by intellectuals in Russia. The activities of Russia in China by Nicholas II were described in an open letter where they were slammed and denounced by Leo Tolstoy in 1902. Tolstoy corresponded with Gu Hongming and they both opposed the Hundred Day's Reform by Kang Youwei and agreed that the reform movement was perilous. Tolstoys' ideology on non violence shaped the anarchist thought of the Society for the Study of Socialism in China. Lao Zi and Confucius's teachings were studied by Tolstoy. Chinese Wisdom was a text written by Tolstoy. The Boxer Rebellion stirred Tolstoy's interest in Chinese philosophy. The Boxer and Boxer wars were denounced by Tolstoy.

In hundreds of essays over the last 20 years of his life, Tolstoy reiterated the anarchist critique of the state and recommended books by Kropotkin and Proudhon to his readers, whilst rejecting anarchism's espousal of violent revolutionary means. In the 1900 essay, "On Anarchy", he wrote; "The Anarchists are right in everything; in the negation of the existing order, and in the assertion that, without Authority, there could not be worse violence than that of Authority under existing conditions. They are mistaken only in thinking that Anarchy can be instituted by a revolution. But it will be instituted only by there being more and more people who do not require the protection of governmental power ... There can be only one permanent revolution—a moral one: the regeneration of the inner man." Despite his misgivings about anarchist violence, Tolstoy took risks to circulate the prohibited publications of anarchist thinkers in Russia, and corrected the proofs of Kropotkin's "Words of a Rebel", illegally published in St Petersburg in 1906.

Tolstoy was enthused by the economic thinking of Henry George, incorporating it approvingly into later works such as Resurrection (1899), the book that played a major factor in his excommunication.

In 1908, Tolstoy wrote A Letter to a Hindu outlining his belief in non-violence as a means for India to gain independence from British colonial rule. In 1909, a copy of the letter was read by Gandhi, who was working as a lawyer in South Africa at the time and just becoming an activist. Tolstoy's letter was significant for Gandhi, who wrote Tolstoy seeking proof that he was the real author, leading to further correspondence between them.

Reading Tolstoy's The Kingdom of God Is Within You also convinced Gandhi to avoid violence and espouse nonviolent resistance, a debt Gandhi acknowledged in his autobiography, calling Tolstoy "the greatest apostle of non-violence that the present age has produced". The correspondence between Tolstoy and Gandhi would only last a year, from October 1909 until Tolstoy's death in November 1910, but led Gandhi to give the name Tolstoy Colony to his second ashram in South Africa. Besides nonviolent resistance, the two men shared a common belief in the merits of vegetarianism, the subject of several of Tolstoy's essays.

Tolstoy also became a major supporter of the Esperanto movement. Tolstoy was impressed by the pacifist beliefs of the Doukhobors and brought their persecution to the attention of the international community, after they burned their weapons in peaceful protest in 1895. He aided the Doukhobors in migrating to Canada. In 1904, during the Russo-Japanese War, Tolstoy condemned the war and wrote to the Japanese Buddhist priest Soyen Shaku in a failed attempt to make a joint pacifist statement.

Towards the end of his life, Tolstoy become more and more occupied with the economic theory and social philosophy of Georgism. He spoke of great admiration of Henry George, stating once that "People do not argue with the teaching of George; they simply do not know it. And it is impossible to do otherwise with his teaching, for he who becomes acquainted with it cannot but agree." He also wrote a preface to George's Social Problems. Tolstoy and George both rejected private property in land (the most important source of income of the passive Russian aristocracy that Tolstoy so heavily criticized) whilst simultaneously both rejecting a centrally planned socialist economy. Some assume that this development in Tolstoy's thinking was a move away from his anarchist views, since Georgism requires a central administration to collect land rent and spend it on infrastructure. However, anarchist versions of Georgism have also been proposed since. Tolstoy's 1899 novel Resurrection explores his thoughts on Georgism in more detail and hints that Tolstoy indeed had such a view. It suggests the possibility of small communities with some form of local governance to manage the collective land rents for common goods; whilst still heavily criticising institutions of the state such as the justice system.

Death

Tolstoy died in 1910, at the age of 82. Just prior to his death, his health had been a concern of his family, who were actively engaged in his care on a daily basis. During his last few days, he had spoken and written about dying. Renouncing his aristocratic lifestyle, he had finally gathered the nerve to separate from his wife, and left home in the middle of winter, in the dead of night. His secretive departure was an apparent attempt to escape unannounced from Sophia's jealous tirades. She was outspokenly opposed to many of his teachings, and in recent years had grown envious of the attention which it seemed to her Tolstoy lavished upon his Tolstoyan "disciples".

Tolstoy died of pneumonia at Astapovo train station, after a day's rail journey south. The station master took Tolstoy to his apartment, and his personal doctors were called to the scene. He was given injections of morphine and camphor.

The police tried to limit access to his funeral procession, but thousands of peasants lined the streets. Still, some were heard to say that, other than knowing that "some nobleman had died", they knew little else about Tolstoy.

According to some sources, Tolstoy spent the last hours of his life preaching love, nonviolence, and Georgism to his fellow passengers on the train. (Source: Wikipedia)

Lightning Source UK Ltd.
Milton Keynes UK
UKHW041030010520
362627UK00006B/849